THE SONG OF
Jackass Creek

By Darby Lee Patterson

Bolton Road Publishing

Bolton Road Publishing
P.O. Box 566
Pollock Pines, CA 95726

ISBN: 978-1-7340281-9-5

Bolton Road
PUBLISHING

Acknowledgments

Without the great fortune of having lived in a forested hamlet near the grandeur of Yosemite National Park this book would not have been written. The people, beliefs and culture of a small town dependent on logging and mining for its existence were embedded in memory so fondly that I wanted to make it come to life again. The characters in my mystery tale are based on many people I came to know and admire during my years as a reporter and publisher in their community. Most of their names have been changed but their personalities ring true. The events, of course, are completely fictionalized and solely the product of the writer's imagination. It's with appreciation to the town of North Fork, California, known by locals as "The exact geographic center of California," that this book is dedicated and to its diverse denizens who made it the unique mountain treasure I called home.

In the same vein I intend for the story to impart the value of lifestyles and beliefs: from families embedded in the culture of forestry to the watchdogs of our environment, from Native Americans sentenced to life on marginalized 'rancherias' to the business owners, large and small, who sustain our small towns.

I am grateful to many people for their help and encouragement in making this book come to life. The late Ms. Mollie Burrows read a draft of the book and declared it, "Just as good as any of those you get at the bookstore!" I considered this high praise from an avid and very experienced reader of mysteries. I greatly benefitted from the help of graphic artist and long-time friend Hal Hammond who told me how awful my first cover design was and proceeded to fix it. My detail editor was my ever-encouraging husband, Randall Hagar, an exceptionally smart, handsome man. If you find any small errors in this edition please hold him responsible. (Yes, I am joking.) The final version of this book was edited by twelve volunteer women readers from Curves Fitness who caught many small errors and few whoppers. They were a 'Village' of editors and their input was invaluable.

Thank *you* for being a reader! Your comments and feedback and an Amazon review are sincerely appreciated.

Darby Lee Patterson
darby@darbypatterson.com

FOREWORD

I have always loved reading a good mystery, one with strong characters I grew to care about and a plot that drove me forward to the end with urgency. Then, somewhere over the last decade, many mystery adventures took a turn. They started focusing on graphic descriptions of deaths and gratuitous violence. Blood was dripping from the pages, body parts scattered, new and grotesque ways of killing were devised. I had a hard time finding mysteries that didn't force me to skip over many descriptive passages.

The Song of Jackass Creek is a return to that more gentle style of mystery writing. Yes, someone dies. After all, it is a murder mystery. But the spotlight is on the characters surrounding the event and the process of uncovering the guilty. If you'd like to be a voyeur in Redbud, population three hundred eighty-six, and get to know the characters who have made this hamlet their home; meet a big city transplant with a storied past and a young boy with big city dreams and follow the story as they tackle a crime that's anything but simple and straightforward, I think you'll enjoy *The Song of Jackass Creek*.

CONTENTS

PROLOGUE

Choker Anderson had been drinking since the afternoon whistle blew at the mill at five o'clock. The first hour, he'd put down several whiskey shooters and then moved on to a couple shots of tequila purchased for him by other guys from the mill who'd heard about the layoffs.

By nine p.m., he'd switched over to nursing a bottle of beer, figuring that if he didn't get home and tell his wife the bad news, she'd hear it from somebody else first and there'd be hell to pay. Choker wasn't alone. There were about a dozen other guys in the Silver Stag who'd heard they'd soon be out of a job. Each one of them had given years of labor to the saw mill and had families and homes in the tiny mountain community tucked in the folds of Northern California. They all knew there wasn't another job for them within a hundred miles, probably more.

In the morning, there would be shockwaves running through the town where one main road held all the businesses and a scattering of small homes. Most of the population lived on modest acreage off dirt roads that cut through the pines and rolling hills and scrub oak. They would hear, and they would know that this was only the beginning. More layoffs would come and the mill, like so many others, would sooner or later be closed down. Redbud would lose its lifeblood and become a community without a soul, home to commuters from the city and transplants from Los Angeles who would never understand the spirit of the mountains.

Choker hated the Southern California transplants in particular. They came up the hill with their fancy cars, troubled kids and – something damn few of the locals had – enough money to build 3,000-square-foot homes on ten and twenty-acre parcels. Now, as he sat peering through the amber that bubbled in his glass, he knew he'd be leaving it all to them: the great, naked outcropping of rock that was shaped like the beak of an eagle; the hundreds of miles of fishing streams where wild brown trout played games with less clever men; the towering pines; and the echoing winds. He and his kind would have to leave or settle for welfare. He watched Hardesty, one of the local Tomah tribe, take a shot with his pool cue and thought about how at least the Indians wouldn't have to leave. They'd have the Redbud Rancheria and its pitiful government dole.

Choker laughed and walked over to Hardesty. He laid his hand on the man's shoulder. "Well, my frien'," he said. "Looks like they got us again. Those folks from the city."

"Hey man, sorry about your job. I'm just waiting for the other shoe to fall," Hardesty answered, dropped his head and slowly rubbed the tip of his cue with a stub of chalk. "Heard they're gonna announce more layoffs in a couple of weeks. It's screwed man, really screwed." He squinted down the length of the cue, shot and dropped the ball in a side pocket. "It's a matter of time for us all."

Choker took another swallow of beer and leaned closer to Hardesty, whose family had worked at the mill for longer than anyone could remember. "You see what they're doin', don'cha? All those tree huggers from the cities pass their so-called environmental laws and they shut us down, chase us out. You know what's next, Hardesty? They come up here. Take over. Make bedroom towns. Sound familiar? Haven't your people been through this before?"

Hardesty picked up what was left of the chalk and worked it on his cue. He was thinking about an answer when suddenly chairs went flying away from one of the round tables that somebody quickly overturned to make room for the men who were shouting and squaring off to fight. Rita Mae, owner of the Stag, bolted from behind the bar holding a tire iron in her fist.

Choker assessed the situation through his alcoholic haze. It was young Birdsong and the Hazlett boy, drunk on their butts and ready to break up the place. Choker knew that Rita would handle it, no problem. He also knew it was definitely time to be moving on, before he did something stupid, like smash one of those city boys sipping imported beer at the bar smack in his clean shaven face.

He walked out to the parking lot, looked over the tiny town, and then up at the sky. It was ablaze with stars, the kind you never get to see in the city. He swore out loud, crawled into his Ford F-150 pick-up truck and headed home.

Choker and his family lived about fifteen miles from Redbud, five miles of which was dirt road that meandered along Jackass Creek and led to his place. There were turnoffs to a smattering of other homes and to a popular camping spot that would be crowded with tourists in a few weeks with the coming of the annual Loggers' Jamboree. That's why the sight of someone walking along the pitch-black road didn't surprise him. Idiots from the flatlands were always doing something stupid. On closer examination, Choker realized he knew this particular idiot and, although he didn't like him one bit, he'd have to give the man a hand. It was a code in that part of the mountains.

"What the hell?" he said opening the passenger door from the inside.

The man looked cautiously at Choker and clenched his fists nervously before stepping forward. Chris Lance had been one of the newcomers who was outspoken about environmental issues and had flat-out said that logging was a lost way of life and that the town had "better adapt or face extinction." This had not made Chris a favorite with the locals. Nonetheless, neighbors still put aside their differences – at least for the time – when there was trouble.

"I ... ahh ... guess I ran over something in the road and then I bounced into a rut. If you could help me out, I've got a spare." The young man seemed a little embarrassed by his predicament. Good, thought Choker. "No problem," he said. "Let's see how bad it's in there."

They rode in silence a short way, having little genuine to say to each other that wouldn't lead to a fight, especially in Choker's frame of mind. They rounded a bend and Chris pointed to a spot where the weeds had been crushed. "There, there it is," he directed. "Pull over anywhere."

Choker shut down the Ford and reached into the glove compartment for his flashlight. He joined the young man on the bank that overlooked Jackass Creek where spring thaws from the high country sent water rushing over granite rocks. The sound filled the night. The melody of the creek changed with the seasons and the weather. Choker had even noticed a difference between its voice in the night and day. In the dark, its tone seemed lower and more resonant, absorbing all around it.

Chris's compact pick-up had bounced into a depression of soft sand. No big deal, thought Choker. He returned to his truck and grabbed a length of chain. "I really appreciate this," Chris said. "I understand we don't agree about everything." He waited a moment. "And I heard about the lay-offs today."

"Bad news travels fast, like they say." Choker really wasn't interested in conversation. "Though, I don't suspect you consider it bad news." He lowered himself under the rear axle of the small truck and wrapped the chain around it. Chris watched with his hands in his pockets. "It's not that I've got anything against you personally," the younger man said. "These are different times. If we don't protect our environment today, it won't be here for tomorrow. Species will become extinct."

"Yeah" Choker shot back, "species like me!" He continued to work at hitching up the two vehicles as fast as possible, wanting to get away from the jerk before his temper got the best of him. "Get in there and steer."

Chris did as told and with little effort, the F-150 pulled the small rig back onto the road. He craned his neck out the window. "Thanks a lot, can I give you something for your trouble?"

"Damn right," Choker said, getting out of the pick-up to retrieve his heavy chain. "You can give me my life back. You and your friends from the city can take your flatland ideas back where they came from."

Chris got out of the truck grabbing his tire iron and jack. "It's easy to blame me," he said. "But I'm not the one who's destroying spotted owl habitat with a chainsaw. It's too many years of logging without regard for the environment."

Choker started seeing red. He wasn't about to stand there in the dark on a dirt road and debate environmental policy with a snot-nose kid he'd just pulled out of a ditch. "Don't make me sorry I stopped," he said and dropped down to unhook the chain from his truck. "I've been out there in the woods with those damn owls since before you were born. Don't even start to give me no lecture about the environment." In disgust, he dropped the heavy chain on the ground.

Now out of the ditch and more confident, Chris positioned a flashlight to focus on the flat tire. "This isn't about you. This is about corporate greed. They don't give a shit about the environmental future. All they want is to clear-cut trees and make money."

Choker stood tall, in the dark resembling a bear. "Son, this operation has been owned by the same family for nearly a hundred years. You don't have a clue what you're talkin' about. That family has given a paycheck to thousands of other families. They made jobs and a way of life that you and your kind just plain don't understand! I'm going home before I say or do something that I'll regret in the morning." Choker crawled behind the wheel, locking his jaws like a vice grip.

"I appreciate the help," Chris shouted again. "Especially since you're apparently blaming me for your bad luck."

Choker sat there for a moment thinking ... bad luck? Bad luck? The layoffs had nothing to do with luck and everything to do with people like him. Choker really wanted to teach this kid a lesson.

He started the big engine and gunned it for effect. He took a deep breath and headed slowly up the road, feeling his blood pressure rise. Even with a few drinks under his belt, he could make mince meat of that green whiner. And, son-of-a-bitch, he'd left his chain back there on the ground.

1 / MOUNTAIN HIGH

By the end of the week, all of Redbud had heard the news about the layoffs and a shadow fell over the town, despite the cloudless sky. The fate of the region was debated in the supermarket, the Christian bookstore, the pharmacy, the hardware store, the Silver Stag, and the post office, all of which lined the main street of town and accounted for more than half of the retail services available. There was also an antique and gift shop, a beauty salon, a well-stocked DVD store, pizza parlor and the lone cafe, each located on abbreviated roads off Main Street that, at a time of optimism, had been the start of more development.

Jesse Kilgore was at the counter in the Eagle Eye Cafe, sipping his mug of steaming coffee and listening to the old timers reminisce about the days when lumber was like gold to the people who settled the rolling landscape. There had been no difference back then, between Indian and white. The mill needed workers and every muscled arm was employed. There was never great prosperity among mill workers and loggers, but families made a decent living. If the dollars never made them wealthy, the riches they drew from living among the ponderosa pines and cedar trees, breathing crystal clear air beneath a brilliant sky, more than compensated for limited wages.

Redbud did, of course, develop its own cadre of well-to-do. There were land developers, business owners, top brass from the lumber company, real estate agents, and others who grew wealthy on the strength of the lumbering industry and the town's natural beauty. Prior lay-offs at the mill had been short. Folks complained, but generally knew that work would come again.

This time was different. The tone of the early morning talk in the Eagle's Eye was dark, like a threatening cloud that promises more to come. Jesse kept an ear tuned to the conversation among the five men. The regulars were settled around the table that was unofficially reserved for the handful of old-timers. Their elbows were up on the table, rough hands clasped around mismatched mugs, and they leaned forward as if to keep their words quiet, although this was never the point. The men intended to have their conversations overheard and repeated around town throughout the day. Jesse liked them and was welcome to join them but preferred this morning to be objectively listening in his capacity as publisher of the local weekly newspaper.

Jesse noted that the news about the layoffs at the mill had energized the group, as if their expertise was needed now more than ever. Daisy, the waitress, owner, and occasional fry-cook at the Eagle's Eye, floated around the table pouring more hot coffee into waiting cups. She made no money at all on this convention of regulars but figured they were part of the local "color" and probably good PR for her place. Their ages ranged from sixty-something to well beyond eighty. Their memories reached back to the days when Redbud had been a wild and booming mill town with railroad tracks connecting to the valley city sixty miles downhill. More than a century before, it had been gold that called men to the hills. Today, abandoned mines carved the landscape.

Down toward the far end of Main Street stood a log-constructed, two-story building that now housed a feed store, real estate office, Thompson's DVD Rental, and, upstairs, Jesse's newspaper, the *Timberline Times*. Sometime around the turn of the century, the same building had been a saloon with hospitality rooms upstairs. It stood perched on log posts and was best known as the Pole Building. Old Charlie, who was the unofficial spokesman for the Eagle's Eye's elders, would selectively take folks down to the Pole Building and show them a spot in the floor where a bullet was lodged.

He'd tell them how a burley logger caught his favorite saloon gal flirting with a miner who'd just struck gold and was scattering it like it was no more than a handful of acorns. Legend says the logger threw the drunken miner on the floor and pinned him down on his back. He put a six-gun to the man's chest and demanded to know where the mine was. In response, the miner spit at him. The logger shot him through the heart. That same bullet became Redbud's only historical site. The alleged mine was never found, though plenty of folks had tried and were still trying.

However, that day in the Eagle's Eye, the men were more concerned about the future than the past. Charlie took his hand off the cup and laid it flat on the table saying, "I tell you, this ain't at all like the other times. This just might be the beginning of the end."

The others chimed in with opinions about what should have been done, what could be done and then agreed that probably nothing would be done. Charlie nodded his head and leaned back once his point had been made. Jesse noticed that the old man's bulbous nose was a little bit redder than usual and figured Charlie had shared another night with the bottle.

Jesse stepped behind the counter and poured himself a second cup of coffee from the burner. Daisy brushed up against him and teasingly said, "Help yerself, why don't cha?"

Jesse smiled at her and thought quickly about how he'd changed. Back in L.A., it had been cappuccino, espresso, and lattes. Reporters in the newsroom even stored their own battery-operated coffee grinders and beans in a desk drawer. Here, Daisy just doubled the amount of Farmers Brothers Coffee to water. Instant dark roast, she claimed. Jesse put the stainless steel pot back on the warmer and slid back onto the stool, guessing where he'd be right now had he stayed in that fast-paced environment. If he were not six feet under, he'd be sipping stale coffee in the newsroom, worrying about how to beat the other metro paper to the day's top story, working fourteen to sixteen hours, and then meeting some buddies for drinks and a little dip into a gram of cocaine. Except Jesse knew he wouldn't have lasted this long. He'd be dead by now.

Instead, here he was, in the little cafe with dulled yellow walls and brown checkered curtains that hung over filmy windowpanes, being catered to by Daisy, a motherly round woman who liked to poke him in the solar plexus when he wasn't expecting it. Here, he was surrounded by plain folk who rolled their shirtsleeves up to work and had hands as rough as #4 sandpaper, who accepted him despite the fact that he'd come from California's Tower of Babel, Los Angeles.

His thoughts turned to the present, to how he would write the story of the new layoffs. Naturally, the metro paper down the hill would get it first. By the time the *Timberline* was out, the news would be days old. It was easy, however, for Jesse, a seasoned and award-winning journalist, to develop a new slant on the story that would keep the mountain communities talking for days.

Over the past five years, Jesse had come to cherish the Eagle's Eye coffee club and, as a writer, regarded them as tribal elders in a quickly disappearing American culture. They were a repository of local history harboring memories that would soon fade with their passing. No matter that a lot of what they said had been said before, or that they had a gift for exaggeration. Here and there were fleeting moments of unintended wisdom.

Charlie, the long retired tree faller with his melon belly, was usually in the company of Flip, who was the long and lanky shadow of Charlie. He was a little introverted and none too bright, but a bona fide member of the unofficial city council. One talked, the other listened, and they both enjoyed a little Wild Turkey now and again. There was old Mr. Merryweather who opened the first real grocery market in town and retired a wealthy man. He could be counted on for an ultra–conservative statement on any and all topics.

Then there was Paul, a white-bearded man of unknown age, who had lived in the woods, off the land, for much of his life. He was an itinerant silversmith by trade, and said little, but what he said deserved listening ears. Jesse suspected the man had a secret past that included an advanced education that Paul clearly didn't want known. Three or four other regulars rotated around the table, each adding to the council of the Eagle Eye.

"What's happening here," pronounced Charlie, "is an extinction. Just like them dinosaurs. You see, the time has come when there won't be no more mills. The city folk who run everything will turn it into their personal playground. Wait and see."

Flip said "yep," and the others shook their heads in agreement or plain disgust at the state of things. Mr. Merryweather cleared his throat and the men looked his way.

"That's the truth. And it's all because them damn liberals cozy up with those tree huggers. Ain't one of them environmentalists would last overnight in these mountains. They'd die of fright before they had a chance to freeze to death and go peacefully. That's the end of this economy," he added for good measure.

The conversation spun around that premise and captured the attention of the other people in the little café. Soon, the dimly lit room was vibrating with opinions and Jesse made a few notes for himself on a paper napkin.

Daisy saw him out of the corner of her eye and brought him a few more napkins. She calculated she was the only one who knew what Jesse was doing and the thought made her smile. She figured it was about time she made the Chicken and Dumplin' special again. It was Jesse's favorite and though the man was young enough to be her son, he was sure easy on the eyes. And how he tightened that belly up every time she gave him a poke!

The debate rose and fell with Charlie instigating more when the talk threatened to mellow. Herb from the two-pump gas station had joined the gathering, warning Charlie to take it easy and not get his blood pressure up, when young Andy Winter burst through the door, wild-eyed and panting.

2 / JACKASS EXCUSE

Andy spoke with the soprano voice of an eleven-year-old boy on an urgent mission, "The sheriff here? Any deputies? You seen Herb anywhere? He ain't at the shop."

"Do you see any deputies here?" Daisy asked, hands on her hips. "Calm down, Andy. And, aren't you supposed to be in school?" Daisy knew the boy's habit of skipping school. He spotted Herb at the table and rushed over to him.

Andy was huffing as if he'd run for miles and, though he was an excitable kid, looked nearly panicked. Sensing this, all eyes turned toward the lanky, redheaded boy who was heading toward Jesse. "Mr. Kilgore, you the newspaperman. You gotta help me!"

Charlie decided the situation called for someone to take charge. He signaled to Andy. "Here, boy. Set here. I'll buy you a cup of coffee and you tell us what's up."

Daisy cringed at the offer of coffee to an eleven -year-old, especially her coffee.

"I cain't, Mr. Charlie. I just seen somethin' awful up at Jackass Creek. Something I can't hardly describe."

Jesse walked over to the boy and joined him at the elder's table. Daisy put a glass of orange juice in front of the boy who ignored it. He turned his head to Jesse and blurted out, "It were hands I saw. Right there in the creek, lodged up against a rock. Two hands and they weren't connected to no body! My God, my Ma's gonna kill me."

The men looked at each other and raised their eyebrows in skepticism, knowing Andy's propensity for tale-telling and his infamously negligent mother. Jesse focused on the boy. "Exactly where were you when you saw this Andy?" he asked.

"'Bout two miles off the turn, I was. Just hidin' out 'cause I didn't want to go to school." He looked around the table for understanding of how impossible school was. "Don't tell Ma, please! She'll get me good if she finds out."

"Just take a breath. Tell me exactly where you were and what you saw," Jesse encouraged. "That's-a-boy, just close your eyes and picture it like it was."

"Yes sir, Mr. Kilgore," And his green eyes shut, barely-there eyebrows creased in concentration.

Recalling details had never been one of Andy's strong suits. "Well I think I was just walkin' long side the road by Jackass, not doin' nuthin', when I came on to this lil' truck sittin' kinda catty-wampus. I looked inside and seen the keys was there. I thought maybe he went down to the creek to fish or somethin' and forgot em'. I figured that since we got so many flatlanders up here with their crime and stuff, I better find him. No disrespect intended, Mr. Kilgore."

"Just go on, boy," Charlie coached, as Jesse acknowledged the exception.

"I looked around a little to see which direction a person might have headed. I saw some tracks leadin' straight down the bank – not a easy way to get there, ya know? Covered with poison oak. I hate that stuff. Once, my Ma …."

"Get back to the subject, Andy," Herb urged knowing how easy it was for the boy to drift like a leaf on a stream.

"Oh yeah, sorry. I was just bein' back there like Mr. Kilgore said. I go down the slope bein' real careful not to touch that stuff. I hollered for somebody a coupla' times. The creek is runnin' pretty good and you can't hear much. So, I went down to the water, lookin' for a rock or sumpthin' to do. That's when I seen these white things waggin' up and down underwater between these two boulders. I waded in a ways, and Hell's Bells, it was a hand. A hand with its fingers flapping up and down at me like it was wavin'. Well, I'll tell you I moved

19

outta there faster than a danged hummin' bird. I run all the way to town and realized I couldn't very well go home, so's I came here. Did I do the right thing, Mr. Herb?"

"You sure did, son," said the distinguished old man who was Redbud's closest thing to a gentleman. "What do you think about that, Jesse? Wouldn't that make your front page?"

Jesse realized no one had taken Andy seriously. The child had gotten darn good at telling tales, due to the regular need for making excuses for not being at school. However, the vivid picture the boy had painted, and the fact that Andy had begun scratching his forearm, made Jesse pause and look the boy in his bright green eyes.

"That's quite a story, Andy," he said gently. "And since it looks like you got a case of poison oak going and wouldn't want to spread it around in school, I'd like to take a ride up to that place and have you show me what you saw." Andy was clearly pleased. Not only had somebody important believed him, but he now had an official excuse for his absence from school.

"Sure, Mr. Kilgore, I can do that," Andy replied, scratching the tiny bumps on his arm faster. The poison oak was beginning to swell into red blotches.

"Sure, he can," Charlie laughed. "Any dang thing but go to school or go home and get the belt!" The other men shook their heads and

20

chuckled at the pair heading out the door. Andy had told many a tale in his eleven years, but this was one of the best. The whole town knew about Andy. Jesse, a newcomer with just five years under his belt as a local, hadn't caught on to the boy yet. But, Jesse was a keeper, they'd decided. Let him indulge the boy.

The pair headed toward the door and Charlie sent them off with, "Hey, Jesse, can you give me a hand later?" The bell on the door tinkled to the sound of laughter as it closed.

Andy had always done poorly in school and was consequently in trouble nearly every day. He didn't mean to make trouble but couldn't do the work and found other places to express his creative energy – like scribbling cartoons on the top of his desk when he was supposed to be reading. The child had found that he much preferred to spend his time with Herb at the gas station. Herb showed him how to make paper airplanes, which pleased Andy because he was very good at it. They also talked about old cars and engines. Andy was learning to love the feel of grease and fear the texture of the printed page. Needless to say, he'd never read one page of Jesse's newspaper but knew the publisher was somebody of note in Redbud.

They drove quickly to the turnoff from the paved road and onto dirt, bouncing over gravel and potholes as Andy pointed the way. But, the truck wasn't hard to locate and Andy breathed an audible sigh of relief, as if he'd begun to doubt himself. Jesse shut down the engine of the Wrangler. "It's right down that bank, Mr. Kilgore," Andy said, pointing to a place where the brush and grass had obviously been disturbed.

"Andy, I'd like you to stay in the car," Jesse said, realizing that the boy would feel cheated out of an adventure. "I wouldn't want anybody to come along and mess with the truck. Could be evidence. Okay?"

Andy wasn't totally convinced, but then considered looking at those hands again. "You bet, Mr. Kilgore. I'll keep an eye on it."

Jesse heard the automatic door locks engage and gave the boy a thumbs-up. The kid was actually scared.

Jesse first went over to the little pick-up. Right away, he saw the flat tire and tools lying on the ground. Then he noticed what from a distance looked like rust all over the truck's fender and hood. After years on the crime beat, Jesse knew blood when he saw it. He stood silently for a moment and then reached to his belt and activated his cell phone. He punched in the number of the sheriff's office but didn't send the call.

The sound of the creek was constant, with highs and lows and ever-changing rhythms, like a tonal drum. Birds cried out their morning calls and Jesse walked over to the crushed trail. He would be careful not to disturb the scene, although he knew that if local law enforcement had to be called, most of the deputies wouldn't be so cautious.

He walked down to the creek alongside the grass that had been flattened, his eyes scanning the area, ears attuned to invasive sounds. The grasses had not just been walked upon, but crushed. At the edge of the bank, where the roar of the creek drowned out all else, Jesse spotted the rocks that Andy had spoken about. He carefully stood on top of a smooth granite boulder that thrust out over the rushing water. There, lodged between the rock and a partially submerged tree branch was the sight that had sent the young boy running for the company of men. The hand was as he had described, flapping with the motion of the clear water, blue-white sentinels seemingly disconnected from anything else.

Jesse punched the "send" button on his cell phone and asked for Sheriff Blair. The scene looked grim and he didn't want a band of cowboys pouncing on it. After briefly describing the discovery and the need for the sheriff to arrive first, Jesse signed off and worked his way along the bank for a closer look. He wasn't ready for what he found. The hand was not, as Andy had described, unattached. The body lay partially submerged, hidden by the outcropping and trapped by the branch.

Jesse had seen a lot in his days as a metropolitan reporter: shootings, stabbings, beatings, strangulations. But the sight of what had once been Chris Lance made him take a deep breath. The water had flushed the blood away from the body that undulated with the movement of the water, leaving gaping gashes of pale pink flesh. It was clearly a brutal beating made macabre by the lack of blood. Despite the damage, Jesse recognized him as the young man he'd recently interviewed at some length for a newspaper story on the timber wars. Once accustomed to the sight, Jesse looked closer and then surveyed the surrounding area. It was good, he thought, that Andy had bolted when he had. It would not be healthy for an eleven-year-old to live with an image such as this.

As he turned to leave, Jesse nearly stepped on the boy who stood transfixed behind him. Jesse took Andy by the shoulders and turned him around. "Thought I told you to stay in the Wrangler."

"I... I... got scared..." Andy stammered. "I kept seein' those fingers..."

Jesse guided him back up the bank, avoiding the trail where Chris Lance's body had likely been dragged. "Well, now you've seen a lot more than fingers," he said. "Pretty bad, huh, pal?" He could feel the boy's body shaking under his hands. It was important to get him to talk.

"I never seen nobody dead before," Andy said.

"I hope you never do, again," Jesse offered. "It's never a pretty sight. This one was about as bad as it gets."

"It was that guy, from them enviros, wasn't it?" Andy asked. "I seen his truck in town."

24

"Looks like it to me," Jesse answered. "Know him?"

"Naw, I stay away from the flatlanders," Andy declared.

Well, that's at least something, Jesse thought. It would have been much worse had the boy been acquainted with what was now a grotesque dead body. "We need to wait for Sheriff Blair," Jesse said. "Keep the crime scene secure."

This got Andy's attention. "Yeah, make sure nobody messes with it, huh? I seen that on TV once. You done this before Mr. Kilgore?"

"When I was a reporter in the big city, Andy. I worked with the police pretty often. I got to know a lot about crime."

"What will they look for?"

With Andy's curiosity piqued, Jesse hunched on his knees and pointed to tire marks that had crushed the weeds. Andy mimicked the posture. Andy pointed to broken branches leading down to the stream and talked about evidence gathering, securing a crime scene. It was a healthier conversation, Jesse figured, than trying to explain the dead body in the creek. It filled up the twenty minutes before they heard the sound of sirens and saw the clouds of dust rise on the dirt road. The sheriff pulled in first, followed by two deputies in a four-wheel drive vehicle. Sheriff Blair wedged his way out of a dusty sedan that he found decidedly uncomfortable. A well-meaning man with a taste for meat and potatoes, the sheriff had packed on the pounds driving the endless labyrinth of mountain roads. He directed the men in the second car to remain inside and approached Jesse.

"You better come with me, Jesse," the sheriff said. "And, boy, you just stay put."

"Yes sir, I wouldn't want to be disturbin' any evidence," Andy responded.

Creekside, Jesse confided his concerns about the department's expertise in gathering evidence and keeping it secure.

"Well, that's why I brought the coroner and my two best men," the sheriff answered with only a trifle of defensiveness. "I know some of the boys get a little over-enthused. I got no training budget, Jesse. Why don't you put that in your paper?"

The sheriff and his men went to work, one of the "men" being a woman deputy. Jesse remained at the scene while the search took place, but kept Andy away from the water. The boy seemed captivated by the whole crime scene process and sat on the hood of the Wrangler taking it all in. Finally, the sheriff called for the department's van to take away the body. Jesse decided Andy did not need to witness this and he packed the boy up for the ride home.

"Are you doin' all right?" Jesse asked the boy, whose face was flush red with excitement.

"I'm fine. I'm doin' just fine, Mr. Kilgore," he answered. "Mr. Kilgore, what would it take to be one of those people who comes to those crime scenes and looks for clues?"

Knowing this was not the answer that Andy wanted to hear, Jesse said; "It'd take a guy going to school and learning enough about science. It'd even take going to college if he wanted to be an expert."

Andy was silent for a moment and looked at Jesse with the first smile he'd managed all day. "Well, I sure do got one heck-of-a excuse for not bein' there today, don't I, Mr. Kilgore?"

3 / HEADLINE NEWS

By mid-day, there was talk of little else in Redbud and the smattering of resort communities that
surrounded it. The murder of Chris Lance, a twenty
-four-year-old environmental activist, traveled word
-of-mouth like a September wildfire. The facts suf-
fered many twists and turns as the story meandered through the ponderosas. The body had been
headless, handless, people said. The news even
eclipsed the lay-offs at the mill, at least for the afternoon.

Jesse dropped Andy off at the trailer where he
lived with his mother. It was noon and the woman
was just getting out of bed. She was, Jesse
thought, the very picture of the western euphe-
mism "rode hard and put away wet." Jesse explained that the boy had made a grim discovery on

28

his way to school and done the right thing by no-tifying the nearest adults. Jesse could almost hear an audible sigh of relief from the youngster. It was rumored that when Andy's mom got high, she got mean. The boy had come to school with some pretty nasty welts, the fellows at the Eagle Eye had said. They felt sorry for the boy and now Jesse knew why.

"The police might want to talk to Andy some more. So, if it's all right with you, I may be back to get him later on," Jesse said, sensing that home seemed to hold little comfort for the eleven-year-old. Andy's mother, who had introduced her-self as Marsha, said she would be off to work at three in the afternoon anyway.

"Go wash that dirty little face of yours," she barked at her son and then eyed Jesse up and down. Marsha appeared to be in her forties, though it was possible she was younger. She brushed her harsh blonde hair back with her hand once she had established that Jesse was, indeed, "good-looking." Years ago, Marsha had been attractive, but her face now told a story of decades of cigarettes and long, hard-lived nights. Dark circles fell in half-moons beneath her eyes, which were green like Andy's, but without the sparkle. She had a provocative way of sliding her hands up and down her hips as she talked.

Having been around long enough to immediately read that kind of body language, Jesse excused

29

himself and headed back to the scene at the creek. He'd called the newspaper's one photographer – Skipper Bell, who was best at taking sports photos – and told him to meet him at the murder scene. As Jesse swung the Wrangler around, he felt a knot in the pit of his stomach. He was having a hard time turning his back on Andy.

The road leading to the crime scene had become an armed camp. Deputies and volunteers with the department set up a roadblock to keep the curious out. Unfortunately, that appeared to include a reporter and photographer from the daily newspaper far down in the valley. Jesse pulled up and joined the debate.

"Deputy Strunk, what seems to be the problem?" Jesse asked, nodding to the daily's reporter whom he knew casually.

"Sheriff Blair told me that nobody, but nobody, but locals that live back here get on this road. Them and law enforcement," Strunk said jutting out his square jaw. "Now, I don't suppose that means you, since you found the body and all, but this fella is from the city!" Strunk said "city" as if it were a curse word.

"I'm sure the sheriff would appreciate you following his orders," Jesse said, "but I think you better let these reporters past or there could be some trouble."

"Trouble?"

"Yeah, Deputy Strunk, these fellas from the

papers won't be the only reporters up here. I wouldn't be surprised if one or two of the TV stations from the valley didn't roll up pretty soon. It's customary to give the press access to places that you wouldn't want the general public to go. Some of that access is even in the Constitution, if I recall."

"You vouch for these guys?" Strunk asked suspiciously.

"I will," Jesse said. "And once we get back there, I'll have the sheriff radio you about the rest of them."

Jesse nodded to the pair from the daily. The reporter was shaking his head. "There's nothing like these small town cops," the reporter said. "Buncha cowboys throwing their weight around. Thanks, anyway. It avoided a hassle."

"No problem," Jesse said, recalling the days when he would have put roadblocks in front of the competition rather than open the door on a good story. But then, he wasn't in competition with a major daily newspaper. Jesse ran a weekly paper and they weren't in the same league. "I'd rather have you get it and get it right, than deal with the sensational stuff the TV guys will be doing. Let me know if I can help."

"Didn't the cop say that you found the body?" the astute reporter asked.

"He did, but he was mistaken. A young boy found the body," Jesse said, and saw an opportunity to get Andy out of the trailer. "Tell you what, let's go back to the scene and do some work. Then, I'll go get the boy and meet you at my office. Say, in a couple of hours?"

"Address?"

"You won't need one. First log building on the right at the end of Main Street."

Unused to such cooperation from a competitor, the reporter said effusive thank you's, hopped in his four-wheel drive, and followed Jesse down the road.

A tow truck had arrived to pull Chris Lance's truck to the yard where it might, or might not, get further analysis. Jesse wondered how thoroughly the pick-up had been dusted for prints. The sheriff was more than a little disgusted when Jesse told him about the snafu with the "Valley Sun" reporter. That's all he needed, bad press. He scurried over to the pair and apologized, trying to explain that some of his people weren't accustomed to dealing with events that attracted the big city press. Out of ear-shot, he quickly radioed Strunk and barked, "I didn't mean the press, deputy! You let them in and be polite about doing it! Draw them a damn map in the dirt!"

"But there's only one road in," Strunk whined.

"Do it anyway," the sheriff commanded.

It took a lot to get the major media up the hill. It wasn't as if Redbud held any real interest. There were no casinos. The local Indians didn't qualify for one yet. Nor was there skiing or nightlife. It was just a long and winding road to a sleepy little logging town. Reporters had been up for the first big environmental demonstration when there had been a fracas between the enviros and a handful of angry loggers. In the five years Jesse had been on the hill, that was the only other time that big city reporters had found the town newsworthy. The sheriff came up to his side.

"I hate talkin' to these guys. They always make us look bad." Just then, two trucks with cameras and remote broadcast equipment rolled up, driving too fast and sending billows of dust into the air. Skipper pulled up just after them, with the same effect.

"This is a crime scene," the sheriff hollered. "Take it easy!" He turned to Jesse. "Guess that's not a good start."

Skipper fumbled with his cameras and bag, and scuttled over to Jesse. "What do you want?" he asked anxiously. He'd never shot anything like this before and his pale complexion (complete with freckles) flushed red with excitement. Jesse instructed him to get a photo of the pick-up being pulled away and the deputies combing the creek side. He also suggested that Skipper get a shot of Deputy Strunk at the roadblock, for goodwill, if nothing else.

Jesse stayed in the background, leaning against a tree and listening. The creek had changed its tone. It sounded busy, anxious.

He turned his attention to two deputies working

as a team. Jesse knew one of them by reputation. His name was Fred Gorring. Locals avoided him in general and the hometown Indians treated him like a one-man, white man plague. Gorring was tough on everyone, but particularly hard on the Tomahs. There were rumors of beatings when an arrest wasn't possible. But no one filed any complaints, least of all a Tomah. The other deputy was young, a newcomer to the small force charged with policing a vast rural area. The mountainous county covered more than three thousand square miles, much of it unpaved roads that surrounded a handful of villages. There were two resort communities on the edge of a lake about fifteen miles from Redbud. That's where most of the action happened, particularly on weekend nights. Sheriff Blair had only twenty-eight men (including the "man" who was a woman) to police the entire area. All the communities, including Redbud, were on the lovely skirt tails of magnificent Yosemite National Park.

Gorring's voice escalated. "Damn, Rose. You know who this is gonna get pinned on? Do you know?"

Deputy Rose just looked at him, waiting for him to answer his own question.

"This is gonna get blamed on a logger," Gorring stated. "Just look at it. There's layoffs at the mill because of those new federal regulations. Those regulations are there because of people like this young buck that got hisself killed. Now, who

34

do you think will get the blame?" he asked, having already stated the answer.

"I guess that's a possibility," Deputy Rose admitted. "But it's a little early to be deciding who's innocent and who's guilty, isn't it?"

"What? What are you sayin'?" Gorring demanded. "I know each and every one of those guys at the mill and out in the woods. There's not a one of them that would do this. They hate those greens, and with good reason. But they wouldn't do that, not beat the hell outta some guy until he looked like pulp! No, this was the work of somebody crazy. Maybe crazy with firewater, the way some of those Tomahs can get."

Deputy Rose turned her head and rolled her eyes. Jesse saw that she was struggling to control herself in the face of Gorring's opinions. He could also see the directions the rumors could take. In a small town already divided, there was trouble ahead and, with minds like Gorring's on the job, regard for the truth and solid evidence would be at a premium.

Jesse herded his photographer around, pointing out possible angles for interesting shots. Skipper wasn't used to taking pictures of anything that wasn't running for a field goal or jumping for a basket. By 3:15, Jesse was back at Andy's trailer, deliberately timing his arrival to avoid the hot gaze of Andy's mother. They drove back to town in silence. Andy seemed to have lost some of his excitement for the day.

"Did you get in trouble for missing school?" Jesse asked.

"Naw, my Mom was mad, that's all."

"Mad about what?"

"She didn't like me coming back home with you."

"How come?"

"'Cause she hadn't put her makeup on yet," Andy said. "It doesn't take a whole lot to get my mom mad. I'm glad she's at work. Hope she works all night."

"But you'd be alone," Jesse said.

"So what? I know how to be alone. I like to be alone." Andy turned his face to the passenger widow and looked out. He was quiet for a while. "The sheriff gonna talk to me? Am I gonna get in trouble?"

"The sheriff will want to talk to you; that's right. You won't get in any trouble 'cause you didn't do anything wrong, except for skip school. And then a big city newspaper reporter is going to want to talk to you, too."

"Me?" This seemed to frighten Andy more that the idea of a talk with the sheriff.

"You were the one who found the body, young man. Could be the TV will want to talk with you, too. Don't worry. I'll be right by you." Jesse saw the boy perk up a little at the thought of being important. This was one reason he'd made the suggestion. Seeing a body like Andy had that morning would be disturbing to any normal adult. It was true that Andy had rallied and been distracted by the police action. But Jesse was worried the vision might come back and haunt his young mind. Andy seemed like a pretty practical fellow, but he was so young.

"Will I be on the TV?"

"Maybe," Jesse said. He wanted the boy to talk more about what had happened and who better to talk to than someone with a camera hoisted on his shoulder? They bounced across the dirt drive and onto the main road. Andy clearly liked to ride in the Wrangler. The wind tossed the boy's hair like little flames and Jesse hoped it might also blow away some memories.

The *Timberline Times* office occupied the floor above what had once been an infamous saloon. Small rooms for entertaining the physical appetites and thirsts of rugged men from the mines and lumber mills had been remodeled into one large room with a small kitchen area and bathroom facilities. Jesse's desk was by a big double window that looked out on the mountainside. His desk was made from a solid slab of redwood cut somewhere around the turn of the century. All the furniture was wood, a symbolic gesture for Jesse, who wanted to leave behind all the trappings of his life in the city. No sleek metal and glass or signs of the twenty-first century, except for four desktop computers, printers, a couple of laptops, and the necessary electronics to keep them all humming.

Jesse had hired a part-time writer and one person to electronically lay out the newspaper each week. Skipper, the photographer, came in on an as-needed basis. He also hired two salespeople to work the circulation area and a couple with a reliable truck for weekly delivery. The newspaper had a long history, although it had gone through many owners. The last had decided to turn the community publication into a shopper, filled with little more than classified and display ads. This angered the locals, who felt a loss. The new owner pointed out that the paper hadn't been important enough for people to subscribe to or for businesses to buy ads. Now, all of a sudden, he pointed out, it was the area's only lifeline! He stuck with his new program and offered free classified ads, hoping to attract display ads from the area's handful of grocery stores. He'd succeeded, but townspeople never forgave him for turning the mountain's only newspaper into a shopper.

When Jesse bought the paper, it was only a matter of a few weeks before the news format was back. He introduced electronic publishing but made few other concessions to modernity. The time honored "gossip" column was resurrected, written by an older woman who knew every local happening without ever leaving her house. He published plenty of sports photos from the local high school, allowed area churches and clubs to publicize their events and – for a small town newspaper – did everything right. That's perhaps why, when it ordinarily took about twenty years for a 'transplant' to be accepted into local culture, Jesse's probation lasted only until folks believed their cherished newspaper was back to stay.

Jesse wrote many of the news items. His journalistic standards remained high, but the locals he'd hired were not trained reporters. It would be nearly impossible, he knew, to attract a professional writer to a newspaper with such low circulation and pay. Instead, he served as a mentor for the part-time young reporter he'd hired, editing her stories and then explaining why he'd made the changes. She was coming along.

Jesse and Andy arrived at the same time as the sheriff pulled up in his cruiser. Skipper was already at the office, downloading photos he'd shot at the crime scene and of the basketball game the night before.

"Andy, you'll need to tell the sheriff what you found this morning. Think you can do that?" Jesse shut off the motor and turned to the boy.

"If I gotta," Andy said. Most of his encounters with law enforcement had been pretty negative, having to do with his absence from school.

Jesse caught the sheriff's eye and nodded to him. "You could talk up there in my office, or I'll bet Sheriff Blair would let you sit in the car with him. You could monitor the calls on the radio and such. What do you think?"

Andy eyed the cruiser with its light bar across the

top and gold star on the door. It was temptation. "We gonna go for a ride?"

"Not just yet," Jesse grinned. "I think I'll go up to my office while you and the sheriff talk. But maybe, if you asked just right, the sheriff might arrange a ride-along one of these days."

The pair walked over to the cruiser. The radio squawked and lit up like a string of flashing Christmas lights that reflected in Andy's eyes.

4 / THE FAST LANE

When Jesse first moved to the mountains from Los Angeles, it hadn't been to break new ground for his journalism career. Quite the opposite. He was sick of the constant competition, the drive of daily deadlines, the immense pressure of remaining a major player in a major media market. That pace had driven him to use a chemical booster to stay hyped up for sixteen-hour days. It started out as a line or two of cocaine a few days in the week and soon became a daily practice. Much, much later in the game he recognized he was crumbling emotionally, physically, and professionally, but was powerless to stop.

Back then, accolades and awards for his writing seemed to float as easily as an ocean breeze off Venice Beach straight into his office. Jesse was a star swimming in deadly stardust. Colleagues who didn't know him well were in awe of his seemingly boundless energy. He could work well into the early morning hours, sleep a few hours and return the following morning, apparently refreshed. He wrote so fast that his typing was one character ahead of the aging computer system at the *Metro Mirror*.

Jesse never relaxed; even a few drinks with other reporters late at night failed to take the edge off. He was driven to out-produce every other writer, and he did, even before the cocaine gave him that extra push of energy. He'd been in the business since his early twenties and worked his way through the small and medium market newspapers, doing it all: sports, business, features, news. Within five years, he landed a job at the *Metro Mirror,* the state's largest circulation daily. There, he made a brief visit to the bottom of the ladder. He was assigned to the daily police log and writing obituaries. But his drive was irrepressible. It took only four months for him to move up to writing short articles and occasionally being sent out on the cop beat. Once Jesse had the forum to display his speed and his talent, he again shot to the top.

His rise to prominence in the newsroom also earned resentment from peers – some whom he'd stepped on to get ahead. Aware that he was making enemies, Jesse tried to balance his professional drive by joining the paper's fast-pitch ball team. Once, in his youth, Jesse dreamed of becoming a major league pitcher. He had the arm and the eye. He had the speed. What he didn't have was a parent to pay for uniforms, fees, and equipment, or to offer him encouragement. But he was killer on the *Mirror* team where winning a few games on the ball field neutralized some of the resentment felt in the newsroom.

Over the next few years, Jesse stayed attuned to opportunities. By the time he was thirty, he could pick the plums from the newsroom assignments. He did this without much regard for his colleagues who had given up any attempts at camaraderie. He seldom dropped by the corner saloon after work or eyed the good-looking women who had their eyes on him. Had anyone asked Jesse what he was chasing, the question would have seemed nonsensical.

Somewhere in his mid-thirties, that question did float into Jesse's mind, uninvited and unwelcome. He wasn't big on introspection, which sounded a good deal to Jesse like a potential for "writer's block." Questions like that might cause him to lose his edge. He had surveyed the newsroom and seen dozens of shining new faces – young faces – cubs in their twenties, all too eager to nip at his heels.

To quiet these thoughts and to boost what he feared was his diminishing drive, Jesse decided to out-produce himself, to remain the alpha wolf of the *Mirror's* newsroom. One line of cocaine gave him the confidence to launch the second-wind of his career. It gave him back the feeling that had fed his ambition for more than a decade: that high energy, cutting edge sharpness that Jesse craved.

His relationship with coke lasted about four years, each year bringing increased dependence and heightened use. Of course, he knew all about King Cocaine, how it was among the most addictive of the so-called recreational drugs and how hard it was to quit. Ironically, he'd written an award-winning series about the people attracted to "The Cocaine Culture, a World of White and Black." He'd talked to users, dealers, suppliers, big quantity buyers who broke the stuff down for the street. He'd then talked to doctors, and shrinks and families torn apart by the not-so-gentle snows that fell upon the streets of L.A. from the cartels of Columbia. The four-part series won a national journalism award and his paper flew Jesse to New York to receive the honors. The Los Angeles Police Department also recognized him with an award because the stories had led to the arrest of a major middle-man pouring stepped-on coke and crack onto the streets of the city's ghettos and barrios.

All this made no sense to Jesse, or to those few who eventually found out about his illicit affair with the drug world. One taste, one journey with the drug coursing through his system and a necessary relationship had begun. And it lasted substantially longer than any relationship he'd had with a woman.

Women, he'd decided, were a distraction. They were nice, but not necessary to reach his goals. He stopped "wasting" his time on softball, satisfied with just dusting off the trophies he'd won over the years. His family occupied even less of his time. His parents were dead. His only sister was long gone and living a Bohemian life on some forgotten island off the coast of Washington state. Jesse saw her life as a waste.

His crash came after several bouts with respiratory infections and bloody noses – a side effect of cocaine use. The burned linings of his nasal cavities had become a Petri dish for germs. The over-the-counter nasal spray he'd chronically used so that he could breathe through his nose quit working and Jesse got sick enough to be forced into a doctor's office. There he learned that his blood pressure was off the charts, his mucus membranes were fried, and the irregular heartbeat he'd been feeling was not, as he had convinced himself, normal arrhythmia. The physician also correctly identified the source of these symptoms. Jesse insisted it had been a one-time experiment and promised never to indulge again. This promise lasted until the next time.

It happened on the 405 Freeway, as Jesse was rolling on a hot story involving hostages, a possible militia member and high-powered explosives. His adrenaline was pumping, as it always did before getting to an active scene. He was driving his sleek, black BMW Z3, weaving in and out of the lanes and keeping an eye out for the Highway Patrol. It was unlikely he'd get a ticket. The cops gave him great latitude. But a stop would lose precious minutes. He had pushed the speedometer up to the far side of 90 mph and was passing a van when the pain pierced his chest. No warning, no numb arm or palpitations, just unbearable pain that stole his breath away and folded his body. He tried to pump on the brakes and steer toward the median strip but a white light wiped out his vision. As he drifted away he heard the distant sounds of crashing metal and screaming brakes. At the blurred edge of consciousness, he saw his sister's face. She was smiling.

After all the surgeries, first to save his life and then to repair his over-taxed heart, Jesse had no choice. He'd been confronted by death: his own and that of the woman he'd sent to the hospital when his car careened into hers. He had defied the dark passage. She had not. Although the doctors knew there had been cocaine in his system at the time of the crash, Jesse would not be charged with manslaughter. He'd had a major heart attack and it would be very difficult to prove the direct causal link. This nuance of the legal system brought no comfort to Jesse. For the first time in his life, he was confronted by a self he'd refused to acknowledge. It was a questioning self, a self that demanded honest answers, one that could not be fooled by rationalizing or inventing excuses. It was a self that would forevermore feel pain. The woman he killed left behind a young son.

After his body healed, Jesse traveled to Bainbridge Island, where he spent nearly a month with his sister, Andrea. They'd gotten to know each other better, although Jesse still could not talk about the cruel reality of the accident. He did, however, let Andrea care for him. He accepted the small gestures of kindness and attention to his comfort, no longer afraid that dependence meant weakness or failure. They had never been close. Their parents had played them against each other as children. The idea had been that competition would foster personal excellence. For Andrea, never as quick as her younger brother, it had fostered jealousy and acceptance of her perceived inferiority.

By the time that Jesse decided to return to life and work, they had repaired some of the childhood damage. He discovered a bond that had existed even before, while they lived their separate lives. It was that inextricable link that brought Andrea's face to his last moments of consciousness on the freeway.

When Jesse was clean and feeling stronger, he made plans for a new life, one that was far away from the source of easy drugs, from the life that had held him prisoner for nearly two decades. It was no longer important to be a meteor rising in the newspaper world, nor would it be safe. Jesse cashed in his retirement, IRA and fifty percent of his stock portfolio to buy the *Timberline Times* in faraway Redbud. He knew no one there, had no career plans, and had, in fact, never been to visit the region that spanned two national parks. His prior vacations had been to more exotic destinations: Barbados, Costa Rica, Bali, and New Zealand. Not surprisingly, he'd returned with top-notch travel stories that were snatched up by a syndicate the minute he shopped them around. All Jesse's vacations had been working ones. Before packing his bags for the mountains, he made one final move to atone for the past. He set up a T-bill account for the son of the woman who died in his crash, an anonymous endowment to be given to the young man when he turned twenty-one. Responsibility for the woman's death would never heal like his broken bones.

5 / SUNRISE SERANADE

In Redbud, Jesse found what he was looking for: the lack of nearly everything he'd ever known. The town, tucked in the hollow of two pine-covered mountains, had one stop sign located at its far end where the road forked to go up the mountain or around the nearby lake. It also seemed to lie in an alternate time zone, punctuated only by the sound of the horn from the mill calling crews to the first shift and – when there was one – the afternoon shift. Best of all, there were no cocaine dealers in sight, no slick suits and fast cars or slippery money trading hands.

Once behind the publisher's desk of the *Times*, Jesse had to reign himself in. Catch himself when he'd felt like a racehorse at the starting gate. It would have been easy to turn the *Times* into the best small market weekly in the nation, or at least the West Coast. It seemed that, in the absence of another newspaper Jesse could have, once again, been inspired to compete against himself.

But it was a different man who waited for the metro reporters to finish interviewing Andy and the sheriff. Never before would Jesse Kilgore have been satisfied to sit on the sidelines, simply listening to news being created. Young Andy's face was flushed with excitement. The TV cameras loved him and, not surprisingly, the boy loved them back. When the media headed back down the hill, the sheriff strapped Andy into the passenger's seat of the cruiser and took him on a short ride before dropping him back at the trailer. Jesse was scribbling his own notes, looking for an angle on the story that wouldn't be old by the Thursday publishing date.

He calculated the murder would become a pawn in the ongoing conflict between loggers and the young group of activists who camped on the outskirts of Redbud. Already there were rumors of a march to the mill in remembrance of Chris Lance and an assumption that a bitter logger was responsible for his death. According to the sheriff, there was little evidence to lead to this conclusion other than the open rivalry that had divided the town for many months.

Jesse made a list of people he would call or visit in compiling the story. Naturally, Big Don Dyke, the mill boss, would be a primary source. It had been Big Don who informed the unlucky workers about the layoff. He'd also been a key player in the earlier confrontations between loggers and the activists. Contrary to what his name might indicate, the boss was a peaceful man, not given to quick anger. But still, few people wanted to challenge the man inside the Paul Bunyan frame.

Of course, Jesse planned to talk more extensively with the sheriff and get some direct quotes from Andy as well. He would have to do the unpleasant task of calling the family of the deceased, and also talking to his friends. Jesse correctly figured that the leader of the local activists would soon contact him and make certain the group's position would be included in the story.

Anticipating where the story would lead, Jesse decided to make his first visit to Mac MacDougald, owner of the Red Mac Logging Company that, among other things, included the local mill and 180,000 acres of forestlands. He called MacDougald at his rambling estate home and made an appointment for ten a.m. the next day. Big Don, at the mill, said he'd be free shortly before noon. Jesse figured he'd drive up to the makeshift settlement of the activists after that. He wanted to give them a little time to cool off after the shock of losing a friend. However, it wasn't long before he heard from the movement. It came in the form of a press release, faxed and emailed to his office and, Jesse figured, every other news outlet within a hundred-mile radius. The contact person was Mark Kingsley, designated public voice of the group. He was an articulate and bright young man who could write short and to-the-point press releases. Had he not had such an obvious agenda, Jesse would have considered hiring him.

The press release began with comments from Mark on behalf of the Save Our Forests for Tomorrow, Inc., (referred to by the public as SOFTI). It expressed deep sadness about the death of Chris Lance, who had devoted two years of his young life to rescuing the forests from the devastation of the mountain's "chainsaw mentality." Without making any direct accusations, Kingsley intimated the murder might have been in retribution for the layoffs at the mill.

"We can only hope that the sacrifice made by Chris Lance did not arise out of the anger expressed by those who cling to the past," the quote read. "Times are changing and we will all have to adapt. Violence will not forestall the inevitable enlightenment of the public regarding our environment." Kingsley went on to call Lance a "martyr for a just cause."

Sheriff Blair walked into the newspaper office just as Jesse was looking over the photos that Skipper had emailed him. Blair pulled off his Stetson and sat down in the chair in front of Jesse's desk.

"Sheeee-ut! We didn't need this." He noticed the letterhead from SOFTI and helped himself to the press release. After digesting it, he said, "A young guy gets killed and then, with no evidence of who might have done this thing, he gets used as a political pawn. First thing, right out the gate. You're not gonna print this are you?"

Jesse laughed. "Not a chance. The day I print a release from any side in a controversy is the day you can take my press pass away from me. This kind of thing is predictable. I would have been surprised if I hadn't gotten this from the group." Jesse identified two photos to use in the next issue. "Anything new?"

"Nothing of substance," Blair answered. "The coroner looked over the body and said the obvious. It looks like the kid was beaten to death. From the imprints on the body, he guessed the weapon might have been a big chain. Other than that, we didn't turn anything up at the scene. There were too many tire tracks from the road bein' traveled so much, and that spot where the kid was found is a fishin' hole. Lotsa people left their footprints. I think our only hope is to find the murder weapon, which is probably laying at the bottom of a deep spot in the creek. Who'd hang onto something like that?"

"I've known some pretty stupid bad guys," Jesse said. "We used to publish a column called *Dumb Crook of the Day.*" He smiled at the sheriff. "Like the car thief who jimmied open the van on Sepulveda, hotwired it, and raced off. Might have worked if the van hadn't been a stake-out vehicle full of cops in the back!"

"Point well taken," the sheriff laughed. "Nevertheless, I don't think we're gonna have much to go on, which is bad because we don't need folks pointing fingers. I've already got some of that happening with my own men."

"Yeah, I overheard Gorring speculating that it looked like the work of one of the local Indians. Where does that come from?"

The sheriff shifted his weight in the chair and grimaced. "Doesn't surprise me. You know I inherited a few deputies with attitudes. That boy is one of them. Isn't a bad cop, but I've heard a few rumors and I am watchin' him. I hear he has something very personal about the locals."

The men talked some more about the case and Jesse knew there would be an additional day to gather any updates from the sheriff, if they became available. The afternoon was ebbing and a slow chill drifted into the mountain air. That was one of the many things that Jesse had come to love about his new home: the changes from day to night, from one season to the next. Southern California never displayed herself with such bold variety. He seldom took notice of nature while he scrambled like a rat in the city, not until she demonstrated herself in the form of a 7.5 earthquake. Even then, in the midst of the shaking and rolling, Jesse was thinking of what the hottest angle on the story might be.

They moved outside and Jesse locked the door

to the newspaper office. The sheriff was half-sitting on a redwood railing, adjusting his hat.

"I s'pose this'll be a pretty big night for little Andy," he said. "I expect we'll see him on the six-o'clock news!"

"The kid was excited all right. I just hope he doesn't have nightmares over this. He's putting on a pretty brave front, anyway."

"Don't you worry about Andy," the sheriff said, shaking his head. "The boy is tough. Has to be to live with that mother of his."

"Yes, I met her this afternoon. Works as a waitress?"

"That and whatever else comes along, if you get my drift. The kid deserves better." The sheriff gave his hat one final twist. "Well, probably see ya tomorrow. Guess we'll both be pretty busy."

Jesse drove home through the twilight, taking the sharp curves on the narrow road with practiced caution. In the five years he'd been covering news in the sprawling mountain area, there had never been an incident like this. There were plenty of fistfights and drunken brawls, an occasional knife fight, drunk driving incidents, trailer fires and forest fires, and a slew of car vs. truck wrecks that ended in fatalities, but never a brutal murder.

The hope that the Sheriff's Department would compile evidence for the conviction in the murder was little more than wishful thinking. Sheriff Blair knew it and Jesse knew it. In fact, Jesse was thinking that the only way there might be a conviction in the case is if the killer confessed. Until this unlikely event happened, there was one thing that folks in the Redbud region were masters at: speculation. Gorring's guess would not be the only one.

Jesse pulled off the pavement and onto the dirt road that led to his cabin and along Jackass Creek. He passed the yellow tape of the crime scene, but all the action was done, press and police gone. He split off on the dirt road toward his own twenty acres. When he'd turned his back on city life, he'd done so with abandon. He'd purchased an experimental four-room house that featured innovation in the form of solar heating, wind generated power, and alternative building materials. Part of his small house was buried in the hillside and grass grew wild over the roof. This technique added heating and cooling efficiency to the structure. The walls were curvilinear, not a ninety-degree corner in the place.

After a year of "roughing it," Jesse had electricity and phone service brought in from the main road, but made few other concessions in his "alternative" lifestyle. He liked to be reminded that it was Mother Nature who was really in charge. His sister had been a big help to Jesse in making the transition to a simpler life and also in being flexible enough to admit that a few modern conveniences were a choice, not a compromise. She'd taught him to make humility part of his emotional vocabulary. Once again, he'd wondered at how poorly – and inaccurately – he'd judged her and her lifestyle in the past.

Now he had a sufficient wifi connection and access to other news websites including the one showing Andy's interview. He continued to refuse to have a television in his sanctuary, although video online came pretty close. What he saw that night was spectacular. Jesse had to admire the ingenuity of the reporters. Since they missed the dramatic shot of the body being carried to the coroner's van, they caught it at the opposite end, being unloaded at the department's morgue. The news anchor had announced that "graphic language could be used in the report and viewer discretion is advised." Jesse found out why. The coroner, a retired general practitioner who had once directed the local little theatre, performed like a veteran. Without making any assumptions about the cause of death, he relayed a detailed description of the condition of the body that Jesse, as a writer and witness, would have spared the reading public. Due to the coroner's theatrical experience, the report included a good deal of Shakespearean delivery. The man had a wide vocabulary and excelled in adjectives. He even found an opportunity to use the word "macerated" in his description of the severe pounding the body apparently received.

Andy's interview closed the segment and Jesse was pleasantly surprised. The boy talked like an educated young person. He described his discovery of the body without once using a double negative or slaughtering the English language. He'd said, "I thought something was wrong and I was scared, but I had to look anyway. At first, I thought I'd found a pair of hands floating in the creek but later I saw they were still attached to poor Mr. Lance. It looked as if he took a very terrible beating!" This, of course, was entrée for the reporter to ask Andy to describe the body. "It was bruised all over, especially on the head. There were big gashes where he had been bleeding but the blood was all washed away and it kinda looked like a trout filet, you know what I mean?" The story then went on to describe the town of Redbud, with its naiveté and lack of serious crime, and its deep rift between old-time loggers and new age environmentalists.

Jesse built a small fire in his woodstove for the night. Soon it would be warm enough to leave the clerestory windows open all night, letting in the smell of Sugar Pine and Incense Cedar and the music of the wind in the trees. He looked forward to the morning, which would bring gentle light filtered through pine boughs, falling on his face from the window above his front door. He never needed an alarm clock. In fact, he never had. In his previous life, he'd worked in his sleep, planning, creating, scheming and ever aware of the passage of time. Then, he awoke out of fear. Now, he slept in empty peace, nudged awake by the breaking of a new day.

6 / LOCAL CHATTER

It dawned like a Prokofiev symphony, glorious and triumphant. The sun cast a gentle pastel glow on the ochre earth and the air still held the crispness of lingering spring. Jesse showered using water stored from his solar system – short and not accurately described as "hot" – and headed out for the Eagle's Eye.

The covey of elders had already gathered. Herb was ordinarily a latecomer because he had a gas station to run. True to tradition, it was Charlie holding forth.

"This is just another nail in the coffin of this town," he was saying. "You ask me, it's directly related to uncontrolled growth and Redbud becoming one of them 'bedroom' communities for the

Flatlanders ... Exceptin' current company." Charlie raised his cup in a salute to Jesse. "There are things happenin' here that wouldn't have happened in a thousand years if we didn't have all this here population growth. What do you think, Jesse? Am I right?"

"Sure seems like Redbud was meant to be a peaceful spot. And I do appreciate you putting up with me, Charlie." Jesse grinned and wondered if the day would arrive when someone wouldn't feel the need to apologize to him after taking a swat at the flatlanders. He grabbed a copy of the Central Valley Sun and put two quarters in the fishbowl Daisy had set by for paper sales. People made their own change as needed. The bowl usually ended up a little ahead when the day was done. The excess was donated to Daisy's church group for charitable works.

"Well, look at it. We've been goin' along and makin' a living up here since I was in short pants." Charlie laughed at this image of himself. He was always clad in a pair of denim overalls that left his big belly free to breathe. Today, Charlie could not hope to see his toes, and a pair of short pants was a comical thought. "When did the trouble start? I've been around for a while and I'll tell you when. It's when those young'uns moved up here and started all that environmental noise. Since then, it's been nothin' but downhill."

Mr. Merryweather, the business owner, cleared his throat. "I have to admit what you say is true.

But it's more than that. A lot of those transplants haven't got any regard for local economies. They don't even understand the concept. Most of 'em shop for their groceries down in the valley, before they even get home and then they wonder why we all seem so poor. No loyalty."

"Those youngsters ain't got no money, anyhow," Flip offered. "Some of 'em ain't got a pot to piss in!" This made the men laugh, because it was a known fact that the makeshift homes in the settlement had no plumbing, although a few portable toilets had been set up.

Daisy emerged from the kitchen and set a cup of coffee in front of Jesse. "Mornin'," she said.

"Mornin'," Jesse responded with a smile.

"Breakfast?"

"The usual."

"Comin' up," Daisy said in her sweet voice that was reserved mainly for his ears. "Ralphy, I need two over easy, hold the spuds, wheat, dry." This she hollered over the clang of pans and the roar of the grease fan.

Ralphy, her oldest son and fry cook, hollered, "Say hi to Jesse for me!"

"Hey, Ralphy," Jesse waved at the pass-through.

"I'd sure like to know how they make it," Mr. Merryweather said. "Seems like none of em' have a payin' job."

"I can tell you about a couple of them," Paul, the silversmith, said. He stroked his long beard and leaned back in his chair. "I've seen two or three of them at arts and craft shows down in the valley. They do pots. Pretty nice ones, if I remember correctly. Sometimes a person can do real well at those shows. It's their bread and butter."

Paul was younger than the rest of the crew, but still white-haired, with a beard that would have done a hermit proud. In fact, there were many weeks on end when no one saw Paul. They'd say he was working but not really understand how making jewelry and pen casings could classify as genuine work. Jesse, who'd already done a feature story on the artist understood quite well how one could make such a living, particularly when one of your major clients was Tiffany's of New York. Jesse adopted a conservative tone in the article, agreeing to keep Paul's success low profile since the Tiffany moniker might encourage the wrong kind of visitor to Paul's workshop . The other reason Paul wanted his anonymity was his chronic habit of pot smoking, which he kept to himself. He cultivated his very own supply and strictly limited the number of people who knew exactly where he lived. That's why when Paul spoke, all the men listened up. He was odd, but in an interesting way. Like what you didn't know about him got your attention.

"Well, I don't hardly see how that can pay the

bills," Mr. Merryweather pronounced.

"What bills?" Charlie croaked. "I hear they're livin' up there free of charge."

Merryweather stroked his chin. "I believe that's part of the old Winston spread," he said.

"I thought that was all left in some trust, or something," Charlie added.

"It was," Mr. Merryweather affirmed. "And the executor of the trust, some flatland, weasel-nosed, liberal lawyer gave them permission to squat. I checked."

This was new information for the men and it called for a chorus of responses. Even Jesse made a note of it on his ever-present, old-fashioned reporter's notebook.

It was then that Herb made his appearance. He came in rubbing his hands together for warmth, and smiling.

"What the hell you got to grin about?" Charlie demanded. "Come on, pull up a chair."

Herb grabbed the back of a mismatched chair from another table and parked himself among the regulars. Daisy caught his eye and headed over with his favorite mug full of black coffee. Herb waited until he could wrap both hands around the hot cup and the steam wafted up to his face. "Cold morning," he began. "But I gotta tell ya', there's never something bad that happens without somethin' good comin' out of it."

"What, you sell a bunch of gas to folks runnin' outta town this morning?" Charlie chuckled sarcastically.

"Better than that," Herb answered and took a sip of coffee. "You know how Andy always comes by my place every mornin'? And how I have to shag the boy off to school, or wherever he goes from my place? Fishin', for all I know. Well, he didn't come by this morning and I got a little worried after all that happened." He lifted the cup to his lips and paused.

Charlie had no patience. "Get on with it for God's sake, Herb!"

"Well, I called his house at the risk of wakin' up that mother of his ... which I did, and she tells me that Andy left for school as usual. Well, then I called the school and they went and got his teacher. Nice woman. Some pretty name like Sofia." Herb looked around appreciating the rapt attention he was getting. "She told me that Andy was in school. That the boy was early! Don't that beat all?"

The men grunted in agreement. They were hoping for news that was a bit more dramatic, although Andy being at school, much less early for it, was indeed an unusual event.

"I expect it was that news on TV last night," Herb added. "And the story in the valley newspaper this morning. The boy did himself proud. Must be one of them 'minor celebrities' at school.

The talk turned to the murder once again. Although no one wanted to admit it, they agreed there was a good likelihood they would know the assailant. There were no strangers in the folds of Redbud's hills. Sooner or later, everyone had to come to town for supplies. People respected the right of privacy for individuals like Paul who wanted to hideout occasionally, but they wouldn't tolerate a person who flat-out ignored the unspoken code of Redbud society. They also agreed, with deep regret, that the guilty party was probably someone from the mill.

Jesse half-listened to the speculations and scanned the story on the front page of the Valley Sun. He was very surprised when he turned to the jump-page, to find a photograph of Andy seated on top of Jesse's desk. The photographer had caught the boy's impish look in a Norman Rockwell moment. It would, Jesse knew, create a few proud moments for Andy.

Jesse checked the time. Already half-past nine. He said his farewells to the boys who had no specific appointments to keep, and headed up the road to talk to the richest man in the entire county. Mac MacDougald had inherited the timberland tradition. His father, grandfather and great grandfather built the business from a family-owned milling operation to a major lumber firm with more than a hundred thousand acres of private timberland in California, Oregon, and Washington. Redbud now accounted for less than one-third of the overall operation and was quickly falling in production. The days when the Redbud Mill kept three full shifts busy were long gone. Now, even the one shift appeared to be threatened.

Mac, as the town knew him (and had known his father and grandfather), built a rambling house atop a hill overlooking Redbud. It was grand without being pretentious. Warm cedar and river rock instead of cold granite. Windows with sweeping views from the backside of the house. Mac and his kin were products of the mountain environment, which didn't approve of bragging or showing off.

Jesse turned off the main road onto a winding drive. About a mile up, an arched gate constructed by a local stonemason framed the main driveway. The house was wrapped in windows and supported by a foundation of artfully assembled river rock by the same mason. Mac had been conscientious about employing local labor to build his house.

Cars could be spotted all the way down at the beginning of the road before they disappeared into the tree cover, and the head of the MacDougald dynasty was already on the front porch waiting for Jesse. He was a strong man in his early fifties. He'd surprised nearly everyone when he chose to remain in Redbud and carry-on the family business. His predecessors had been seat-of-the-pants lumberjacks and businessmen. After a couple of years of travel on his own, young Mac had returned to California and gotten himself a Stanford education. Everyone expected that Mac would be off to

66

bigger things, a more stimulating business environment, but he chose to stay on the mountain.

Jesse pulled around the U-shaped drive and parked his car. Mac met him halfway.

"Jesse, good to see you, though it's not the best of circumstances." The two men measured the same height, a couple inches over six feet. However, while Jesse had the body of a man who worked to maintain muscle, Mac had the frame of a mountain-bred logger: sinewy, rather than buff, with skin weathered by the sun and hands callused from manual work. He still prided himself in being able to ride into the woods with a crew and put in a day's labor. Mac's dark curly hair, peppered with gray, framed the cheekbones of a Scots Highlander. Bright blue eyes met Jesse's.

The men shook hands and went inside to Mac's study, a spacious wood paneled room with a rock fireplace that covered an entire wall. A vast picture window opened up over the valley and framed the town and mill below. The house was tastefully decorated and one hundred percent male. Mac had never married, making him the most desirable bachelor on the mountain, a distinction he found both amusing and a little embarrassing. They sat down in leather easy chairs and talked about the murder and the layoffs. Mac expressed his deep regrets over both events and Jesse let his digital recorder take notes. Mac was articulate and educated, easily quoted for stories. Finally, the conversation steered in a more useful direction. Jesse was looking for the bigger picture. How it all fit into place.

"Off the record?" Mac asked.

"Off the record."

"You know this is where my family started. Our roots are here. It's the last place I'd want to shut down. But I gotta tell you Jesse, Redbud has become a real problem for us. You see, my granddad and dad took real caution to make certain the company wouldn't be depending upon timber from public lands. Granddad bought up thousands of acres and my dad kept it as private forestland. My dad in particular had an uncanny sense for which way the political winds were blowing. He said that any operation that depended on cutting for Uncle Sam would be in big trouble. So he expanded our holdings so that we can sustain our own without getting in bed with the government. We're in such good shape that last year we only cut two percent of our forestland to meet our timber goals. Mostly, we're in the business of managing our forests for health and sustainability. We don't need federal timber sales to survive."

"That's why you didn't fold when so many of the other independents here and in the other Pacific Northwest states couldn't make it." Jesse had heard the story before. "Why do you suppose you're having so much trouble here then? It's your own land."

"Damned if I know," Mac said getting up to

pace in front of the great window. "Maybe it's just the political climate, or the climate, period. It's warm enough for relocated Southern Californians yet cold enough to feel like a new life in the mountains. They're creating issues, Jesse, where there aren't any. Hell, I'd be crazy to cut the few old sequoias I've got or that old growth redwood at the coast property. I've got plenty of trees for lumber. I'll tell you, sometimes I'd like to kick those enviros in the butt. They just don't get our life up here. And don't you quote me on that."

"We're off the record, remember?" It was keeping true to that statement that helped build Jesse's reputation. Never, even in his man-eating days, had he betrayed that simple three-word promise.

"And while we are, let me tell you what really gets me going. It's how they're using this spotted owl thing to achieve very narrow political ends. Look into it, Jesse. Look at the new research about where the bird lives and hunts and breeds. It's all politics. Makes me think about running for office."

"You serious?"

"Half-way. I'm not ready to say, yet. But you'll be among the first to know. I'll even wait for your publishing day, so you can scoop the valley folks." Mac grinned tantalizingly but the sound of the telephone pierced the moment. "Mac here." He listened and Jesse saw Mac's body language change. "Yes, call the sheriff but ask him to come alone. Just him. I'll be right down there." Mac gave Jesse a glance. "I expect that Jesse from the paper will be over there too. Just keep the trucks inside and the drivers quiet. I don't want them to say one word to those dang people."

He put the phone back on the cradle and leaned both arms on his desk. "I've got a pretty big bunch of picketers outside the gate to the mill yard. They apparently won't move aside to let the loaded trucks out. Jesus, what a mess!"

"I didn't think there were enough of them to pull something like that off," Jesse said.

"These aren't just the locals. Big Don said they bused up a bunch from the valley. There's a mob." Mac grabbed his leather jacket and car keys. "I'll tell you, Jesse, there are definitely times that I've seriously considered the offers I've been getting on this place. Hell, the insurance alone is killin' me."

The men hurried to their separate rides and Jesse filed Mac's last comment away. He'd remember to ask more about those "offers." Before starting the Wrangler, Jesse took advantage of the altitude to use his cell phone, which had spotty reception down in town. He reached Skipper at the office and told him to get over to the mill with his camera.

There were three entrances to the mill. One for the public to come and go and two for trucks either leaving the mill loaded with logs or returning empty. Most of the crowd was gathered outside of the exit for loaded trucks and a smattering – about a dozen people – stood by the gate for the empty trucks in case a driver tried to get out that way. There appeared to be close to a hundred people, mostly young, carrying signs and wearing expressions of excitement, anger, and righteousness.

Jesse parked his car near the visitors' gate and walked over to the crowd. They were chanting, "Chainsaws, no! Let trees grow!" and pumping their signs into the air. A young man wearing a red checkered wool jacket, not unlike the ones favored by loggers, quickly noticed him. Jesse recognized him as Mark Kingsley. Mark was in his mid-twenties, soft-spoken and a dedicated environmentalist. He had tousled, dark auburn hair and ruddy skin that was used to the outdoors. His complexion contrasted with his hazel eyes, giving the young man a slightly exotic look that set him apart.

He'd told Jesse he had come to Redbud to "make a real difference." Jesse respected the young man's intentions and had observed the same dedication among other true believers in conflicts and stories past. Mark was a good kid with a cause, who wasn't afraid of going public.

The young man lowered his sign and walked up to Jesse. They nodded in greeting to each other. "Want to tell me what brought this on?" Jesse asked, already knowing the answer. Many of the signs bore the name of Chris Lance followed by: "Cut down, May 20, 2005."

Mark easily went into his message for the

media. Jesse recognized the language from the press release. He pulled his recorder out of the pocket of his jacket.

"We are making a statement here about the terrible price that we continue to pay so that the rich can get richer at the expense of the environment," Mark said. "Chris Lance was cut down just like the trees we are trying to protect."

"Why do you think there is a connection?" Jesse asked.

"It seems a little too coincidental that on the day when business at the mill takes a bad turn, one of our people gets murdered. We aren't saying that a logger did it, but there is a lot of anger up here and most of it is directed at us."

"Mark, let me ask you this. How are you going to feel if it turns out that Lance was killed for entirely different reasons, something completely unrelated?"

"To tell you the truth, I don't think we'll ever know who did it."

"Why is that?"

"I don't think that law enforcement in this town is going to look very hard. If it had been a logger who had been killed, they'd be all over our place, looking for someone to pin it on. But we know whose side they're on. We're used to it."

"What do you hope to accomplish here, today?" Jesse asked.

"We want to bring attention to the depth of the problem with the industry in this state and how far they will go to stop us."

"That's a pretty radical statement."

"Murder is a pretty desperate act," Mark said.

Jesse spied Skipper rolling up in his beat-up yellow Gremlin. He figured it was one of the last running specimens in the state. "I'm going to ask my photographer to take a few shots," Jesse said to Mark. "Don't give him too much grief, okay?"

"No problem. You're not the enemy."

Jesse signaled to Skipper to get busy, walked back to his car and silently admired Mark and his cohorts for standing by something they believed in. He had never had that kind of conviction. Even as a young man, he'd been a reporter focused on "objectivity" and getting more than one side of the story. Oh, he'd had his personal opinion plenty of times, but he never had a passion for anything, except for getting quotes like the ones he'd just gotten from Mark.

At the edge of the young crowd stood Tommy Thompson, half-sitting on the fender of his Mercedes SUV. Thompson owned the local DVD store, a couple more in the valley and a stretch of property adjacent to the mill. Because the environmental group had gotten permission to camp out on land next to his, Thompson had built a rapport with the young people.

Even though he was a good fifteen years older

than the protestors, he had a way with them, having gotten to know them at his store and in passing. Their "encampment" adjoined the west border of Thompson's land and Tommy didn't want trouble. He raised his index finger in salute to Jesse who returned the homegrown gesture.

Tommy was a short, stocky man who reminded Jesse of the Welsh miners who once answered the summons of the Gold Rush. Soft facial features balanced his broad chest and big biceps. Tommy looked tough, but saved it for business. It looked like Tommy was keeping a post on the sidelines, waiting to move in and talk a little sense to the young people, if necessary. Jesse gave him a thumbs-up and felt comforted that someone would be monitoring the action.

Inside the mill, the tension ran thick. Mac stood behind his desk, consoling Big Don. There was a marked contrast between the two men. MacDougald was trimmed and polished and, although he wore a flannel shirt and blue jeans, looked ruggedly elegant. Big Don Dyke was about two inches taller and half again as wide as his boss. He wore work boots caked with mud and a pair of Stihl Saw suspenders that arched across a modest belly. His face was weathered and hands raw from a lifetime of working the woods. But what Big Don was known best for was the size of his heart.

"Jesse," Big Don said in greeting. "Guess this hasta be in the papers?"

"I'm afraid you might hear from more than the *Timberline,* Don. I think the valley folks might find this interesting after what happened yesterday."

"That's all I need."

Mac took charge. "I'll handle the press. You take care of our drivers. Get out there and tell them that under no circumstances are they to make any moves against those kids. Tell them to go ahead and go home. Quietly, with no verbal exchanges on the way. They'll all get paid for the day."

He turned his attention to Jesse and waited for the recorder to appear. "For the record, I want to extend our shock and sorrow over the death of Mr. Lance. We sincerely hope there is a good arrest in the case and the perpetrator is brought to justice. We also believe there is no connection between this operation and that horrible event. We understand how his friends and colleagues up here feel a need to express themselves. I also want to say that I am personally looking into what this company can do in memory of this young man. Not because we bear responsibility in any way, but because it is what we would do for any of our neighbors."

"What do you have in mind?" Jesse asked.

"Once again, Jesse, you will be the first to know."

Just then a screaming horn from the mill erupted in three long blasts. Mac's posture turned rigid and Big Don dove for the phone. He punched a red button. "What!" he shouted. There was short pause. "My Lord, ... you called the Doc and the fire department?" Another pause. "I'll be right there. You did the right thing." He swung around to face MacDougald.

"There's been an accident. One of our sawyers went into the planer. They think he's gonna lose a leg. There's a lot of blood but he's conscious. Our guys got him in a tourniquet already and they called all the right people. I'm going down." Mac nodded and Big Don moved faster than a man his size ought to be able to.

Jesse immediately saw the potential for more trouble. "You know, when the kids out there hear a siren coming up the hill, they're going to think it's coming for them."

"Son of a bitch! I didn't think this could get any worse," Mac said, rubbing his brow. "Can I ask you a favor, Jesse? I know it's not in your job description but if I go out there or send one of my people, they won't believe it, and we need help to get here without any delay."

"No problem." Jesse was out the door and carrying the message. "Tommy's out there already, but he doesn't know the details. I'll get him to talk to the kids. They know him. I'll go tell Mark Kingsley myself. We just talked."

Mark didn't want to believe it. "This is just a diversion to get the trucks out," he guessed, when

Jesse told him the news. "Take my word for it. The owner sent all the drivers home and a man's life is at stake. Do you want to take that chance?"

It was then that Thompson stepped in to do his thing. "I heard," he said, nodding to Jesse and looked at Mark. "Smart thing to do would be to cool it. If a mill worker in there died cause your friends had been a barrier to medical help, it wouldn't help your cause much."

Mark was silent for a beat and then got it. "I'll spread the word. We won't get in the way."

Jesse figured the group would stay because there was still the possibility of more press showing up. Big press. For a rag-tag bunch of kids they were pretty media savvy, he thought.

Jesse and Thompson moved away. Jesse admired the man. If Redbud had a "leading citizen," Thompson would be it. He sat on the school board and probably could've been elected mayor, if the town had a mayor. "Thanks Tommy," Jesse said.

"I just want to keep the heads out here cool," Thompson explained. "How's the guy inside?"

"Pretty bad. They're working on him. News travels fast."

"Yeah, I heard it from a driver. Hope he's okay. Know who it is?"

"I don't. They called local emergency, but it looks serious. I don't think we can handle it up here."

"I'll say a prayer, Jesse."

7 / THE STAG SCENE

John Didion, the local volunteer fire chief and former Army medic in Vietnam, had raced up the hill to administer emergency medical attention, but Redbud wasn't prepared to deal with the gravity of the injury. MacDougald used his head (and influence) to convince the nearby Forest Service operation to send their helicopter to transport the man to the hospital in the valley.

Didion kept Begae talking. Sure that he was dying, Begae sent a heart-felt message to his wife and kids - then another to Big Don. "He said to tell you it wasn't his fault," Didion later reported.

As he stemmed the bleeding, Didion told the man he'd live to be a hundred. Said he'd repaired "way worse" injuries in Nam. It was positive chatter to make Begae's spirit stronger than his failing body.

The sheriff also arrived and he and Jesse stood in the "saw room" where the accident had occurred. Between the protest outside and the emergency inside, operations had all but ceased for the day. Mac and Big Don had sent the crew of sawyers home, but not before Jesse overheard the men wondering about what had happened. They knew their jobs were dangerous. Working with high speed steel blades that rotate at 6000-plus rpm's involved risk, even with plenty of state safety regulations and an owner who insisted on exceeding those requirements. It wasn't unheard of that a sawyer lost a finger or sustained some injury. But falling into the saw? That needed some explaining. This was the worst accident in the mill's recent history – at least since the early 1980s when a man fell to his death from a cat-walk.

Sheriff Blair and Jesse approached the pit area where the 36-inch saw blade stood silent, painted with blood that had already turned from red to rust. The floor was littered with sawdust, also violently colored by the accident. A waist-high wooden wall and an elevated walkway sur-rounded the area, separating the workspace from foot traffic. The metal gate to the saw area was open wide.

Sheriff Blair leaned over and examined the gate. "Check this out, Jesse."

The latching mechanism was like a deadbolt. It had to be turned and then slipped out of a catch on the railing. It was designed so that it couldn't be left in the open position, with a spring that shot the bolt back into place as the gate automatically swung shut. Jesse and the sheriff looked down at the broken edge of the bolt, raw and shiny like a new wound.

"It looks to me like this was sawed off, Jesse. See those striations?"

"If it had snapped off, I think the break would've been clean," Jesse said. "Suppose we can find the broken-off end?"

"Worth a try," the sheriff said. "It's been pretty trampled here but we might get lucky. Let's start by the gate and work our way back." No grid work or crime scene investigators for Redbud. Jesse had adapted to the hometown methodology.

The men dropped to their hands and knees, and felt and sifted the layer of sawdust and chips that covered the floor. It was possible that the end of the bolt had been removed entirely but Jesse figured that finding it might indicate what kind of implement had been used to cut it – information that could be useful in a trial. His fingers moved carefully through the debris. The alcohol smell of new cut wood wafted up his nostrils.

The sheriff, owing to the size of his belly, moved slowly. "Best not to mention this to anyone, yet," he said. "Shee-ut, my knees weren't made for this!"

They worked their way about two feet from the railing when the sheriff kneeled back. "Got it!" He held up a two-inch piece of machined metal. One side was jagged and sharp.

Jesse let a handful of shavings filter through his fingers, leaving behind an embossed cigar band. "Good work," Jesse said and for no good reason slipped the colorful band into his shirt pocket. "If you get some official word on that by dinner tonight, give me a call. We put the paper to bed about six. Otherwise, it's off the record."

"Appreciate it, Jesse."

It was early the following morning when Jesse finally got a report on the injured mill worker. It originally looked as if the man might die, but thanks to Chief Didion's heroic efforts, emergency surgeons had pulled him through. Later, Didion told Jesse that he'd seen much worse on the battlefields of Vietnam, but admitted the lumberman's injuries could easily have led to death. Blood loss was severe, but that was something Didion had dealt with all too often.

A phone interview with Begae's surgeon in the valley affirmed Didion's actions. He told Jesse "If the volunteer chief hadn't been so competent, the man would have, at the very least, lost his leg and, most likely, his life.

Jesse scribbled his notes and was pleased. He had a great quote and even better news. Ben Begae would live. But, the prognosis for a full recovery was not good. The doctor speculated that millwork was probably not an option for his future. There was still a chance the leg would have to be amputated, but at least Begae's wife would have her husband and the couple's two children would have a father. However, behind the news and looming across his mind like a storm cloud, was the awareness that Begae's fall into the saw might not have been an accident. Furthermore, the young father was probably not the exact target. A weakened bolt could have broken against anyone's weight. It appeared that someone intended for an "accident" to happen and didn't care to whom or how severe.

Sheriff Blair called from the valley with the same topic on his mind. Expressing relief that Begae would make it and pride in the volunteer fire chief, he told Jesse in confidence about his short conversation with the injured man.

"He was pretty drugged up and in pain," Blair said. "And he knows that he's damn lucky to be alive. So, before he nods out, he calls me over and says quiet-like, 'That gate busted right open. I just leaned on it a little and lost my balance.' Said he didn't want to get Dyke in trouble or anybody else, but wanted me to know. Said he thought it might be sabotage by the enviros in response to Lance's murder. Then he was out like a light."

Blair said he planned to be back in the early afternoon and report the severed bolt to MacDougald. But, given the already volatile climate in the town, he would suggest that the information be kept confidential. Jesse agreed.

By nightfall, the sheriff and Jesse were in the Silver Stag. Jesse sat down at the end of the long bar, nursing a cup of Irish coffee. The bar was hewn out of walnut that had been brought in by wagon during the glory days of the region. Pitted and stained and burned by countless cigarettes and cigars over the decades, it was a mute repository of history. The wall behind the bar was covered with mirrors and bottles of everything from the cheapest whiskey to imported liquors that were rarely poured. But most remarkable was the woman behind the bar.

Rita was firmly in middle age, and it seemed she started her life that way and would remain there. She was taller than most of the men she served and her shoulders, nearly as wide. She wore her hair pulled straight back from her face in a loose ponytail and wore no make-up. Rita was a combination of no nonsense and one hell of a sense of humor. She had the physical confidence to handle the fights that predictably sprang up toward closing time, and could swing a mean baseball bat that even the drunkest men respected. She once told Jesse she kind of regretted never having married and having children, but figured the bar and its loyal customers were plenty family for one person. This wasn't said with any self-pity, just stated as a simple fact.

Sheriff Blair was sipping plain black coffee and

sitting on a wooden barstool next to Jesse. They were waiting for Rita to get caught up on drink orders. A group of men and a handful of women from the mill had drifted in for a quick one before going home. The beer flowed and a handful of fancy drinks were concocted. The jukebox was playing a new piece by Tim McGraw and Jesse found himself liking it. In L.A., the mere thought of country music had been off-putting. He looked around. For the Stag, it was a quiet crowd. The events of the week were putting a damper on after-work revelry.

The watering hole was decorated in vintage taxidermy. Animals from Redbud's extended backyard shared the gallery with those from afar, glass eyes staring down from the walls and rafters of the expansive room. The head of a grizzly bear with bared teeth and a six-pointed buck hung next to the head of a cheetah, the latter courtesy of an old WWII soldier who had picked it up while stationed in North Africa. All manner of fowl, small critters like fox and squirrel and pheasant decorated the walls. In various stages of deterioration, the small animals had been stuffed whole, set in supposedly natural poses. But the centerpiece of the Stag was a floor-to-ceiling fireplace, built of local rock that still held veins of gold.

Rita worked her way toward the men, wiping the bar with a white towel as she moved. It was the custom in Redbud, even if you were the sheriff, to open a conversation with pleasantries, questions about family, the weather. Anything but come to the point. But Rita wasn't much for formalities.

"Guess you're here about the other night," she said, mopping up the ring that Blair's cup had left on the bar. "What can I tell you?" She favored Jesse with a smile that, on someone else might have been coquettish.

"Well, Rita, you can tell me, exactly as you remember, what happened on the night the kid was killed," the sheriff said. "Who was here, what did they do? There's no tellin' what little detail might help us."

Rita began to reconstruct the night, saying that she could tell the minute the mill crew came through the front doors that something was wrong. She'd been through a number of cutbacks, and felt the pain and fear like it was happening to her too. She identified the handful of men who had gone a little over limit with drinks that night, including Choker. "It's guys like him that I feel really sorry for," she said shaking her head slowly. "All his life, all he knows is the mill and the woods. I don't think the guy even graduated from high school, but he's been able to make a living for that family of his. I hear his one son is pretty sharp, getting scholarships and all. Guy like Choker isn't going to find another job. And, somehow, I just can't see him on welfare, or whatever they call it nowadays."

"Did he have any trouble?" the sheriff asked.

"Naw. He just drank a little too much. Talked

to Hardesty a little and hightailed it home. About nine, if I recall. Anyway, it was right when the fight started. Guess he wanted no part of that."

"Fight? Details, Rita," Blair said.

"It was those two hotheads from the Redbud Rancheria. Hazlett and Birdsong. They got into it about the mill layoffs. I think Hazlett got the boot and Birdsong didn't. I don't know why they were arguing. There's not two years of difference in their ages, but they're shoutin' about 'seniority.' Of course, Hazlett was drinkin' tequila shots. I told him not to. Said I'd tell his aunt. But that didn't stop him."

Jesse listened – he kept quiet when Blair was working – and pictured Hazlett. A remarkable combination of Native American and Irish. Straight red hair, dark skin, and hazel eyes that changed from green to brown, depending on the light. The kid could ride a horse like a rodeo star. He proved it last Fourth of July when he leapt bareback onto an Appaloosa and scattered the tiny parade on Main Street. Shouting war whoops, pulling the horse up onto its hind legs in a Lone Ranger salute. Of course, as he often was when not working, Hazlett was bombed.

"They started to fling chairs around and turned over that table in the corner. But I was on 'em. Convinced them to knock it off or take it outside. Then, I called Hazlett's Aunt and Birdsong's brother. I told Hazlett I called his aunt and he was outta here like a shot. Birdsong's brother came and got him about fifteen minutes later. Other than that, no action all night. Most folks were pretty stunned by the mill news and didn't need any more trouble."

"You see that young Lance at all?"

"Not in here! You kidding? Last time I saw him he was coming out of the store and getting into that little pick-up of his. About three in the afternoon. What a shame." Rita leaned toward Jesse and Blair and lowered her voice. "You know, those kids don't mean to hurt anybody with their ideas. I think they really believe they're doing the right thing. This environmental thing is like a religion to them; God bless 'em. But they just got a lot to learn." That said, Rita scanned the bar. "I'd better get back to pourin' and wipin' and listenin' to sad stories."

"Thanks, Rita. I appreciate your time," the sheriff said and raised his coffee mug to her.

The two men sat at the bar for a while and talked quietly about the circumstances of the case. Earlier in the day, the sheriff told MacDougald about the cut dead bolt. The broken piece that he found in the sawdust had been sent to the county seat for microscopic examination. But Blair knew what they'd find. He'd been in law enforcement long enough to recognize that the metal had been sawed through. MacDougald was very concerned, the sheriff reported.

"I tell you Jesse, the man's head was reeling. He said that meant that somebody in his own shop had done it. The saw rooms are locked at night. They had some trouble with guys coming in after hours to use the tools so Mac has the place sealed up after the last crew is out.

"Isn't there a guard, too?"

"Sure is. After they started havin' troubles and those protesting kids got a little brave, Mac hired a security guy. Stays on through the night. And, he's got a dog. A Queensland. You know how sharp and protective those things are."

"So, either way, on shift or overnight, it would be pretty hard to saw off a bolt."

"Right. And here's an extra problem," the sheriff said. "If we go in there askin' around, folks will know that something's up. I'd like to keep this quiet as long as possible."

Jesse had been around Blair long enough to read him like a book. "You've got an idea."

"I do. And it requires, as usual, your complete discretion. The newspaper hat has to come off."

Jesse's curiosity was piqued. The sheriff trusted him to go on an interview like the one he'd just conducted with Rita and suddenly he's talking about "discretion"?

Blair sat straight and looked Jesse in the eye. "I'm thinkin' about sending in our new Deputy Rose. He took a sip from his already-empty cup.

"Okay, I'll bite. Why?"

"Well ... and this is the sensitive part and I

can't tell you everything ... but Rose might look like an 'affirmative action' hire. That and lookin' like a rookie kid. But she's not. She's got seniority and experience under her belt. So, I figure that everybody is pretty much going to discount her. Underestimate her. I'll brief her and she'll know what we know. I'll send her in to talk to the crews. They'll think its routine, maybe training for the new kid, her being a woman and all, and they won't pay her much mind."

"Well, it might work if she's as good as you seem to think she is. In fact, back in the old days when I wanted information that I couldn't get, I admit to sending in a good-looking intern to ask my questions. Usually worked. So what's this Rose's first name?"

"Sorry, Jesse. I've told you more than I intended already. Why? You interested?"

"Hell, no! She's a baby. I could have a daughter as old as her."

Blair erupted with a belly laugh that sent little shock waves through his body. Jesse saw Blair's rotund tummy quiver like Jell-O.

"You'd be surprised, my man. You'd be surprised."

Just as the sheriff was swallowing his amusement and patting himself on the back for what he didn't tell Jesse, the front doors banged open and framed Deputy Gorring, standing like a six-gun cowboy in a dime western. Gorring strode into the bar carrying a garbage bag. The recently mentioned Deputy Rose entered quietly behind him. After making certain all eyes were on him, Gorring walked across the plank floor to his boss.

"Got a little somethin' for you," he announced, and dropped the bundle on the bar with a loud clatter.

Blair paused and looked at Gorring. "Maybe you should tell me what's in the bag."

"Right." Gorring cleared his throat. "I have every reason to believe this here is the murder weapon. It's a standard towing chain that was tossed clear to the opposite bank of the creek. It was sitting in ten inches of running water for more than twenty-four hours, so there's not much chance of evidence bein' on it."

Jesse glanced at Rose in a new light. Her face was stoic and she was doing her best to blend into the background. Without being obvious, Jesse examined her face for signs of age he hadn't seen before.

"So, how'd you find it?" Blair asked.

Jamming his thumbs under his woven leather belt, Gorring said, "I thought we needed another look around the scene so we went back this morning. Dang! It took a long time but at about three this afternoon we found it! About fifty feet downstream from where the body was, only on the other side. Bingo!"

Jesse checked out Deputy Rose's expression.

Not a clue to what she was thinking. Apparently, this had been a one-man operation.

"I'll tell you what," the sheriff said, placing his hand on top of the plastic bundle. "This is just real valuable evidence and we sure do want to look at it. Just not right here and right now. How about you leave it with me? And, by God, damn good work!"

"Thanks, Sheriff. I gotta say that Deputy Rose was in on the search, too. Hope it's the breakthrough we're lookin' for."

The admission that the woman had played a role in the find must have been a hard one for Gorring, Jesse thought. Rose herself seemed intentionally disconnected from the dialogue.

Dismissed, the deputies left and shortly after, Jesse and Blair were standing in the parking lot of the Silver Stag. The sheriff was still driving the uncomfortable sedan. He popped the trunk open and checked the parking lot for people. No one. He dropped the plastic bag into the trunk and gently rolled down the edges. From the light at the top of the trunk they saw a dull, but clean chain. "How many folks up here you figure own a chain like this?" the sheriff asked rhetorically. "For whatever good it'll do, I'll send it off to the lab." He slammed the trunk shut on Choker Anderson's chain.

8 / CONVENIENT ARREST

Jesse spent Tuesday putting the paper to bed. In its past manifestation, this activity had been labor-intensive for the owners of the paper. Full-sized paste-ups of all the pages had to be delivered over fifty miles away to the web press printer. In the old days, layout artists, typographers, and editors had to hustle to meet strict deadlines. Back then, work at a newspaper had been physical.

In a way, Jesse hated to see those days disappear. But publishing was a competitive business and he wanted more than a hobby. Jesse had immediately installed PCs with powerful publishing programs. He worked with the printer down the hill to set up electronic publishing and the results had stunned everyone, including himself.

The cost savings were tremendous and the time ... well, the electronic process took days off the publishing schedule.

For Thursday's paper, Jesse wrote an up-to-date account of the murder, trumping the daily with details about the scene and background that the city reporters hadn't thought to investigate. He'd also been able to break the news about the discovery of the chain. He was very careful to keep the sheriff's proprietary information to himself. Jesse wasn't even tempted to use it. In his new life in Redbud, friendship and integrity were far more important than a big scoop. He'd also written up the incident at the mill along with an account of the protest outside.

One thing that had become important to Jesse was a new style of writing he'd discovered after coming to the mountains. He hadn't wanted to do it. The council at the Eagle's Eye had convinced him he had to. It was an editorial column that was one hundred percent opinion. His opinion. Jesse had never done editorial writing before. In L.A., he aimed for the kind of objectivity that would win prizes, not hearts.

Of course, he was not objective about his stories. He had lots of feelings driving the style in which he wrote. He became very subtle and effective in packing a story with attitude discernable only to himself and a select few.

But now, his weekly column was a forum for opinion and he experienced an unexpected freedom and, yes, power, in writing it. The town, Charlie had patiently explained to him, needed a focal point. When the newspaper had become an advertiser, that center was lost. After all, they had no official mayor or city council. An opinion column by the publisher would motivate folks to talk about civic things. To care out loud about Redbud. Surprisingly, Mr. Merriweather agreed. Of course, he was afraid that, with Jesse being a flatlander and, worse, from LaLa Land, he might tend to be too liberal. Nonetheless, he felt the concept was entirely accurate and he was willing to take the risk.

Jesse, knowing that acceptance would be the key to his future in the town that didn't suffer outsiders easily, acquiesced. It was the birth of Jesse's respect for the council of elders. This week, he used the opportunity to try to pre-empt the polarity that was brewing in the town. He wrote about jumping to conclusions and gave a couple of extreme examples from his past as a big city reporter. He hoped his words would move even a few people to reconsider the direction in which public opinion had been heading. This was a new kind of winning for Jesse and he was grateful.

The *Timberline* would be delivered from the printer's in the morning, dropped at rural homes by pick-up trucks and hand delivered by the local ambassador who walked the town throughout the afternoon. It would contain the good news, the bad news, Alice's column – badly written but cherished by the townsfolk – the new column by Jesse, great sports shots by Skipper, and a story also written by Skipper, that called for some gentle editing.

Alice was an elderly woman who, Jesse felt, could not write her way out of wet facial tissue, much less a paper bag. However, her columns contained vital information that no one else could gather. Who had visited whom. Who had a baby or a birthday. Who had an operation or an unfortunate encounter with the law. It was the *National Enquirer* of Redbud, without super-imposing photos of one celebrity's head on another's body. It was honest and it was true. Alice Forest worked the phones like the best big city gossip pros, and her column was critical to the readership of the *Timberline*. Jesse was so damn glad he had recognized that and just let Alice's column run with very little editing, even when a great deal was needed to pass journalistic muster.

Leaning back in his oak office chair, he felt the combination of satisfaction and fear that came with the publishing of every paper. He hated like hell to find the mistakes, and they would be there. The publishing of each paper was like a birth. Perhaps a minor birth, admittedly, but he felt tremendous pride of authorship. The phone interrupted his drifting thoughts. It was Blair.

"Jesse, I got a situation. My cowboy is ridin'."

"I'm guessing that means that Deputy Gorring has made some moves on the case?"

"Right. Now, ordinarily, I would reward this

kind of initiative. But I know where it's comin'
from. Gorring is none too fond of the Tomah and a
little too eager. I think he's heading down a dead-
end road. Meet me over at the Rancheria?" The
Rancheria was a loose collection of homesteads al-
lotted to the Tomahs by the much hated federal
government Bureau of Land Management in the
early 1900s.

Jesse locked up the office and went down to
the dirt parking lot where Ginny and Rob, who delivered the paper to distribution points, were load-
ing copies of the *Timberline Times* into their pick-up
truck. Jesse stopped to give the couple a hand with
the last few bundles, thanked them for their work,
and jumped into the Wrangler. It would have been
refreshing, he thought, if the whole thing had
moved in a less predictable direction. Of course,
Gorring had his mind set on the murderer being
one of the locals and he'd conveniently found Hazlett to pin it on. Jesse wondered about what evidence the deputy might have that wasn't available
to himself and the sheriff.

The Rancheria was up a hill just to the north of
town. It was hidden by a stand of ponderosa pines
that towered so high into the mountain sky they
seemed to brush the clouds. The beauty of the forest was dazzling to Jesse, and he often wondered
how he'd lived so long without experiencing the
blessings of nature. However, he knew the great
pine trees were not there for beauty, but because of
the scene that lay behind the stand of trees: the

ramshackle lean-tos that some of the Indians called home. The trees had been spared from the chainsaws to block the view of poverty and blight.

Although some of the Tomahs had built family homes on the lower part of the six hundred acres vested to them, the newer construction had been done further back from the road, a little up on the hill where there were vistas to be had. The section closest to the road was an eyesore. Wooden shacks were roofed with tarpaper and corrugated tin. Windows were boarded up or covered with plastic. Carcasses of old cars were scattered everywhere, acting as convenient shelters for the packs of dogs that roamed freely.

This poverty was unmatched, even in the big city ghettos and barrios that Jesse had visited. It was shameful because of the history that created it. It was a poverty of spirit that had been stolen by the U.S. government. It was a sign of human betrayal and it made Jesse angry every time he saw it. He pulled onto the road that wound through the lower quarter, as the locals called it. He drove slowly, looking out for children and puppies, occasionally raising his hand to acknowledge a man or woman sitting outside on overturned plastic buckets. He sensed tension in the air, knowing that Gorring, and perhaps the sheriff, had already been through and folks knew something was up.

Jesse spotted the patrol cars up near the demarcation line where squalor ended and the landscape slowly transformed. There was a collection of small houses, old but maintained, and the residents had eschewed the urge to collect old cars and junk piles. It was clear the people were still poor, but they did not live as if they were in despair. This, alone, Jesse found amazing.

The sheriff was leaning against his Bronco, in conversation with Gorring. Jesse looked at Gorring's car and saw that, in the back seat behind the cage, there was a young man with long, red hair. The deputy had apparently nabbed the Hazlett boy. In the front passenger seat sat Deputy Rose, who appeared to be talking to the prisoner. Jesse looked then at the frame house with its peeling paint and waning respectability. Framed in the front door was an old woman, small and dark, with her shoulders rolled forward and arms crossed. She stood stoically, not watching anyone in particular. Just waiting.

Anna Sister Longreed had been an elder of the tribe for as long as anyone could recall. No one, including Sister herself, knew her accurate age. She was there when the loggers had come up the hill and first built their houses and stores. She was a child when the white school was built and the Indian children were beaten if they spoke in their native language. Sister had lived a lot of history and emerged wisened by the years, seemingly without any enduring anger. She was sought out as a counselor, and many people believed she had special powers. Jesse, who once would have scoffed at such an idea, found himself in agreement.

98

Perhaps, he thought, Sister was summoning those powers now to free her nephew from yet another encounter with the law.

The sheriff nodded to Jesse, who got out of his truck and waited for a sign that it was okay to approach. Blair gave him a wave and he walked over to the men, glancing at Sister and giving her a respectful nod.

The sheriff was dismissing Gorring. "You take him over to County. And Gorring, I'd better not hear you laid one hand on that boy." Blair paused and looked the deputy in the eye. "Be best, I'd think, if you let Rose book him through. You stay a mile away."

Gorring smirked. "You think a lil' gal like her can control that wild one?"

"Better than you appear to control your mouth," the sheriff shot back. "Not a finger, you hear me?"

"You got it." Gorring strode back to the patrol car. The deputy had a way of swaggering when he walked, leading with his chest and turning his feet slightly out. Part of a practiced arrogance, Jesse thought.

The sheriff shook his head in exasperation. "I came out here prepared to cut the boy loose. Figured Gorring was engaged in a little wishful thinking."

"You mean he actually has evidence enough?"

"It's thin," the sheriff replied, "but I'd be remiss

if I didn't hold Hazlett while we did some more investigating. Gorring went over to the hardware store and talked to old man Jeeter. For a change, Gorring didn't stack the deck ... I mean he didn't go in there and say, 'Any Tomahs bought a chain, lately?' Says he asked Jeeter who had bought a chain in the last couple months. Asked him to write down a list. Well, it was a pretty short list. Bernie at the feed store bought one. Mrs. Einsbrook, that widow over by Three Corners. And Hazlett."

"That's enough to arrest him?"

"Not nearly, but it set Gorring on an expedition. You know Hazlett drives that old International? It's a joke around here about how he runs four different brands of tires on that thing. Never can afford a whole set so he gets re-treads and mixes 'em up. Well, Gorring goes back to the creek where we found Lance's truck and looks for, guess what?"

"Tire tracks."

"Yup. Of course, even though we roped it off, there were tire tracks all over the place from before. But when you're lookin' for something real specific, it gets a lot easier. Gorring found a set that matched Hazlett's about fifteen paces from where that little pickup was. That's evidence that Hazlett was there."

"What does the kid say?" Jesse asked.

"Says he's not talkin' to anybody. He's been

through this drill plenty of times before. I believe he has the mountain record for getting busted. Small stuff, usually. Almost always associated with getting drunk."

"Rita said he was drinking pretty hard that night."

"Yeah. Poor guy just got laid off."

"Sounds like you don't want Hazlett to be guilty, Sheriff."

"Tell you the truth, I don't. He's a rabble-rouser and he's lost. Got a serious drinking problem and he's only, what, twenty-three? His family has been through enough." Blair glanced up at Anna Sister, who still stood in the doorway, even after Gorring had driven away with her nephew. She was, as before, staring into the distance as if seeing something unrevealed to other eyes.

"And both Hazlett's parents are gone, right?" Jesse asked.

"Father killed in a logging accident when the kid was about four. Mother committed suicide when he was twelve. No wonder he's a handful. Sister, here, has tried to guide him. He does respect her. I've seen him helping her out, taking her to the store, fixing this old house of hers. But he just can't tame that wild side and his drinkin' doesn't help."

"There will be a number of people who'll think this case is now closed," Jesse observed.

"Yup. Folks on all sides. The enviros won't like

that it's a Native American, but Hazlett was also a logger, so who knows? The handful of rednecks up here will be satisfied it's an Indian."

"How about you?"

The sheriff examined the pointed toe of his dusty black boot. "I don't think he did it. My gut tells me he didn't, but my head tells me I gotta pursue all the evidence, like it or not. I suggest we keep a very open mind on this."

Blair told Jesse he was sending Deputy Rose to the mill that afternoon, without Gorring, and that he'd be following up, asking more questions of people at the Stag and around town. "If you could maybe poke around here ... talk to the kid's friends ... see if anyone saw him later that night, I'd appreciate it. You know they don't take too well to this uniform. Bad history up here. I want to change that, but it's gonna take time." Blair carried the burden of those thoughts on his shoulders as he drove back into town.

Jesse stood and watched him roll down the hill, thinking the sheriff was right. It was too easy to pin the murder on Hazlett and the kid was all that Blair had described. Wild, but kind. Lost, but perhaps not forever. Jesse knew a lot about being trapped and lost, and he wanted to help.

As a newcomer, he'd made a good connection with the community. He'd gotten on well with the Tomahs and done several articles about their culture and celebrations. He'd been invited to attend ceremonies that were generally off-limits to outsiders.

The drumming, the chanting and singing, the dancing and language of dreams had reached deep into Jesse's soul and touched a place that had been unattended. Now, he looked at Anna Sister and watched for a sign that he might approach.

She turned her head toward him almost imperceptibly. Jesse walked to the stairs and looked up at her and, out of respect, waited for her to speak to him. Anna Sister's face was etched with time and her eyes were small flames that burned with a knowing. Her hair was silver and pulled back to the nape of her neck, where it was gathered in a beaded barrette. She hugged a small blanket around her thin shoulders.

They stood in silence for some minutes and then, without looking at Jesse, Anna Sister spoke. "This will not happen to my sister's boy. His spirit is wild and free, like the water that cuts through this place. It goes over the rocks, around the land. It bends and flows and it cannot be stopped." She extended a bone-thin arm and her gnarled, brown fingers traced a landscape in the air. "He is Running Water. That is what his name means in our language, the name he took of our people." She was silent again and Jesse waited. "I know you understand," she said and looked at Jesse. "He is water and he has fire in his belly. You have burned with this fire, too," she paused. "My nephew did not murder that young white man."

"I will ask questions, Anna Sister. I'll go talk to your nephew, too, if you think it will help. The sheriff isn't assuming he's guilty, either."

"Sheriff Blair is a good man. But some of his people are not good. "

Jesse also thought about something else she'd said. Only Blair knew about his former drug addiction and then not in great detail. He was mystified, yet not unsettled, by her insights. "And I'll see if I can get some legal help for your nephew, other than the public defender."

Anna Sister looked at him again and nodded, her expression never changing. She turned and went into her house.

9 / The Wild One

Although Jesse had all the respect in the world for the old Indian woman, he needed to hear the story from the kid himself. He stopped back at his office for messages, hoping there weren't any delivery problems. Ginny and Rob's truck was about twenty years old and, in the absence of "Triple A," Jesse had performed many a rescue. He also called the elementary school and inquired about Andy. Andy, he was told, was still collecting interest on his television appearance. He'd been in school, on time, all week. It was a classic "mixed blessing," Jesse calculated. He called the Sheriff's Office and Blair said he'd be welcome at the jail. Hazlett had just been processed. He'd been cooperative, but not talkative. The kid, after all, knew the drill by heart.

105

Jesse drove down the hill to the Gold County jail facility just on the edge of Goldrush, a small city and county seat. Not fifteen miles away, but in a different county, was the valley's major metropolitan area, Westfield, home to four television stations and the daily newspaper. Had the murder happened in Westfield County, law enforcement resources would have been abundant and the personnel better trained. Gold County was like a neglected stepchild when it came to state and federal funds for crime fighting. When Blair ran for office, he'd promised to change that.

From Redbud to the valley, Jesse traveled down a winding two-lane road that passed through enough natural beauty to feed the soul a bountiful meal. The drive took him about a half-hour and he'd spent the time thinking about his curious reaction to Anna Sister and her people. Jesse was a skeptic, by nature and by professional training. He'd never been willing to suspend logic and let go. That was the thing about cocaine. It seemed to sharpen your edge, not dull your sense of the moment. It heightened that feeling of rubbing up against reality and moving fast, a sensation that Jesse loved. He realized now that it hadn't made him a better reporter, but at the time, he felt like he was moving at warp speed. Living high, sinking low, burning out.

But that didn't compare to the feeling he got when sitting with the Tomah men around the drum circle. Or when he closed his eyes and listened to the singers. He'd been able to let himself drift, float on the tones and words he didn't understand. At first, he'd tried to snap himself back to "reality," then told himself that to write a really good story, it was okay to surrender to the moment. Finally, he'd realized it was just all right to surrender, even without a goal in mind. It was safe and it felt good. It was reality. These were things he didn't entirely understand and, in a way, liked it that way.

Jesse pulled into the paved lot in front of the sheriff's station just as Deputy Rose was climbing into a patrol car. They'd never spoken before, but were aware of each other from unavoidable encounters in the small community. Blair had piqued his curiosity about her, so Jesse welcomed the opportunity for some one-on-one.

"Deputy Rose, we haven't formally met," he said, extending his hand and gifting her with a smile that, he'd been told, would melt snow. "I'm Jesse Kilgore, publisher of the *Timberline Times*, which I think you already know."

She took his hand with a firm and dry grasp, a good sign. "Of course, I know who you are. I've been looking forward to meeting you."

"Any first name attached to 'Deputy Rose'?" he asked out of burning curiosity.

"Not for the record," she said. "You can just call me Rose."

Definitely getting the idea that this was a

domain to which he didn't have the password, Jesse laughed and said, "Right. Rose. Wonderful name!" He paused. "How's the prisoner?"

"He's scared," she answered and Jesse recognized that she might be older than twenty-nine. "And, I'd bet my favorite dog that he didn't do it."

"Can I have a few details?" he asked, wondering just how many dogs Rose had.

"First, let me say that the sheriff let me know that he and you, well, talk. He said it's okay to keep you up on the case." She paused and gave him a look of suspicion. "Frankly, it's the first time I ever heard of a lawman trusting a newsman. But, whatever the sheriff says."

"I guess we all do things differently up here," Jesse responded.

"You got a point there. So, the Hazlett kid. I know that he's had a lot of experience being a guest in this particular jail. I understand he's a chronic hell-raiser. But, right now, he's experiencing some genuine fear."

"I have to admit, I've never seen Hazlett in that state. Usually – at least when he's bombed – belligerent is about as far as he goes," Jesse said.

"I suspect you're right. But I trust my intuition, and the kid who was talking to me is scared and ... I think, probably innocent."

"Did he have any comment about the evidence? The chain, the tire tracks?"

"Yeah. He said he could explain."

"Did he?"

"No. He's not stupid... and, for a change, he was sober. He's not talking without a lawyer. I didn't push him for details... didn't want problems, if it came to a trial. You won't have the same problems."

Jesse was looking at her as she talked. Around the crystal clear, blue eyes were lines as thin as a spider's web. And her confidence and comfort with the law were much too firm for a rookie, though she looked young, innocent.

"I have to get over to the mill," she announced. "If I find anything, I'll tell the sheriff and see where it goes from there." She ducked into the patrol car and looked up at him through the open window with eyes the color of new denim.

***

The inside of the county jail was the color of dull despair. The walls were a dusty hue, lying somewhere between beige and gray. Metal desks and worn Formica countertops completed the institutional ambience. Jesse was ushered into a ten-foot square interview room that held a table and two chairs, all bolted to the concrete floor. Hazlett was escorted into the room by a guard that Jesse recognized from visits past. The men exchanged nods as the officer led Hazlett to the other chair. The prisoner's legs were in shackles, his hands in cuffs. The guard stepped silently outside the door that led to the belly of the jail. "I'll be right outside, Jesse. Just give me the word when you're done." He didn't appear to have any worry about Hazlett. After all, this particular prisoner was a regular guest.

Jesse and Hazlett greeted each other like relative strangers. The young man kept eye contact at a minimum, a natural response to the situation and to his culture, where eye-to-eye was an implied threat and indicated a level of disrespect.

"Your aunt asked me to talk to you," Jesse began. "She's very worried about you."

Hazlett slowly shook his head. His long hair was loose. He couldn't wear it back in the ponytail that was his style because the jailers stripped him of any potential "weapons." Elastic hair bands qualified.

"I don't want the old woman hurt," he said. "This is all wrong." He looked up then at Jesse, into his eyes. "I done a lot of things. I made her real sad. But I sure didn't kill that white boy." He bowed his head as if in shame, fingers intertwined on the table. "Do you think you can help me?"

Jesse paused. He wasn't prepared for this level of responsibility. He was a reporter, not an advocate. But this was Redbud and a new life with new rules.

"I told Anna Sister I would try," he said. "I need you to tell me about that night. I need you to believe that I won't write about this. I guess I am asking you, without much justification, to trust me."

"If Sister asked you to talk to me, that's enough reason."

Jesse leaned forward, his elbows on the cold tabletop. "The night that Lance was killed. I want you tell me everything you did from the minute you left work until you went home and went to bed." Jesse already knew about part of the night from Rita. He was interested to see if the stories matched.

"Well, ol' Dyke called me into the office about four, just as the shift was ending. He had to drop the bad news to everybody who was gettin' laid off. Shitty job. All day long, the guys at the mill were waiting to hear their names called. Said it was like being on death row." Hazlett shifted in his chair and the chain holding his ankles scraped on the concrete. "Us, being out in the woods, we got the axe when we got back. Crappy thing is, if I wouldn't have been off for four months last fall – cause I was doin' a little time in this place – I would've had enough seniority to have made it through this round."

"So, you left the mill at what time?"

"Doesn't take long to say 'adios.' Dyke told me, I turned around and got the hell out. Must've been about four-thirty. I went right over to the Stag with everybody else who got laid off. Stayed there 'til about nine or so. Lotsa people saw me. You can ask."

"Anything unusual happen while you were there?"

111

"Yeah, but it wasn't nothing. That baby Bird-song come in about six. He made it through the day and still had a job ... guy is younger than me. Pissed me off. We started to get into it, but ol' Rita blasted from behind the bar with that tire iron of hers and it was over."

"So. What was your condition?"

"I'd been drinkin' pretty steady, but slow. I guess you'd say I was basically shitfaced. But I knew it and I didn't want no more trouble, so I left."

"And went where?"

"Well, here's the hard part," Hazlett said and pulled his hair back from his face. "I went over there by Jackass. See, I thought I was doing a good thing by leaving and going to sit by the creek for a while to try to get a little straight before goin' home." He cupped his forehead in his hands and closed his eyes. "Shee-it, I saw that enviro's pick-up sittin' there alongside the road. I figured that's all I'd need. To get into it with one of them. I was just gonna' turn around and get outa there."

"Was?" asked Jesse.

"Like it's not bad enough. I was starting to drive off and I see a perfectly good chain layin' along side the road, little up from where the pick-up was sittin. Damn!" Hazlett was shaking his head over his bad luck or stupidity. "So, I jump outta my truck and pick the thing up and throw it in the back. I just had bought one of those suckers new, just two weeks before and some sonofabitch stole it outta' the back of my truck. I figured it was one of those 'gifts' a guy gets from the universe now and then.

Anyway, I drove straight out and I went home to sleep it off."

"Did you tell the sheriff this, or anyone?"

"I'm not as dumb as I look. I need a lawyer for this one. I ain't said nothin' except that I didn't do it."

"Where's the chain now?" Jesse asked.

"When I heard the guy was beaten to death with a chain, I got rid of it. Jesus! It's gotta have my fingerprints on it!"

Jesse felt like he had to extract every detail. "And ... where is it?"

"I don't exactly think I should tell you... or any-body. That could be the nail in the coffin that peo-ple like that pig Gorring are looking for."

"You know they found a chain? In the creek, a little way up from the body."

"I heard. But that one doesn't have my prints on it and the one that I found does. Wouldn't Gor-ring love to find that?"

Jesse decided not to press the kid any harder. He asked him to recall if there were any other de-tails he'd noticed during his trip to Jackass. "I'll see what I can do about getting you a lawyer," he told Hazlett. "If it's any consolation, there are quite a few people who think you're innocent. You've got some friends out there."

"I done a lot of stupid things," Hazlett said, looking up at the ceiling. "Funny, that night I was going to Jackass, I was going to wash myself in the running water ... wash it all away. I was actually gonna stop drinkin'. Isn't that what you call 'ironic'?"

Jesse left as the guard was leading Hazlett back to his cell. He believed the man. Not only did the brutality of the crime seem incompatible with Hazlett's history, the story he'd told was too dangerous not to be true. If he had been guilty, why put himself at the scene and admit that he'd picked up a chain? There would have been a far safer story to tell.

In the years that Jesse had been living in the mountain community, he'd picked up a kind of vibe that many of Redbud's residents shared. He felt it as he steered the Wrangler back up the hill. Although an occasional trip to the valley was necessary – and about the only source for fine dining and entertainment – there was always a sense of disquiet, a touch of uneasiness that disappeared with the return trip home. Now, as he wound the curves, hugging the grassy shoulder to make plenty of room for any unexpected rig hauling logs or lumber from the mill, he felt the pull of home. It was a sensation – indeed, a place – he'd never

114

before known.

He crested the last hill that overlooked Redbud. There below him lay the town, embraced by ponderosa pines and cedars, engraved with winding roads and meandering Jackass Creek. The landmark that lay at the far end of the little valley was the inverted cone of the mill's burner that sent swirls of white smoke into the sky. For some, it was a historic symbol of vitality; to others, it was an environmental eyesore. Each time Jesse mounted the hill and was met by the scene, it was like seeing it all for the first time.

He drove slowly through town, watching out for dogs, cats, kids, and Redbud's "ambassador," Sally, who delivered the mail to all the businesses, even though she didn't work for the post office. Sally had a way of getting distracted and standing in the middle of the street gripping her upholstered bag of mail.

Pulling into the *Timberline* parking lot, he was confronted with two familiar faces. Tommy Thompson was unloading boxes of DVDs from his van and Andy was perched on the railing of the porch that wrapped around the building. The men greeted each other and Jesse gave the Redbud high sign to Andy.

Thompson wiped his forehead with the back of his hand. He was perspiring from the effort of shuffling the boxes into his store on the lower level of the building. "My kids are off at a track meet in Westfield," Thompson explained about his crew of young workers. "I'm too old for this kind of work. How are you doin', Jesse?"

"I'm fine, Tommy. Events around here have been keeping me pretty busy."

"Shame. I just hate it. I heard about the Hazlett kid. That aunt of his doesn't need any more trouble. Tell you the truth, I find it hard to believe he did it. Just not his style. In fact, I hate to sound like I'm stereotyping, but it doesn't sound like any of the Tomahs."

"Well, I share your opinion, and I did just talk to him. Could be he's a classic victim of circumstance."

"He'll be a victim of more than that, if some people have their way." The men discussed the prejudices in the town and, when Jesse suggested that a good lawyer might facilitate justice, Thompson surprised him. "Leave it to me. I have a connection with a nonprofit group down in the valley. They've got funding, and they target minority communities. I'll make some calls."

"That's good of you, Tommy," Jesse said. "I'll let Anna Sister know and I'm sure she'll be grateful."

"I'm a little concerned about how this will play out for the town. I don't think anyone wants an innocent man convicted, especially when he's one of our locals. Even that group of young ones camped out by my place were disappointed when they found it was a Tomah. It's not politically correct, you know."

Jesse laughed. "You seem to get on with everybody, Tommy. That's a gift!"

"Some would call it phony," Tommy smiled. "But I try to look for the good in everybody. I'll make that call and let you know."

Jesse motioned for Andy. "Let's help Mr. Thompson here, come on and lend a hand!" Andy hopped off the rail and sprinted over. He grabbed a box that was almost half his size and led the parade into the store. After the van was empty and Thompson had handed Andy a five dollar bill, the boy followed Jesse upstairs to the newspaper.

Andy sat in one of the wooden office chairs that could spin around in circles, which is what he did as Jesse listened to his voice mail. "How come you're not dizzy?" Jesse asked, hanging up the phone.

"I don't get dizzy," Andy stated and stood up to prove his point. Steady as a rock.

"So. I hear you've been going to school."

"Yup."

"Nice job you did on the TV."

"Yup."

Getting the picture, Jesse fell silent and waited for the boy to talk. He sometimes used this tactic in interviews when there was something the subject did or did not want to say. Andy poked around the items on the top of a desk. Jesse just leaned back and looked at the boy, smiling.

"I've been thinkin'," Andy finally said.

"Yes?"

"I've been thinkin' about that TV man that came up here and put me on the news. That reporter guy," Andy said looking very serious. "I been wondering if that might not be more fun than bein' a mechanic."

"For the right person, I suspect it would be," Jesse said.

"I was thinkin' I might be a mechanic like Mr. Herb, maybe get a job here at the mill when I get older," Andy explained. "But traveling around and seeing exciting stuff and talking on the TV sure does sound better."

"Well, to tell you the truth, the way you handled yourself on that interview, I'd say you have a talent for it."

"You think so? All the kids at school said it was pretty cool. I even gave a speech about it."

"You spoke right up. By golly, I heard you even spoke good English! How about that!"

"Oh, I know how I'm 'sposed to talk. Just 'cause I don't git good grades on tests and stuff don't mean I ain't listenin'." Andy smiled, fully aware of what he'd just done to the English language. "So, what's it take to be one of them reporters?"

"Other than how you talked on television in contrast to how you are talking to me right now?

118

A guy would have to be able to read pretty well, write pretty good, move fast, and always be thinking."

"I can move fast – faster than anyone in my class – and I am pretty good at thinkin'," Andy boasted. "Guess I'd have to work on the other two."

"If you want to do that bad enough, you will," Jesse suggested. "You might start out by watching some reporters on television. Watch the evening news. Look at the big national reporters on the news and then at the local ones. See if you can figure what makes them good."

"I can do that. It would almost be like a homework assignment that I actually did."

"Well, you can't get away from it. You're going to have to get educated one way or another. It's up to you, buddy."

"Heck, I know. I just get bored with school sometimes. I don't know why I'm there."

"Well, maybe now you'll find out!"

"Huh?"

"To make Redbud stand up and look at Andy Winters, news anchor for NBC in, what, ten, fifteen years?"

"Yeah. Maybe." Andy slid off the chair and headed for the door. He turned. "So Mr. Jesse, you won't say nothin' to Mr. Herb about me maybe not wantin' to be a mechanic, will you? I think he was maybe countin' on me."

"Not a word. But I've got a feeling that Mr. Herb would be pretty proud of you whatever you did, so long as it was good and honest work. Thanks for your help down there," he added.

"No problem. I got me five extra bucks. I like that Mr. Tommy. He always has money." Andy slammed the door and made the windows rattle. Jesse sat down at his desk, answered his e-mails, checked the news feeds, and closed up the office. It was downtime in his publishing cycle, a little breathing room before the whole process began anew. He sat looking out the window that faced a thicket of manzanita. Just beyond was the dancing Jackass Creek that fell from the high country, fed by the snow pack of the Sierra, cold and clean. Jesse could see shining glimpses of the water when sunlight hit it just right. He thought about the secret it might be singing if only he could understand the words.

Before heading home, he stopped to visit with Anna Sister. He wanted to give her some encouragement, no matter how small and, truth be told, just be in her presence to figure something out, something far away from his knowing.

***

At the same time as Jesse was driving to the Rancheria, Choker was sitting at a table at the far end of the Silver Stag. From there, he surveyed the cavernous room like he was seeing it for the first time although, in reality, he'd been a regular for nearly 20 years. The massive elk head that hung over the river rock fireplace looked menacing tonight and the other varmints that had been slowly disintegrating over the decades were giving him the creeps. Why don't they take those ratty things down and give 'em a decent burial, he wondered. As a hunter himself, Choker had no real objection to the animals being stuffed and hung as trophies. It was the current condition of these particular prizes that he found disturbing. And then, it was something else all together. He'd had good reason to be thinking about disintegration.

He took a pull on his bottle of beer, hoping to get drunk enough so that recent events slid into a hazy past. He'd been doing a lot of that lately, worrying his wife, who blamed it on the layoffs. But it was more than that. It was having been with the Lance kid just minutes before he was killed. It was knowing that the killer had probably been watching them as Choker helped to pull the kid's truck out of the ditch. It was figuring that it was probably his chain that had been used to beat Chris Lance to death.

Choker felt no relief that Hazlett had been arrested. For starters, Hazlett had still been in the bar when he'd left and he'd seen no headlights behind him on the road. Not only did Choker think the Indian wasn't the type to beat a man to death with a chain, he didn't think the timing would have been right. Hell, the fight was just starting when he left the bar.

Thinking that an innocent local man was in jail and worrying that, if he were to talk to the sheriff, he might end up there as well, put Choker between a rock and a hard place. Laid off and in jail? Never in his wildest, scariest dreams did Choker imagine he'd be in such a place after so many years of hard work and being (mostly) a straight-up guy.

During the last few days, he'd kept himself busy with the job all the jobless did in Redbud. He cut and split firewood. The physical work felt good, but when it was done, Choker was left sweaty and without a future, so far as he could see. By late afternoon, the demons came to visit him and he was obsessed with thoughts about what he might have done differently that night. What he should do now and how he couldn't make himself do it. What he would do for money if the mill held the layoffs through the coming season? This felt very personal to Choker, who measured his worth by his ability to provide for his family. He was fifty-four, for Christ's sake! What did they expect him to do? Take up computer science?

His wife, Mary, said for him to take it easy. They'd been through layoffs together before and survived. The work always came back sooner or later. But Choker felt something in his bones about this one. With each passing day, his thoughts grew darker until he merely went through the motions of the day in order to make it to a respectable hour and return to the Stag. There, he methodically got the demons drunk so they slurred their message and tripped on their tails. After a couple of hours at the bar, Choker could talk to people again and play a game or two of pool. To most folks, he seemed like his old self, only drunk a lot more frequently.

10 / THE CAFÉ COUNCIL

Jesse spent the morning planning the next week's paper. He looked at potential stories and made assignments for Skipper and his young reporter, Katherine. He called his stringer, Alice, to tell her how nice the last column was and to inquire about her new great grandbaby whose birth had been announced in flowering prose in her latest column. He called the ministers from the two local churches, a Methodist and an evangelical Baptist, to remind them to get their next week's work in by Monday. He called the local veterinarian to get his "Critter Korner" rolling, and finally, the local real estate agents, who took turns writing about how to buy property in the mountains. All this one-on-one attention was necessary because, outside of Skipper, the delivery team, the reporter and (of course) the printer, no one was paid.

By late morning, Jesse was ready for a little socializing and walked the length of town to the Eagle's Eye. The breakfast crowd had long gone and what was left was the core of Redbud's council: Charlie, Paul, and Mr. Merriweather. Herb was at the gas station working his regular shift. He would be in at noon for lunch, however, simply putting a "closed" sign on one of the two gas pumps. Regular travelers to the town knew not to count on getting gas between noon and about 1:30, give or take a half-hour.

Sally was handing Daisy a packet of mail and talking a mile a minute. Sally liked to keep up on the news and was always asking someone's opinion as an excuse to give her own. Seldom coming up for breath, she pontificated on government, politics, health care, and the price of prescription medicines. The last topic was dear to her heart because Sally had a variety of maladies, both physical and emotional. She was prone to long bouts of depression, which she covered up by talking almost constantly. She had a tic on the left side of her face that made it look as if she were incessantly winking and she walked with limp. None of these conditions stopped her from making her regular "ambassadorial" rounds with the mail. Business people paid her a few dollars for the service that they really didn't need since the post office was less than three blocks away. The rest of her monthly income came from disability payments and – some people said – from a healthy inheritance left to her by her mother. Redbud took care of its own.

"Mr. Jesse," she said and became flustered. Jesse had this effect on some women, causing them to flirt against their will. "My, well. You must be so busy. There's so much news. Seems like something is happening every minute of every day. I don't know how you keep up." She fumbled in her bag and pulled out a packet of mail. "I can give this to you now if you want. Or I can just take it up to the paper. But I don't know about those steps today. But I sure can if you want me to. Whatever is convenient for you."

Jesse reached out and accepted his delivery. "This will be just fine Sally, and I thank you kindly." He smiled at her, which seemed to stop the thought she'd been about to express.

"You have a very successful and abundant day," she said and ambled out to the street, heading for the drug store where she'd spend some focused time talking medicine with the pharmacist.

Jesse pulled out a chair at the table next to the old men. They'd long since lost interest in their coffee. New blood, however, perked them up. "Daisy, bring that pot over here, will ya?" Charlie asked. "Give Jesse here some java. Looks like he could use it."

Mr. Merriweather set the agenda. "Well, it's not lookin' good for our local boy, is it now, Jesse? I heard a deputy found a chain and then I heard that the Hazlett boy bought one from Jeeter's Hardware just the other day."

"Is that right?" Jesse responded.

"They find anything on that chain?" Charlie asked, not wanting to talk specifically about blood.

"I'm afraid I haven't heard," Jesse said, wondering if Gorring had done some bragging on his own.

"Cain't be anything on it, can there," Charlie ventured, "if they found it in the creek! This time of year, water goes through there like a high pressure hose."

Paul, an authority on the unexpected, chimed in. "That's usually the case. But nowadays they have very sophisticated equipment that will pick up tiny traces of evidence on very corrupted material."

"Hell, how you know that?" Charlie challenged.

"I got a dish," Paul said.

"Don't believe everything you see on the television," advised Mr. Merriweather. There was no cable television in the region and few folks had satellite dishes. It came as a surprise to the men at the café that Paul, the recluse, would be the one to have this window to the world.

"I don't. But I do know something about science and that's entirely possible. They are doin' absolutely incredible things with trace evidence and genetic footprints. They can get your DNA off that cup you're holdin'. Or off from your hat band thirty years from now. They'll know it was you who wore that ratty old hat practically to death. Think it belonged to a poor man!"

Everybody laughed as Merriweather removed his trademark blue cap with 1978 Republican Convention and a donkey's rear end embroidered on the front. Mr. Merriweather was about as far from poor as any man on the mountain, with the exception of MacDougald and, maybe, Thompson, who was "new money".

"Well, I for one, hope the kid didn't do it," pronounced Charlie. "Oh, he's trouble. But he's the kind we understand. Remember that time he rode through the VFW ceremony bareback? And I mean bare – back!"

Paul found this particularly funny and went into a laughing fit that – given his very bad smoking habit – turned into a coughing fit.

"Remember when he 'borrowed' Bernie's mule to pull his Jeep out of the ditch up there by Laughing Meadow? That ol' mule pulled it out and then Bernie got his hands on the kid. I'll never forget that, Jesse. You should've seen it," Charlie recalled. "You know, Bernie is this big guy. Wearin' a patch over his eye and lookin' mean as a rattler. But he's got a heart of gold. So, instead of callin' the sheriff (it was Rockford back then and he was a mean SOB to the locals) Bernie just goes and gets the mule. Grabs the kid by the ear and takes them all back to his twenty acres. I hear the

128

kid thinks he's gonna die."

Charlie was doing everything he could to keep from falling apart with the memory. "The next thing you know, the mule is hitched up to the plow and young Hazlett is ridin' behind him, plowing up Bernie's entire garden. Bernie's there along the fence makin' sure the work goes on till he's satisfied. And, that Anna Sister, she's right there at Bernie's side. Arms folded. Lookin' like she's almost proud of the young buck for his work."

"Ask me," said Paul, who was in an unusually talkative mood, "Hazlett's more afraid of that old woman than he is of anything."

Merriweather chimed in. "That might be a damned good thing."

Merriweather's language told Jesse that this was a very important topic. The conservative business owner rarely resorted to any sort of cursing to deliver his point.

The old man slipped his cap off revealing a mostly bald head. "I gotta tell you, I don't like how things are progressing here. Nothin' has been the same since those kids came up here and caused all that trouble," Mr. Merriweather pronounced.

Paul, having been a flaming liberal for much of his eclectic life, felt obliged to speak up. "Well, you can't just stop time. I won't call it progress and I admit that Mac up at the mill has done nothin' to deserve this, but things just change. That's the nature of life."

Merriweather snorted. He'd learned to like the bearded neighbor who hid out for long periods of time, despite the fact he suspected him of partaking in a certain illegal drug and harboring leftist leanings. "And Mac deserves even more credit," Merriweather said. "I know for a fact that he's been offered darn good money for that mill property and the timberland around it. He'd never have to earn another dime in his life, and neither would his kids or grandkids. But, by God, he's hung on to the operation 'cause he knows it keeps this town alive."

All eyes were on Merriweather, who had just added new information to the collective database, but it was Jesse who spoke. "How long has this been going on? The offers, I mean?"

"Started about a year ago, little after that logger got ripped up so bad from the spike those enviros buried in that big ol' cedar. I thought he'd sell back then. But he bit the bullet and told those city slickers 'no deal.' Good man. Must be a Republican."

That brought a chuckle from his colleagues. "Yeah," laughed Paul. "Nowadays they call it 'compassionate conservatism.'"

Charlie wasn't pleased with being out of the limelight and challenged Merriweather. "So, where did this so-called offer come from?"

"I am not at liberty to reveal that," Mr. Merriweather said. "But it may have not been the first and it certainly wasn't the last." He shut his mouth with determination and folded his arms across his chest.

The look on Charlie's face said he wasn't satisfied with Merriweather's inside information. It was, however, known that the old man had his personal network for news, developed over decades of building trust and family relationships throughout the mountain community. It didn't harm his credibility in this matter that his niece was married to MacDougald's nephew.

The ring of the café's phone interrupted the discussion and Daisy grabbed it. "Eagle's Eye Cafe," she announced. "Food you want to pounce on!!" (This was the result of an advertising executive who had gotten drunk at the Stag early in the day, stopped by the cafe to sober up and had offered Daisy some free marketing advice.) After a pause she said, "Yes sir, he's here." She gestured to Jesse and handed him the phone, whispering in his ear just loud enough so that everyone with passable hearing could understand, "It's the Sheriff."

Jesse took the phone and gifted Daisy with a grateful smile. It was why she loved him. He just never forgot to be charming. "Sheriff," Jesse said.

"Jesse, Deputy Rose just finished talking with the crew at the mill. I think she might have some material to chew on.

"Wouldn't hurt for us to meet. The Eye is probably not the right place. You name it."

"How about my office? Where are you?"

"I'm down in Goldrush. Deputy Rose is with me. Give me thirty minutes."

Jesse knew that meant Blair would be running his deck of lights and breaking some speed limits. He returned the phone to its cradle and faced the men who had fallen completely silent during the call. They were unabashedly staring at him, clearly waiting for an explanation. "Gotta go. Put that coffee on my tab, Daisy?"

"You bet, Jesse. Everything all right?"

"Just fine. The sheriff is just looking for some old information from a paper about a month ago. Threw his out."

Charlie slowly turned his attention back to his coffee cup. "You sure ain't no liar, Jesse," he laughed. "That's for certain."

"Oh, leave him alone," chided Daisy. "We need more honest men up here. "Them's what you call 'little white lies,' huh?" Paul laughed. The men looked at each other and smiled.

"Well, whatever it is, Jesse, I'm sure we'll know soon enough," said Charlie.

"I have no doubt," said Jesse easing the door shut.

The sheriff kept to his appointed half-hour and barreled into the driveway, sending dirt flying up in clouds. Deputy Rose jumped out the passenger door. "That was some ride, Sheriff!" She was smiling, so Jesse, who had been perched on the deck railing, assumed she meant that in a positive way.

Blair scooped his hat up from the seat and grunted in response. The three walked in silence to Jesse's office. Jesse had sent Skipper on a mission to take a photo of the "teacher of the month" at the local elementary school. Katherine was writing from home and the office was empty. He perched himself on the edge of his desk. Blair sat and Deputy Rose stood.

"For starters, I got a report back on that chain we found," Blair announced, leaning back to make himself comfortable. "Clean as a new penny. In fact, the lab said it probably was new. Seemed like it had never been used, right off the showroom floor."

"I guess that's mixed news," Jesse said. "Bad 'cause it sounds like the chain that Hazlett bought. Good 'cause there was no trace of blood. What did the lab say about that?"

"They said that even with the running water, they probably would have found something, specially where the links join. But they can't make any conclusions."

"Does that weaken the case against Hazlett?"

"Could," Blair said.

"Are you going to cut him loose?"

"Not just yet. We still have the tire imprints, and he admits to buying a chain. We'll have to get it over to Jeeter and see if he can identify the brand. They all look alike to me! Anyway, not to worry. The lawyer showed up today."

"So soon?"

"Yup. Twenty-four hours. Somebody's got some pull."

"Thompson said he had some connections in the valley. I guess they were pretty good."

"Damn good. And the gal brought a trunk full of designer clothes along with her."

"What do you mean?" Jesse asked.

"Deputy?" Blair said raising his eyebrows at Rose.

"Well, she doesn't look like a storefront lawyer, anyway. I mean, since when can they afford Jones of New York? She's very polished," Rose said. "Not a ragged edge on this counselor. Not at all what I expected."

"Tommy mentioned there were grants for the defense of Native Americans," Jesse offered. "Said that money wouldn't be a problem."

"One can wonder if her skills are as sophisticated as her choice in clothes," Deputy Rose said and promptly looked down at her boots.

What is this, thought Jesse, a little female competition? He was amused.

"Part of what Rose here is sayin' is relevant," the sheriff quickened to add. "Hazlett's got a bail hearing coming up in two days. The gal will have to be good to get one of the judges up here to get it low enough so as somebody in his family can afford it. Hell, there's not a one of them that's got any property to put up."

"That's so. Kinda stacks the odds against him from the start," Jesse observed.

"Them that's got, gets," the sheriff said. "Anyway, Rose here spent a few hours at the mill yesterday afternoon. My sense about that was pretty good. They didn't take her real serious. But they did want to talk to her. Go ahead Rose, tell Jesse what you learned."

"Well, I gotta say this was about the most macho group of guys I've had the pleasure of questioning, aside from bull fighters, but that's another story. So, after we get through the preliminaries – that include them checking out my body – I start asking about procedures and getting a sense about the atmosphere at the mill. Fact is that nobody saw anything happening to that gate. And there are so many people around during working hours that sawing off the bolt just wouldn't be possible unless you had Houdini himself on the crew."

"What shifts were they running?" Jesse asked.

"They had a six-to-three shift and then a noon-to-nine came on. The place was pretty well shut down by eleven. There's mop up and security after the last shift leaves. So I figure the chances of the bolt being sawed during working hours are pretty slim. Plus, every one of those guys was just floored by the idea that it could have been him. Or her. There are two women in the operation.

They said they were lucky it wasn't them who fell through that gate. I talked to most everybody. They were aching to talk. This has been traumatic, really out of their expectations. Now, I have to say they are thinking accident because they don't know what the sheriff found."

"So, what does Deputy Rose do?" asked Blair. "She thinks about those windows of opportunity and goes out and finds David Fossey, the security guard."

"And this was really interesting!" she said to Jesse. "And you really ought to go out there and do a story. Amazing and unexpected." Jesse straightened up and listened intently. "First off, the family lives in this old house. Two stories. The living room is occupied by the uncle, who is in a hospital bed. I swear, I watched and I could not see the old man breathing. But the rest of the house is decorated with these paintings ... amazing Hollywood paintings by the older brother, Alfie. If this guy were in L.A., he'd already be a legend! Anyway, the other brother, the disabled guy that rides around town in a golf cart, has built this tree house that's like an estate for pigeons. He lives up there, too. Pulls himself up the limbs with his arms and sleeps in the perch, taking care of these homing pigeons. His name is Leonard, but they call him ... get this ... Lucky Strike."

"Would you mind cutting to the chase, Deputy Rose?" Blair asked.

"Sorry," she said, corralling her enthusiasm. "Turns out that the family history is intimately connected with the mill. The father who produced this interesting progeny was a real dark spot in the mill's history. He was a logger who was in the wrong place at the wrong time. Seems that a tree was felled, went down and hit another tree – and this is another 'believe it or not' – hit another tree where there was a lightning strike a few years back, that broke off and landed on father Felix. His legs were severely damaged. MacDougald's dad did his best to make it right. Gave him a good sum of money and took care of the family. But Felix had a gambling habit. And his disability payments made it possible for him to visit Reno."

"You say there's three at home?" Jesse asked.

"There was one girl that moved away the minute she was eighteen. There's another son, the youngest. Name's Rupert they tell me. He's in state prison. David says his brother is innocent. Twenty-five years in Folsom for armed robbery."

"When you think about how they grew up, that's not a bad average," the sheriff said. "With that many boys, I'd have figured more trouble with the law than what they had!"

"The boys at home seem disinclined toward

137

violence. I don't know what happened with the youngest. He was about twelve or thirteen when Felix died. Said it was a heart thing. He ate crap and didn't move around much since he was in a wheelchair. Not much exercise in pulling the lever of a slot machine."

"So David, the guard? What's he like?"

"Nice guy, it seems. Likes to have his days free so he can write. Into health foods. Doesn't drink or prowl around at night. Not bad looking. And anything but dumb. Good vocabulary. I think he's not formally educated, so it has to come from his reading and writing. Says that late afternoons are best for him to write and the hours of the job work out perfectly. It also works with the family situation. He's got a shift with the barely-breathing uncle."

"What's your feeling?" Jesse asked. "Could somebody slip past this guy?"

"Honestly, I don't think so. He's not your typical security guard type, who always wanted to be a cop but, for one reason or another, couldn't get in. He's ... well, I think they used to call them 'peaceniks.' The guy is more of a lover than a fighter. Matter of fact, that seems to run through the whole family."

"What do you mean?" Blair asked. "I've known those Fosseys for forty-some years and I never would've described them as tribe of 'lovers.'"

Deputy Rose laughed, looking at the sheriff

with something that approached affection, Jesse thought. "What I mean is, if you look at the family, what with the artist and the son who lives with those birds, and the way that David likes to write, plus the way he cares for that dog, you've got to admit there's not a lot of macho mentality being passed along to the male side of the family," she said.

"Come to think of it," the sheriff said, "their dad was a real reader. Like, literature, I mean. He used to sit over at the Stag and talk about Shakespeare and some such. Nobody understood a damn thing he was sayin'. But he always had books with him. Fat books, if I recall. And I believe the mother was an actress. Come from some real artsy-fartsy stock, those kids do."

The telephone on Jesse's desk rang. It was one of Hazlett's cousins. Seemed like most of the Tomahs considered themselves related and Jesse had yet to figure how lineage was calculated. The young man told Jesse he was calling on behalf of Anna Sister. She was asking that Jesse come see her in the morning, early. Jesse pretended to check his calendar but knew there was no way he'd turn down the old woman. He said he'd be at her house by eight a.m.

"Well, that's interesting," observed the sheriff. "What do you suppose that's about?"

"Guess I'll know in the morning," Jesse said. "And guess I'll do the writing that I'd planned to do in the morning, today."

"I think the publisher here is telling us he has to get to work," Deputy Rose said to Blair.

"We got our business done anyway," Blair said. "Think we'll take a quick trip over to the mill, talk to Big Don before heading down the hill." He hesitated. "You will, of course, inform me if there's anything I need to know."

"Always," Jesse promised. "She probably just wants a little reassurance about her nephew."

11 / GATHERING THE SPIRIT

Anna Sister prepared her mind and body to be strong. She sat in the window of her little house that overlooked the lower part of the Rancheria. Her home was the demarcation point between surrender and hope. Above her were houses built by young families, with most of the men employed at the mill or in the woods. The houses were not big or fancy, but they bore the look of people who cared. Flowers and bushes had been planted here and there. There were garages or carports for the automobiles. Junk piles were contained and kept to a minimum. A smattering of families had also built traditional structures, hemispherical thatched dwellings where they taught their children the old ways. The dome-shaped huts looked curiously compatible with new construction and the surrounding of cedars, pines, and manzanita that hugged the hillsides.

Anna Sister looked out down the dirt road that wound through the Rancheria to the main road, leading to town. From there, she could see wooden shacks bending slightly to the ravages of wind, time, and neglect. Roofs had been patched with pieces of scrap tin and bright blue tarps. Windows were covered with milky plastic or bed sheets or not at all. Most of the dwellings did not house families but rather a collection of the young, who had yet to find their way, and old, who would never find it. Bottles and cans littered the ground and community dogs scampered around scavenging for edible scraps. This, the old woman thought, was not a good home. It was a place where the spirits of her people were restless and, even, doomed. It was a place haunted by a past where people got stuck as if their feet were rocks, too heavy to lift and walk away. She feared her nephew would end up on the lower side of the hill. But, she also knew his spirit was like the river, running free and rich with life. The song of that spirit had been quieted by drinking and a despair that he himself didn't understand.

She had a plan. It would be the last time she gathered her resources together in this way. She was too old to engage the body and mind and determination at will. She preferred to listen now to the voices around her: the great birds, the wind, the rain, the laughter of young children.

With the dawn, she would ask the white publisher to take her many places. Her day would be spent in a world that, although not unfamiliar to her, was not her world. She would force her frail body to stand tall and she would speak with the language the white teachers had taught her. Anna Sister watched as the sun fell behind the mountain where the eagle's eye looked down on the valley. Even though the great rock was many miles away, she could see it as clearly as when she had climbed to its base as a young girl. She dropped a handful of dry sage into a bowl that had been crafted out of local rock. Putting a match to the fragrant herb, she sung softly to herself. The song and silvery smoke and the aroma filled the room and drifted out the window. She emptied her mind of thoughts.

The next morning, Jesse drove slowly into the Rancheria, so as to kick up little dust behind his tires. Instead of choosing his now-customary western shirt and jeans, he'd dressed carefully. Coming from the city, Jesse was never a slouch in his attire. Contrary to the image of scruffy reporters, Jesse had dressed as smartly as the TV reporters. That obsession changed when he moved to Redbud. But this morning he'd thought about it and, to show respect for the Indian woman, he'd worn a newly pressed shirt and thrown a professional shine on his Tony Lama boots.

Most of the lower half of the community was still asleep, having partied long into the morning hours. Only a few children and the ever-present dogs hustled about. As Jesse pulled in front of Anna Sister's house, he saw that the front door was open and took it as a welcoming sign. He found the elder sitting at a small wooden table, her hands folded in front of her. Anna Sister, too, had taken care with her appearance. Gone was the loose dress and shawl that she characteristically wore. Instead, she'd chosen a simple, tailored black dress that reached below her knees. A black leather purse lay on the table, an item Jesse had never before seen in her possession. Anna Sister seemed to rely on deep pockets to carry her treasures.

Her pewter hair was pulled tightly back into a bun at the nape of her neck. She turned to acknowledge Jesse and a beam of sunlight flashed off the strands of the silver necklace she wore. It was Native American in design, though not from the Tomah tradition. From her ears dangled matching earrings that danced as she turned her head. Jesse was stunned by the transformation. Anna Sister had lost 20 years from her face. And, when she stood to greet him, she held her shoulders straight with the pride of a strong woman.

"I thank you for coming, Jesse," she said with a slight bow of her head. "It's always my pleasure to see you," Jesse responded. "And, if it's not forward of me to say so, you are looking very lovely this morning. You look as if you have been visited by the fountain of youth."

Anna Sister smiled and motioned for Jesse to sit opposite her at the table. "I have important things to do today," she answered, as if this explained the remarkable transformation. "I hope that I can count on you to help me accomplish them."

It wasn't a question, Jesse knew. It was a command. For a moment he wondered what it was about this small woman that was so powerful that he would no more resist her than he would a second chance at life.

They sat at the table together for more than an hour. Anna Sister talked, Jesse asked a few questions, and the sun rose higher in the sky. The smell of sage lingered in the room and Jesse's head felt clearer than it had in decades. He gently touched her elbow as they walked to the Wrangler. The old woman no longer looked as if she needed supporting and she lifted herself into the high rise vehicle. As Jesse shut the door and walked around the car, he glanced at the shadow of the woman in the passenger's seat. Why me, he wondered.

Their first stop took them to the Tribal Center where Jesse sat on the front porch and watched the sun moving behind Eagle's Eye Mountain. He hadn't visited the rock himself and planned to hike up this coming summer. But in his mind's eye, the rock was etched in great detail, the natural formation with its beak jutting out and great eye watching all that lay below. Watching the Tomahs centuries ago as they hunted deer and wild boar, and gathered acorns and reeds. Watching as the European settlers swept over the valley with a fever for gold and something they called civilization. Still watching today. Jesse looked down at his clasped hands. He could not go inside the tribal house because the elders had convened at the behest of Anna Sister. So, he waited quietly under the watchful Eye.

Anna Sister herself was considered an elder, but the circle of men had separate roles from hers. She seldom met with them all at once, although she was aware that modern Indian women were welcome in the circles of certain tribes. She asked for their prayers and, as Jesse sat staring out toward Eagle Eye Mountain, he heard the chant rise from the log building and his heart beat with the steady, slow rhythm of the drum.

Anna Sister emerged from the log structure and led Jesse to the Jeep. Their next drive took them high above the mill to McDougald's place. Although she had never before visited, Anna entered like visiting royalty and was treated with due respect by Mac. From the richest man on the mountain, she extracted a commitment to post bail for Hazlett. She then outlined the entire chain of support that would assure him her nephew would not run. If it pained her to ask for the white man's money, she did not show it. Anna Sister conducted herself like a compassionate negotiator, business-like and assured.

Mac placed a call down to the mill. By the

time Jesse and Anna arrived, Dyke was in his office waiting for them. Dyke and Anna Sister had had many encounters, from the time he'd pulled a younger Hazlett out of an overturned truck to more celebratory times, such as when Hazlett won the axe-throwing event at the annual Logger's Jamboree. They shared a mutual respect, but Anna was about to ask for more. Mac's call had cleared the way for Dyke to do his part. While out on bail, he'd be given his old job back and be under Dyke's watchful, sometimes intimidating eye. Jesse participated in the negotiations infrequently. It was the old woman's show and he'd already agreed to play his contributing role.

Finally, they headed down the hill to the County Jail. Anna maintained her energy and posture, sitting up straight and tall on the twisting road down the mountain. She and Jesse had not talked, for it was no longer necessary. They rode in suspended in the moment.

The old woman asked Jesse to be with her when she spoke to her nephew about the plan and extracted his promise not to betray her trust.

Hazlett, like Jesse, had noted Anna Sister's changed carriage and appearance. Unlike Jesse, he'd said nothing but seemed to feast his eyes in amazement. Anna Sister clearly had his attention.

But as she began to speak in her quiet and authoritative way, Hazlett hung his head. He knew what it had taken for his aunt to do what she had done. He looked into her eyes only when making the promises she demanded from him. Once the commitment was clear and Jesse had served as witness, Anna Sister asked him to leave her alone with her nephew. Another twenty minutes passed before she emerged from the jail and they headed up the hill with the sun falling in the sky behind them. Jesse wondered, but didn't ask, what she'd said to the young man. What magic had she given him to sustain him through the trials that were sure to come?

On the journey back to the old woman's house, Jesse could sense Anna Sister changing. The energy she'd displayed throughout the day was spent and she slouched a little in the seat of his car. He walked around to the passenger side door and extended his hand to help her from the seat she'd easily mounted earlier in the day. Anna Sister took his hand without shame. Jesse noticed that her shoulders had rolled forward and her back hunched a bit. He helped her up the steps to the front door where Anna Sister turned and clasped both his hands inside hers. "I thank you, Mister Jesse, for what you have done today and what you have still to do," she said. "I won't go out again. You will come to see me if you want to talk."

"I'll do my best, Anna Sister," Jesse responded.

"I know that you will. And Jesse?"

"Yes?"

"I know your name. Someday soon, you will know it also.'

She removed her hands from his. "I am tired now." With that, she turned her back and went inside to the stillness and shadows of her home.

12 / ELDER INTERVENTION

Anna Sister had sealed a partnership. Her visits had been methodical and determined. Each piece had created an order. The process had taken extraordinary strength because she'd done something essentially against her nature. Anna felt strongly about her people maintaining what little power they had left, including solving their own problems within the community. However, so deep was her belief in her nephew and so immediate was the situation, she'd made the hard choice and moved purposely forward with a plan. She gave thanks that the men she talked to were good men. They had proven themselves to have good character.

Two days later, Hazlett appeared before Judge

Winifred Begae, who was rumored to be a distant relative of the local Tomah Begaes. The lineage was always difficult to determine because the natives of the mountain were given European surnames. Not only were the Tomah names difficult for the white settlers to pronounce, they had only one name and that didn't fit the way the newcomers did business. Consequently, there were white European Begaes and there were one hundred percent Tomah Begaes and a flock of mixed-blood in between. In Redbud, nobody much cared. People were judged on individual character. Bigots didn't last long, though rednecks flourished. This was an interesting distinction that had taken Jesse a few months to understand.

MacDougald, Dyke, Jesse, Blair, Deputy Rose, and two elders from the council were at the court proceedings. Before the hearing, Jesse met with Hazlett and his attorney whom Thompson had arranged - Camilla Roarke, a strikingly well dressed, confident woman. She was briefed on the plan and later introduced to the others who would carry it out. Her argument to Judge Begae was simple, clear, and persuasive. She cited the lack of substantial evidence, the fact that her client had no prior felonies or arrests for violent behavior and, finally, his lifelong connection with the community. Where Hazlett could run, given his background and roots, was limited to a range of about ten miles, she told the judge, seeing as he had no vehicle (the truck was in impound) and the eyes of the entire community would be on him. Her argument and check of $25,000 bail from MacDougald convinced the Judge. Hazlett was on the streets of Redbud by noon, Friday.

Hazlett had been out a week and was behaving himself. Dyke kept the young man in his sight every hour of every working day. On the weekend, he hired Hazlett to do odd jobs around his ranch: fence mending, fixing the roof on the horse barn, bringing bales of hay down from the loft. But it wasn't the days that folks who'd invested money or time in Hazlett were worried about. It was the nights that haunted him, calling him to the camaraderie of sharing a bottle with his friends at home. The drink – gin was the cheapest – filled an empty place somewhere between his belly and throat. He hated drinking for what it did to him and, at the same time, loved it for the same reason. He'd come to believe that to fight it was helpless. It owned him.

This was a phenomenon of addiction that Jesse understood only too well. That's why he volunteered for the hard part. He got Hazlett at night. All night. The first week wasn't bad, owing to the fact that Hazlett had a little over a week of sobriety behind him, thanks to being in jail. But this had happened before, for longer periods of time and at the first opportunity Hazlett had tied on a major homecoming drunk. This time, there was more at stake. It wasn't a few months in County; it was years to life in state prison. And it was something else. It was the look on Anna Sister's face when she'd come to see him. It was what she'd said about the people. Still, the tips of his finger ached when he thought about the feel of a smooth, round bottle and the clear alcohol slowly burning its way down his throat, making its way to his brain, where it softened the edges of the world. Where it made him laugh and be gleefully dizzy. Gin had been his closest friend. Jesse knew this urge and although he no longer craved cocaine, he remembered his "friend" well, a deceptive friend that slowly steals a man's power like a charming embezzler. He also remembered that one of the best ways to get past the daily urge was to be busy and fill up the hole that was in the heart. Jesse took Hazlett to AA meetings in the nearby town of Pinehurst. Hazlett took Jesse to a meeting of the tribal elders on the Rancheria.

Together, they met with attorney Camilla Roarke. Deputy Rose had been right in her assessment, the lawyer had a definite air of stature. This was no storefront rookie right out of law school. Jesse's curiosity piqued. He mentioned this to Rose when they had a chance meeting at Herb's gas station.

"And you thought I was just being catty," she joked.

"I guess I underestimated you," Jesse answered.

"Most people do," she said. "Nobody knows better than I that looks can be deceiving."

The sun through the poplar tree that hugged Herb's white stucco gas station threw dancing shadows on the deputy's face, a faint scar ran along the line of her chin. Jesse had been too good a reporter for too long to miss a clue. He wondered if she'd had cosmetic work done, maybe something related to her elusive past.

"Anyway, we are on the same page about the lawyer," Rose said. "On one hand, I'm glad she appears overqualified for the situation. On the other, she doesn't seem like the type to dedicate her professional life to pro bono work. Unless she's independently wealthy, which could be the case, it would take more than a month's salary to pay for just one of her suits."

"Do I hear that 'meow' again?"

"Didn't want to disappoint you," the deputy quipped and sped away in the patrol car.

13 / ROOTS OF CONFLICT

The young outsiders arrived in vans, trucks, campers, and on foot, having hitch-hiked up the hill from the valley. They came from the Golden State and north, from Oregon and Washington. They made rainbow splashes of color wherever they went. For Jesse it was a déjàvu of the '70s, with brilliant tie-dye and mellow earth tones. There were necklaces and earrings on both men and women. Long skirts, braids, and new style Birkenstocks decorated both genders. New to this generation was a festival of body art: tattoos and piercings that made the locals wince and wonder.

The range of ages was surprisingly wide and Jesse thought he recognized a senior hippie from an interview long past. The memory brought back the image of Timothy Leary, whom he'd interviewed while in the California Men's Colony on charges of drug possession and sales. However, most of the crowd consisted of twenty-something, wrinkle-free idealists.

Jesse interviewed several from the flock celebrating the arrival of summer and protesting what they saw as the irreversible loss of wilderness. He learned they'd come from throughout the West with a large contingent from the concrete forests of the Bay Area and the redwood forests of Humboldt County. Some were politically motivated, having heard about the death of Chris Lance, and were convinced of the evils of MacDougald's "empire," as they called it.

Serving as the local event organizer, Mark told Jesse the gathering was meant to pay tribute to a martyr and to honor the change of seasons in "what was left of the natural environment." Jesse accepted another copy of the press release he'd already received by e-mail and through snail-mail. If nothing else, he thought, the group had heightened media awareness.

The weekend camp had been an annual event since Jesse arrived on the mountain. The old timers said it was in retaliation for the mid-July Logger's Jamboree, when wood chips sailed through the air like bullets as woodsmen proudly showed their skills in competitions. This year, however, the weekend's attendance had exploded, going from less than a hundred campers in years past to at

156

least three times that many. As usual, they pitched their tents on the property adjacent to Thompson's. And, as usual, Thompson was unfazed by his colorful neighbors. He said he'd sat around the campfire – though the fires had been in stoves because of the encroaching dry season – and listened peacefully to acoustic music from guitars, mandolins, and fiddles. One woman, he said, had brought a lovely ruby red concertina that sent melodies echoing far into the night.

Strictly off the record, Thompson confided to Jesse that there was a bit of marijuana being passed around. He, of course, did not imbibe in any kind of intoxicants, including beer.

Thompson said he wasn't sure who owned the eighty-plus acres next to his. He'd lost track of it after a long string of transactions that included corporations and court actions. And, he reported, he didn't care, so long as his neighbors respected his property rights.

"These kids, Jesse, they just need something to believe in. Our parents had WWII and the American way of life," Thompson offered, turning philosophical. "This younger generation here, they don't even have the advantage of good ol' time religion. These trees and the environment, that's their altar. In my opinion, the best people believe in something, instead of nothin'."

"Are you agreeing with their point of view?" Jesse asked, anticipating the answer.

"No way! I've been here long enough to know

that MacDougald's no industrial rapist. He's the salt of the earth. Been damn good for this town and, so far as I can see, he hasn't hurt these forests one bit. Matter of fact, Jesse, when the company was working contracts with the Forest Service, those stands were a hell of a lot healthier. We didn't have any fires like that one we had back in '96." Thompson paused and relaxed his delivery. "I am just tryin' to understand." He cocked his head and assessed Jesse. "You were young once, right?"

***

Jesse drove back to his office, mulling over Thompson's words. Yes, he had been young once, and he'd believed in nothing. Nothing except his need to rise, to prove himself, be validated through performance and rewarded with accolades and headlines.

He shook off that thought as he sat in front of his computer and wrote a lively story he hoped would enlighten the local folks who feared the strangers, using a lot of Thompson's quotes. As an opinion leader in the community, Tommy's tolerance would go a long way to reassuring mountain folks that their way of life was not in jeopardy. He'd intentionally left Skipper behind when he'd returned to town, figuring the photography would go better without his middle-aged presence. Skipper returned to the office about ninety minutes after Jesse, looking flushed and excited.

"I got some shots in here you are not gonna believe!" he said, slamming the office door behind him so hard the glass rattled. Skipper's face was again flushed with excitement and his strawberry blond hair disheveled. Ordinarily self-conscious about his appearance, the young photographer's shirt was streaked with sweat and dust.

"Whoa, Skipper. I haven't seen you like this before," Jesse said, "Not even after Auburn won the regionals!"

"Yeah, well, that was sports. This is, I dunno, something else." Skipper plugged the camera into the computer on his desk and nearly a hundred shots loaded onto the screen.

"What happened to 'One Shot Skipper'?" The boy was trying to make his trademark by taking only one shot of a subject.

"There is one shot, just of about a hundred different things. I mean, I didn't just shoot like crazy like I do during a game. I took some time and I thought about it. It was like doin' a painting or something. Like, I got to choose the shot. I didn't have to shoot just to catch something fast. I had this killer natural light, filtered through the trees. Perfect!"

"Great. I can't wait to see them," Jesse said. "We'll use as many as possible if they're as good as you say they are. I'm glad it didn't cause a problem with you being there with a camera and all."

"Problem? Like, the opposite," Skipper said. "They were either too stoned to care or they were posing. Incredible! I was, like, invisible. Like a fly sitting on a rock. Nobody cared." Skipper began to open the pictures in Photo Shop and work them.

"Hell, they even talked like I was deaf or sumpthin'." He studied the screen and cropped a photo, adjusted the color and checked the resolution. "I even heard that some of those eco-terrorists are here. What's the name?"

"Radical Organization for Our Roots - ROOTS," Jesse answered.

"Yeah, well, I heard that some of them are here. Nobody seems to know who they are, 'cause it's kinda undercover. But they were sayin' that some of the group came up from the Bay Area and SoCal." Skipper reached into his vest pocket and dropped a pile of fliers and leaflets on Jesse's desk. "Picked this stuff up too, in case you didn't see it."

"Interesting," said Jesse, paging through the materials. He pulled out a thin booklet. "Let's see those images. Sounds like you did a helluva job."

Skipper gave a thumbs-up and focused on his work. Jesse smiled. He was surprised and pleased. He hadn't expected the young man to be excited by much of anything. Skipper was one of

the locals, trapped by circumstance and essentially uneducated. But he had a natural talent for the
nuances of photography, although he'd never displayed any real passion for the art. Believing in
something, Jesse remembered, having a passion.
This is a good thing.

He leaned against the edge of his desk and
flipped through the pages of the SOFTI pamphlet
Skipper had given him. It was photocopied on two
sides and stapled together to bind the pages, obviously a cost-saving measure. On page three he
found the source: "Published by ROOTS." This, he
thought, was definitely interesting and wondered
how he'd missed it. But, due in part to his age,
Skipper likely got to places that Jesse wasn't entirely welcome. He read over the beginning of the
second chapter, titled "Eco Defense."

> "Dress to blend into the environment,"
> it said. "Camouflage clothing and earth
> tones are best. Wear footwear that allows
> quiet and easy movement and running if
> necessary. The point is to be able to hide
> and remain undetected in areas where log-
> ging activity is happening. So long as they
> know we are out there, they can't cut trees.
> They only have to get a glimpse of you and
> they will stop. Make sure you carry rations
> with you in case of an extended standoff.
> Stealth is the tactic at all times.

> "Don't carry anything unnecessary.
> However, a camera or a video camera may

be crucial equipment. The media love these action shots and will pay money for footage, no matter how or where you get it. Your photos or video could be worth more than a million words and any profits could help to finance the movement. We have the advantage here. Anything the industry says will be viewed as pure PR. It won't be believed or broadcast. And, be assured, the rapists of the environment won't be using video. Basically, they are too uneducated to use it!"

The last paragraph spoke volumes to Jesse. There was more than idealism in the words. There was an arrogance, coupled with a veiled attempt to manipulate.

The booklet read like a guerilla fighter handbook. It instructed protestors on how to spike trees, chain themselves to heavy equipment, passively resist arrest, and how to entice loggers to make the first aggressive move. This was not done with hurling insults and curses, the writer advised, but by making sure the working men knew they were sub-humans. "Cro-Magnons," according to the pamphlet. It said that polysyllabic words and practiced sneers often enraged loggers who had "limited command of the English language."

Additionally interesting for Jesse was the section devoted to a biography of the group's anonymous leader. It described the individual as a pioneer in environmental activism. In prose that made the person sound like either a secular saint or a combat hero, it explained that he'd been forced underground fifteen years ago but still directed the movement from undisclosed locations.

The piece then went on to appeal for donations to continue the cause. In closing, it claimed "The end will justify the means."

In tone, it was not unlike literature Jesse had picked up in some charismatic churches where people rolled in the aisles in ecstasy and talked in tongues. There was a Website listed and Jesse jotted down the URL, and a P.O. Box located in Los Angeles. His skills using the Internet to do research were finely honed from many years of using technology to get an edge on the competition. He sometimes wondered what it would be like now, with high-speed lines and nearly unlimited access to information from databases around the world. Running down the background on ROOTS and its mysterious leader sounded like fun, a personal challenge that would bring some attention to his small town paper. Unlike his glory days, he felt driven by curiosity instead of demons.

As Skipper worked his magic on the raw images, Jesse jumped on the Web and began a journey that started in Los Angeles.

14 / WILDFIRE WEEKEND

Charlie had two mules. Every year, he trailered them over the mountain to Bishop for the annual Mule Days Festival. Only one of them, Blossom, was fit for competition, being beautiful in the way that only other mules and their owners recognize. Blossom regularly returned from the trip with another blue ribbon to hang over the mantle on Charlie's fireplace. Jasper, the other mule, Charlie hauled along just so Blossom would have proper company. It was Charlie's habit to go back to his place after lunch, do some chores and feed his animals – a couple of Nubian goats, a gaggle of leghorns, his dog Shep, several cats and the mules – before returning to the Eagle's Eye for dinner. Herb came over to the café as soon as he closed the filling station for the night, which was anytime that seemed right under the current conditions. Flip, having no animals to care for and only a lonely single-wide trailer parked on a cement pad, was often the first to show up. Merriweather seldom made the dinner hour, having a wife and established home to return to at the close of the day. Paul dropped in once and a while, depending on his work at his silversmith's bench.

Thus it was that Flip was waiting at the group's table, staring into his coffee like it was a book, when Jesse walked in. "Flip," Jesse said, removing his hat and nodding.

"Jesse," Flip said with a lift of his chin. Jesse walked over to the coffeepot and helped himself. Herb walked in gently closing the noisy café door and wiping his hands on his clean, blue work pants. He acknowledged Jesse with a nod and took his place across from Flip. Herb had often said that working in a gas station was no excuse for walking around like a grease monkey. His uniform was always clean and creased in the right places. Jesse thought of him as the town gentleman: Mr. Manners of the Mountain. Herb held up his coffee mug and looked at Jesse. "You mind, since you're holding the pot?"

Jesse smiled and brought the pot, along with a pitcher of real cream over to the table. "My pleasure. You can leave me your usual tip." The three men laughed since tipping among the regulars was strictly limited to advice.

"Have a seat," Herb said.

"Might do that for a bit, thanks." Jesse turned one of the chrome-legged chairs around and straddled it. "I'm on a project, needed a little of Daisy's coffee to keep me going."

"I'm not even going to ask what, 'cause I know you reporters don't talk," Herb stated, emptying a generous amount of cream into his cup.

"I'm surfing the Web," Jesse offered. "I've been all over the state in the past two hours and am about to do a little foreign travel."

"That's all Greek to me," Herb said.

"Me, too," Flip added and looked at Herb. "You seen Charlie?"

"Not since right after lunch. You're right, he's late. He's usually here before me. That good lookin' mule of his must've bit him."

Flip sniggered, "Yeah, in the butt." Daisy walked out from the kitchen, rolling her hands and arms in a clean towel as if she'd just done surgery.

"See you all helped yourself, again," she said. "Doesn't get you out of leavin' your usual tip. Where's Charlie?"

As if on cue, Charlie yanked open the door and immediately started shaking his head. He lowered himself into his chair with everyone waiting for him to speak. "Daisy, give me a cup of the fresh stuff," he said, looking down at his folded

166

hands. After a pause, he looked up at the others, one by one. "I am here to tell you, we are in a world of hurt. Do you know why I'm late getting here?" he asked, not even anticipating an answer. "I have spent that last forty-five minutes scraping Choker's sorry butt off the bank by the creek, into my truck, and home where the man belongs."

Charlie held out his cup as Daisy poured thick, dark coffee that may or may not have been fresh. At the very least, it was strong.

"Whaddaya mean?" Flip asked. "I seen him over at the Stag earlier on and he seemed fine!"

"Yeah, well, that must've been a few hours ago. To get as drunk as he was, it takes some extended time." Charlie sipped from his cup and made a face. "Thought I said fresh."

Daisy overheard. "You'll get fresh if you don't watch it!"

Charlie acted as if he hadn't heard her. "So, I get done takin' care of Blossom and Jasper. That Blossom gets prettier every day, I swear. Anyway, I'm drivin' out from my place and makin' that turn where it comes close to the creek. You know, where they found that boy's truck. So, I see Choker's pickup and it looks like he left the lights on. Why he'd have the doggone things on in the daylight, I don't know. So, I stop and shut the lights off. Then I start thinkin' that maybe Choker isn't feeling too good or something. Or maybe he's fishin'. I dunno. I just decided to go look for him. Danged if I don't find him

down there where they found that body. He's sittin' leaned up against a poplar, looks like he's
sleepin'. Except when I try to wake him up, it ain't
easy. Smelled like a one-man brewery, he did. I
realized he was passed out. Had a quart of Coors
in one hand and a half pint of Jack Daniels in the
other."

"Shame," Herb said slowly shaking his head.
"He's a good man. Good family man."

"So, what'd ya do?" Flip asked.

"I threw some cold Jackass water on his face
and shook him good. He came around, more or
less."

"He tell you what he was doin', getting' shitfaced in the middle of the day?" Flip had been
known to do the same in his more youthful past.

"Well, I got him loaded in my truck – had to
leave his there," Charlie explained. "And he mumbled about how things will never be same. Said he
was sorry, for what I don't know. He cussed out
the enviros some and conked out again. I delivered him to Jenny."

"Poor woman," Herb said. "This must be tough
on her, seeing Choker go through this."

"She's strong. Woman has to be to live with a
man working in the woods for twenty years. But,
yeah, I could tell she had a lot on her mind,"
Charlie said. "We put her ol' man to bed and I
took her to get his truck. She said she was getting' pretty worried about the drinkin'. They've

been through a few layoffs before, but nothing hit him like this one did. Said she just didn't understand." Charlie took a swig of coffee.

"You heard anything about more layoffs, Jesse?" Herb asked quietly. "Strictly off the record, I mean?"

"I believe there won't be any more this season, but that's just an educated guess," Jesse answered. And, (off-the-record) word from MacDougald that any more cutbacks in labor were to be postponed until things stabilized in the community.

"So, how's your boy?" Charlie asked Jesse, letting a smile cross his face. "Is he behavin' himself?"

"If you're referring to Hazlett, he is, indeed. Goes to work in the woods during the week and over to Dyke's on the weekends. It's working out pretty good," Jesse said, draining his cup of coffee. "I'm picking him up after the meeting with the elders at the Rancheria. Gives me a chance to do some more work on the computer tonight."

"That's a mighty fine thing to do," Charlie said. "Any of us can tell you what a handful that boy's been. I, for one, sure couldn't take him on."

"I've got plenty of help. And don't tell me that if Anna Sister asked you for a favor, you'd decline," Jesse said, laying a dollar on the counter.

"Nope, can't say I could," Charlie said.

"That woman is small but mighty!"

"Amen to that," said Herb, holding out his cup for Daisy.

"Every one of you is a soft touch," she teased. "You talk tough, but you're a pack of pussycats."

Had the bell on the door of the Eagle Eye not clanged so loudly, there would have been some good-natured banter, but Andy Winters appeared with his red face streaked with soot.

"Mr. Herb, Mr. Jesse! It's a fire. Up at the camp-in. Call the chief!" The men all stood.

They heard no sirens.

Daisy was heading for the phone. "Where is it, boy, exactly?" she asked as she dialed Didion's number.

"It's toward the back edge, where it butts up against the Forest Service property," Andy sputtered. "Just got goin'. I tried to get to Mr. Thompson's phone first, but he wasn't home, so I run all the way down here. The campers up there are tryin' to put it out with buckets and stuff."

Daisy relayed the information to Chief Didion. Jesse stood behind her with his hand outstretched. She hung up and handed him the receiver. Jesse dialed. "Skipper, get up to the camp. We've got a fire." Then he strode to the front door with Andy trailing right behind.

"Where do you think you're going?" Herb shot at the boy.

"With Mr. Jesse. I know right where it is and the fastest way to get in. I was there," he answered.

Jesse stopped. "Where's your mom?"

"I dunno. Probably at work over by the lake."

"You'll do everything Jesse says, won't you boy?" Herb looked directly into Andy's green eyes.

"I will, Mr. Herb. You can count on that." He looked up at Jesse. "Okay?"

On the way up the hill, Jesse made it clear to Andy that he was to stay in the car. This was a second (and final) chance. The first time, he'd disobeyed. It was a short drive, so the instructions had to be clear and brief. "Fires are unpredictable, Andy. One draft, change in the wind, new fuel ignites and the flames behave like they're alive. One minute you can be safe and the next, you're surrounded. You'll just have to believe me on this. I've been in plenty. Too many."

"Yes, sir. I will stay in the car. Can I have the window rolled down?"

"You can. And, Andy, I won't go far from the car but I am leaving the keys in the ignition. I am doing this in case something happens out there and I absolutely can't get back here. I don't want you stuck if there's a life-threatening emergency and you need to get away fast. Promise me you won't even think about it for any other reason except that you haven't heard from me in way too long."

"Promise. I promise, Mr. Jesse." Andy reached into the glove compartment and removed a small digital recorder. "Can I use this?"

"Sure," said Jesse, who hated to depend on tape recorders. "What for?"

"I dunno. Just anything I might think about while I'm sittin' there."

They pulled onto the dirt road that led steeply up the hill to Thompson's place and veered toward the camp. Jesse turned right at the first fork in the road and the climb became even steeper. In the far distance, Jesse heard the wail of a siren.

"Look, up there," Andy pointed to a glow in the trees where light flickered low to the ground. "It's back on the far side. Was just in the tall grass when I beat it outta there. Hope it don't get onto the trees. That'd be bad! It's already dry. They'd go up pretty fast."

Jesse recalled that Andy must have been about eight years old at the last time a big fire hit the forests surrounding Redbud. The barren destruction had lingered long after and, in some places, still showed deep scars on the landscape.

"Here, turn up that road on the right. It's an old logging road. Take us right straight back there," Andy shouted.

"How about Didion?" Jesse asked. "Does he know this road?"

"Heck, yes. He helped when they fixed it up after the logs was out. They called it 'respiration' or something," Andy said.

"Restoration?"

"Yeah."

Jesse pulled over by the cut-off. "What are you doin'?" Andy asked.

"Taking no chances," Jesse answered, and pulled a battery-operated flare out of his kit in the back of the Jeep. He positioned it at the turn, took a piece of notebook paper and quickly drew a right facing arrow on it with a black marker for Didion's eyes and set it underneath the flashing light. He could see more dancing flames now and sped closer to the clearing where tents and vehicles sat in smoky silence. At the edge of the clearing, Jesse stopped. Through the encroaching night and smoke, he saw that a group of people had formed a chain from the narrow, running stream to the area where the fire burned low, but seemed to be spreading from its far edges. Each bucket of water that was tossed on the fire sent white smoke into the air. Shouts of urgency traveled along the human fire line. Around the tents and small RV's, people were scurrying to pack vehicles with bags and boxes, ready to evacuate. Some cars were already leaving, kicking up dust as they sped away down the main access road. Jesse got out to study the scene, assessing what he might do. He heard the sound of sirens coming closer, the big whining bellow of the fire truck and the high-pitched wail of police and other emergency vehicles. The Forest Service would also be sending crews. There was a network of emergency notifications that blasted out to the crews. Jesse pulled well over to the side of the road and soon Didion's big red truck screamed from the one lane road into the clearing. The volunteer chief was often the first to make it to a scene, largely because he drove the five-ton truck like it was an MG. He lumbered to a halt by Jesse.

"Jump on back!" he shouted. "I might need you!"

Jesse grabbed his hard hat from the back seat of the Jeep and his gloves, emergency equipment for a reporter in the mountains. He leapt onto the side boards of the truck and wrapped his arm around the steel bar. Didion had two other men up front. Jesse pointed a gloved finger at Andy.

"Counting on you!"

"I'll call in and have the next truck pick Andy up." Didion shouted.

Jesse had been in dozens of fires during his career as a reporter. From house fires to forest fires and industrial fires fed by explosive chemicals. Never before had he been recruited to fight one. Of course, he'd always tried to be helpful to emergency personnel, knowing that follow-up interviews would be easier if he was seen as an ally. However, the news media in the city was generally looked upon as an impediment to emergency work and, mostly, he just tried to stay (conspicuously) out of the way. But then, he'd never had his home on fire before. The closer they got to the flames, the more Jesse felt his adrenaline rise.

Just short of the fire line, Didion slammed on the brakes and shouted orders for the men to dismount. They grabbed the brass nozzle on the fire hose and dashed toward the flames.   The chief told Jesse to get behind the man in front and hang on. The water burst forth more violently than Jesse had anticipated. It was going to take some strength just to do his small part. Smoke burned his eyes and filled his lungs. Didion was unfazed by the black smoke as he sprinted forward. Behind them, more emergency vehicles sped onto the scene. Torrents of water showered the flames that had spread to cover dozens of acres. On the far edge, squat manzanita were glowing, a hot-burning wood that was the bane of fire fighters. Just beyond the brush and manzanita was the forest, tall ponderosa pines and invasive, shorter firs. Under ordinary conditions, a low fire wouldn't reach to the crown of big trees and the bark would insulate most of the trunks from the fire. But the forest had been untouched for nearly a decade, owing to a new hands-off policy from the feds and the Forest Service. Consequently, the floor of the forest was thick with woody debris and rife with spindly firs, kindling for a crown fire. This was the fear as the men pushed further into the flames, working toward the perimeter and the danger zone.

"We lost it over here!" Jesse heard someone shout. Masses of men moved toward the direction of the call, concentrating water and effort on the hot spot that had flared up in the stand of trees. Jesse saw a small group of men suited up in yellow, flame resistant Nomex and breathing masks. They were members of the local Forest Service "Hot Shot" crew. A low fire like this wouldn't ordinarily call for the elite of fire fighters but, fortunately, a group of them lived in Redbud, at the ready for any local fire. They pushed past other crews and disappeared into the billowing smoke, pulling coils of hose behind them. Jesse held on to his post, following the hose wherever the lead fighter pulled it. The immediacy of the threat overcame the discomfort of the smoke.

Andy watched the action as best he could, craning his long, skinny neck out the car window. He saw the movement of yellow and red and green uniforms in and out of the smoke. He heard the shouts and wished that he could help. But he made a promise, which Mr. Herb had told him was a man's true measure. It seemed like the fire was moving closer to the forest and Andy saw the backs of men who were attacking the dangerous direction of the flames. Maybe it was a wind, like Mr. Jesse had said, that blew the flames. But Andy, and the other folks at the encampment, had also seen a finger of fire moving stealthily in the opposite direction, toward the tents and cars. People were fleeing, driving out the main access road and deserting the camp. Andy watched and waited, and finally turned on the car radio. The news station from the valley came in faintly. He heard a brief report about a "grass fire" up near Redbud. About twenty acres were burning but the fire was mostly under control, the report said. They must be looking at a different fire than I am, thought Andy as the finger of flames became a fist. He shut off the radio and listened. Like Jesse said, how dangerous the fire would be depended on lots of things. He wet his finger and held it in the wind. It was blowing away from the camp, into the forest where the men were. Maybe the grass fire heading his way would burn itself out.

When the explosion happened, Andy jumped so high that he hit his head on the roof of the Jeep. Immediately, he remembered the other thing that Jesse had said. The fire depended on fuel. Fuel, like propane that campers used for their stoves. At the far end of the encampment, a tongue of fire had reached a lone tent and probably, a tank of propane. The tent and everything in it was a bonfire of angry flames. Andy wasn't worried that there were people inside because it looked like everyone had run away. He could hear the roar of the fire as it consumed the fuel like a starving monster. The sound died down and once again he heard the men in the distance. Some of the campers – mostly men but also many women – had stayed on the fire line, backing up the local crews. They, too, had put their attention on the threat to the forest. Andy wondered if maybe he should go get someone. But he stayed put, eyes zeroed in on the outbreak in the camp.

As the din died down and his brain stopped shouting at him, Andy heard another sound. It was like a hurt animal, a yelping dog, a child crying? He focused on listening. It was a cry. A human cry. Andy craned his entire upper body out of the window of the Wrangler. Like radar, he turned his head to catch the direction. The sound was coming from one of the tents nearby. No more hesitation or thinking about obeying. Andy was on the ground and running to the pup tents. He ripped open the doors looking inside, trying to keep the fire in the edge of his vision. In the third tent, blue nylon already bearing black dimes of melted material from the ash in the air, he found a girl curled up in a sleeping bag, locked in a fetal position. She looked to be about five or six years old, dark-haired and dark-skinned.

"Come on, we gotta go!" Andy shouted and grabbed her arm. The girl screamed again.

"No, no! My dad!"

"Where's your dad?"

"Out there! In the fire!" she screamed.

"Okay, then he's fine. He's with the fire fighters and we have to get out of here."

"But he told me not to leave!" she cried.

"Yeah, well, I heard that too. Now come on, he doesn't know you're in danger. He thought you'd be safe. He wants you safe, doesn't he?" The girl sniffled and nodded, then crawled out of the bag.

Andy yanked her by the arm and they ran together toward the Jeep. The fire had snaked its way toward another tent. More fuel, wondered Andy as fireworks erupted from the tent. Real fireworks. Sparkling flames and whirling flames and high pitched whistling sounds. Sharp pops and bangs. They never, ever, had fireworks in the mountains. Not even on the Fourth of July. The second tent sent up violent flames and ignited more grass between the campsites. Andy hoisted the little girl into the Jeep. He rolled up the windows to keep out the smoke and looked at the encroaching path of the fire. There was no way to tell what was inside the tents or what fuel would go next. He made a decision.

He quickly tested the distance between his foot and the gas pedal, and brake. He checked his ability to see through the front window while touching the pedals. It was close. It would be hard to see and use the pedals at the same time. However, Andy knew the car would move forward without his foot on the gas, depending upon where the idle was set. Mr. Herb taught him that. Reverse would work the same. Only stopping might be a problem. He knew about changing gears from park to drive and to reverse. The other letters on the shifter were a mystery.

Another tent burst into flames. No explosions, but it was enough to convince Andy about the rightness of his plan. He turned on the key and the Jeep made a terrible grinding sound. The girl was

still crying and he wished she'd be quiet. He needed his concentration. Andy slouched down in the
seat, put his left foot on the brake, and turned the
key. The Jeep roared to life. He sat up and looked
out the rear, shifted the gear clumsily to reverse,
and the car jumped back. He steered as best he
could and then dove down on the seat and hit the
brake. The Jeep stalled out and Andy started the
process again, urging the gearshift into drive. He
pushed on the gas with his right toes and the Jeep
bounced forward, finally settling into a crawling
motion that had them heading toward the logging
road. The girl was crying, "Daddy, daddy!"

Andy shouted that she needed to be quiet and
sit up and look out for trees. "This is the first time
I've ever really driven," he shouted. Behind them,
the cooking tent exploded, tossing banquets of fire
across the camp. The girl's tent slowly melted into
a sad, blue heap. They drove through the trees at
about three mph, Andy hanging onto the steering
wheel with bright, white knuckles. "This drivin'
ain't as much fun as I thought it would be," he
said. He told the girl to help by keeping her eyes
on the road, figuring some kind of job might quiet
her down. After what seemed liked many miles of
driving, though it was only a little more than a single mile, Andy saw the flashing light that Jesse
had left behind. He peered through the darkness
for a place to pull over, off the road, in case more
emergency vehicles were coming. It looked clear
enough on the right, behind the light. He steered
in that direction, craning his neck to keep an eye

on the road as he reached for the brake. He hit his blind spot where the eyes couldn't see the road and the foot couldn't reach the brake. He made a swift jab at the floor and the Jeep lurched to a stop, right after hitting something.

Oh well, thought Andy. Don't have to stay in the car anymore. He got out to check the damage. He'd run into a stump and dented the fender. The black Wrangler was sitting a little 'cattywampus' on the edge of the road. The girl was crying again. Andy was climbing back inside the car just as he heard the sweet sounds of more sirens coming up the road and the beating of the Forest Service helicopter overheard. They were sending in the heavy equipment, Andy thought. We're saved. He hung his top half out the window again to direct the oncoming vehicles to the short cut to the new hot spot.

***

Hazlett and the men at the tribal center learned early on about the fire. Ronny Littleriver was one of the volunteers and his wife called him right after Didion phoned the couple's house. Ronny hustled out of the meeting and met the tanker truck in the parking lot. The meeting went on, guided by Ben Johnson, the elder who'd left the mountain, gotten an education, and returned to his people, an unusual occurrence in the world of reservations and rancherias. Hazlett had tried this course before, talking about his demons to the elders and hearing about the spirits that guided their people from the beginning of time. The words about guides and seers, mother earth, the coyote stories, the eye of the eagle, hadn't seemed real to Hazlett. But this time, there was a whisper of truth reaching Hazlett's soul. It was still vague, like a fairy tale meant to soothe or teach a child. Yet, somewhere between the words and images, he experienced a knowing. He decided to be patient and listen.

He left the meeting and drank in the late evening air that continued to ring with sirens. He looked to the northeast and saw billows of white smoke rising from the hill. They are getting hold of it, he thought, realizing that Jesse would be up at the fire with no way to contact him. Hazlett knew that Jesse would not let him down. He knew this about a lot of people in town and still hadn't cared enough to change. If Jesse wasn't there to pick him up, there was a damned good reason. He looked around to assess the situation. He headed down the dirt road of the Rancheria toward town. Somebody would give him a ride to Jesse's place once he was on the blacktop. Hazlett walked and listened. Listening was his new mantra, something he'd never quite learned to do.

With the sound of birds and wind and the fire weaving in and out of his conscious mind, he arrived at the main road. He bounced back to the immediate need, a ride to or near Jesse's cabin.

The road that led to Thompson's place and the one to the Rancheria were no more than a block apart. Hazlett looked to the east and saw a red Nissan pick-up with a small camper sitting at the turn up to the camp and the fire zone. The guy in the driver's seat was covered with a map. Clearly some flatlander looking for a way out. Hazlett figured they could exchange service-for-service. He walked the short distance to the truck.

"Hey," he said. The young man in the truck jumped, surprised. "Didn't mean to scare you, man. Thought you might need some directions?"

"Yeah, sorry. I was concentrating on the map," the man said. "Name's Johnny, and I sure could use some directions outa here. This place has gotten a little crazy."

"They call me Hazlett," he said and extended a handshake to the traveler. "Tell you what. There's pretty much one way outta here and it goes by where I am stayin' at the time. Fair trade?" Hazlett could tell the guy was assessing him. Looking at his red hair, yet Indian features. This was a risk for the city boy. Hazlett looked like danger, yet represented a group that his peers were trying to defend. Native Americans and their sensibilities about the world.

"Get in. Let's help each other," Johnny said.

Hazlett climbed into the cab. They rode together in silence until they reached the center of the town and pulled into Merriweather's Market. "I need something for the trip down," the boy said. "How about you? Can I buy you a beer or something?"

"No thanks. I'm kickin' the habit. I'll just wait right here," Hazlett said. "We Indians are a patient lot." Hazlett gave him a smile. Whites sometimes had no sense of humor.

"Coke, Pepsi?"

"Nope, can't stand the stuff," Hazlett said.

"Okay, I'll be right out," Johnny said, leaving the keys in the car. "Listen to the radio if you want."

Hazlett was feeling good. Taking command for maybe the first time. He watched the white man disappear into the fluorescent lights of the market, a brand of light that felt violent to Hazlett. He fiddled with the radio dial and, finding nothing bearable in the handful of choices, settled for quiet. He watched as old man Merriweather left the store clutching a canvas bag under his armpit. Hazlett gave him a respectful nod and Merriweather nodded in response. Hazlett knew the old man was as conservative as a summer's day is long. But he also remembered that painful time right after his mother had left, that Merriweather had personally delivered bags of groceries to his empty shack. Yet, in a town of little more than five hundred souls, they'd never spoken. For a moment, Hazlett thought that was pretty strange and, without conscious words, vowed to thank the old man at the next opportunity.

Johnny emerged from the electric doors – the very first on the mountain – hugging four bottles. Two were Budwiesers and the others Hazlett didn't recognize.

"These are for me," he said hoisting up the Buds. "And these are for you. Non-alcoholic beer. Sorry, they aren't cool. But I want you to notice that I didn't buy Coors. I remember what they did to your people and the Mexicans back in the early '80s. Anyway, I heard about it and they're on my blacklist."

Johnny was so filled with goodwill that Hazlett accepted the bottles. Not only was he thirsty and broke, he was extremely proud of his eighteen days of sobriety.

"Hey, is it cool to pop one and drive," Johnny asked like a naughty kid.

"Just keep it down when you drive through town and don't break any laws," Hazlett advised, twisting the cap off his beverage. "But I'd wait till we get away from the market. Old man Merriweather doesn't take to any kind of drinking in his parking lot."

They drove peacefully along the main road, Johnny being mindful of his driving and nursing the beer. Whatever the conflict that had lit the spark between the flatlanders and the mountain men faded to insignificance. Johnny and Hazlett were talking easily, like two young men who'd known each other for years, rather than minutes. They pulled up at the turnoff to Jesse's place, the road that followed Jackass Creek and gave way to spider leg dirt roads and property hidden in the pines.

"Thanks, man," Hazlett said, extending his hand in the brotherhood handshake. Johnny's hand met the Tomah's palm and their eyes locked. Hazlett slammed the door and patted it like an additional sign of lasting connection. Short, but intense, given the circumstances. The wheels of the Nissan spun in the dirt and sped away. The night closed in, darkness tinged with the aroma of fire.

Hazlett knew the road even without the light from the crescent moon playing among the branches of the trees. He absentmindedly sipped from the bottle and walked to the turn that led to Jesse's driveway. Except for the discomfiting smell of smoke, it was a peaceful night with only the sound of rustling leaves and the hush of wind singing through the tall pines. Hazlett was never afraid when walking in nature, day or night. It was being inside the constructs of men – schools, courtrooms, supermarkets, the county jail – that shook his countenance. Perhaps, he thought, that's why he didn't mind bars. The light was colored, subdued. Not harsh and violent.

He walked quietly, keeping his senses alert for the creatures of the night, snowy white owls, coyotes, big cats. He'd seen his share walking in the woods and they, on occasion, had seen him. They

186

were like cousins from the same distant family, undisturbed by the other's presence, respectful of their territory. Hazlett took a last pull on the bottle, pleased with the flavor of the substitute beer. He stopped at the fork leading to Jesse's drive and stashed the empty behind a stump. Thinking that it might not be smart to take the other home with him, he sat on the remains of the old cedar and downed the second. He covered both bottles with dried leaves, planning to retrieve them the following day for the trash bin at work.

He stood up, feeling slightly dizzy, and made his way along the road. By the time he'd turned up Jesse's drive and opened the iron gate, he was feeling ready to drop. Getting sick? He felt his forehead. Food poisoning? The non-alcohol beers? Hazlett was staggering by the time he rounded the last curve to Jesse's cabin. His head was hung low and that's why he didn't see the car parked in the drive until the headlights blasted on and drowned him in a yellow beam.

"Havin' a little private party?" Gorring snarled. Blinded by the lights, Hazlett couldn't see the deputy, but knew the voice like a recurring bad dream. He tried to speak, but only mumbles came out as Gorring grabbed him by the elbows and slammed his body against the patrol car. Hazlett felt his temple crack open. Hands cuffed behind his back, he lifted his head to protest. Gorring grabbed a shock of Hazlett's hair and jerked it further back.

"You got something to say, boy? Looks to me like

there ain't no question about you being drunk. And resisting arrest. That's a violation of your bail, isn't it, chief? Now, I suggest you make it easy on yourself and just cooperate. I wouldn't want to have to force the matter, know what I mean?"

Hazlett could feel the warm blood draining down his face. Even if he had wanted to speak, words didn't seem to come to his lips. He felt oddly numb.

"You know the drill, boy," Gorring ordered. "Let's be goin' back to your second home." He yanked roughly on Hazlett's arms, pushing him to the car door. "Pity it's so dark and your keeper is off at the fire. It's just you and me. And you're drunk!" Gorring ripped the door open, slamming it against Hazlett's body. He grabbed a fistful of his hair and forced Hazlett's head down so that he fell across the back seat. Gorring slammed the door shut on the man's left ankle. Hazlett passed out.

***

By the time Jesse got home, it was the early hours of the morning. He'd been on the fire until nearly eleven and then had to locate his car and the boy who'd driven it away. Fortunately, the damage to the Wrangler was cosmetic and Jesse was able to drive home after reuniting the little girl with her father. Andy had been waiting long enough for the adventure element of the night to mellow. He'd spent the last hour dwelling on how much trouble he might be in for disobeying Jesse and crashing the car.

Jesse, however, had seen the scorched earth where he'd first parked the Jeep and was deeply relieved to find the vehicle and Andy gone from the scene. He listened carefully as the boy reported the events that had led to his decision to drive out. There was no need for Andy to embellish his story. The truth was high drama all by itself. By the time they arrived at Andy's trailer, Jesse had the boy calmed down and told him he'd done the right thing. He was not in trouble. It had been bad judgment on his part, Jesse said, to let him ride along. Andy should be proud of himself. He'd saved a life that night.

Andy acted as if this was news. "What you mean that lil' thing of a girl? She was screamin' so bad I had to go find her. She prob'ly would've run out in time."

"You most surely did," Jesse answered, walking Andy up to door of the single-wide. There were no lights on, inside or out. "Your mom home?"

"Naw, she comes home later. Sometimes."

Jesse poked his head in the trailer, letting out the smell of old food and stale cigarettes. "Mrs. Winters?" he called and listened.

"She ain't here, I tell ya. Her pickup would

be here if she was. Don't worry about me, I can take care of myself," Andy said with a yawn.

"I don't doubt that," Jesse answered, thinking how it wasn't right that a kid does a brave act, lives through a forest fire and arrives home to nobody. "But, tell you what. I'm going to leave your mom a note and I want you to come stay with me tonight. Okay with you?"

"Guess so."

By the time they rounded the last bend in the road to the cabin, Andy was deep in sleep. The moonlight cast a gentle glow on the boy's face and Jesse thought about trite references to children as angels. Looking down at Andy's freckled face as he carried the boy into the cabin, the comparison no longer seemed like bad prose.

He tucked Andy in on the leather sofa, wrapping him with a soft blanket and gently placed the boy's head on a down pillow. Jesse eased open the door to his small study to peek in on his other charge. Hazlett wasn't there. Jesse took a long deep breath, thought of any number of good reasons the kid had stayed elsewhere. Fought away the obvious conclusion and decided it was late enough. He flashed on the fact that his gate had been open when they drove in. Jesse always kept the gate shut. He'd handle it all in the morning.

15 / TWO FOR THE ROAD

Choker had been on the wagon since Charlie poured him into bed. He was feeling only slightly better about life when he heard that Hazlett was out on bail – some of the guilt was gone. But, a complicated duel still played out in the recesses of his mind. He suspected that Hazlett hadn't committed the murder. In fact, the kid had still been in the Stag when he'd left for home. But that didn't prove anything. For all he knew, the Indian left right after him. Hell, he had been as pissed off and drunk as Choker. But dislike those city-bastards as much as he did, Choker could never kill one of them, except that night he'd been pretty damn drunk. And, there was the matter of the chain. What if it had been his chain that was used to kill the kid? They'd pretty much have to suspect him.

191

How in the hell would he tell Jenny and their son? Too much. It was just too much at one time.

Anyway, so long as Hazlett was out, there was nothing to worry about. Choker decided he wouldn't let it get as far as the trial before he spoke up. Till then, well, he'd just ride it out. He'd spent the past few days bucking up wood he'd cut from his property. He wiped sweat from his brow – the sun already felt hot, like August, even though it was only late May. He toyed with the idea that maybe there was something like global warming going on. Every summer seemed to start earlier and hotter than the last. It wasn't that Choker was anti-environment. It was just that he suspected the motives of some of the so-called leaders of the movement. They had cushy jobs and six-figure salaries – never having to leave their high-rise, air-conditioned digs to bother with the inconveniences of the environment they were trying to rescue.

The phone rang inside the house and Choker hesitated before revving up the chainsaw. He allowed a couple of minutes of silence to make sure that Jenny had caught the call and set back to work. The McCullough roared to life and Choker cut through a 12-inch log like it was butter, wood-chips flying up and sticking to his wet skin. He shut the saw down and picked up the splitter. Jenny appeared in the doorway, folding her arms across her chest and looking at her husband. This, she thought, is how I like to see him – a sweaty, mussed-up working man.

192

"That was my sister," she shouted. "That crazy Hazlett kid got himself arrested again."

Choker froze and walked closer to her. "Said he got drunk as a skunk, resisted arrest and they took him back to county. Just terrible. I really feel sorry for his Aunt. She's had so much to bear with him," Jenny said.

"Shit!" Choker ripped the leather glove off his left hand, threw it to ground and stormed into the house.

"Honey ... ? What's the matter?"

Within minutes Choker was in the shower and feeling clear about what he was going to do.

Jesse first heard the bad news after he'd dropped Andy off at school and stopped in at the Eye for coffee-to-go. To their credit, the men didn't rub it in or do any "I-told-you-so's." They managed to describe in some detail the events of the arrest and how Hazlett had gotten himself pretty messed up. Stitches on his forehead and a fractured ankle.

"I should've knowed when I saw him with that Hippie," Mr. Merriweather said. "Sure looked like beer bottles he was passing into that truck from where I sat." They lamented the terrible fate that had lately visited Redbud and postulated on the causes.

Jesse took his leave, anxious to get to the office and have a private talk with Blair. In the back of his mind was dread about the talk he knew he'd be having with Anna Sister. He put a lid on the heavy paper cup and carried it by the rim.

What the coffee lacked in flavor, it made up for with heat. Pulling into the newspaper's lot, he was met with the sight of Deputy Rose, one hand on her holster, tapping her foot in impatience. Without more than a mutual nod, they went into the *Timberline* office where they were alone. "This really sucks," she announced, dropping into a chair.

"You're telling me? We've got so much on the line with this kid, I don't know where to begin. Honestly, I thought we were over the hump. I had a feeling ...."

"Hazlett says he had two non-alcoholic beers – at least that's what he thought they were. Talked to him first thing this morning. Poor SOB is a mess. All beat up and sick as a dog."

"From two beers?"

"Non-alcohol to boot. Says he can prove it. Asked me to ask you to go by the tribal house and check on him. Ask the elders about his sober condition when he left. Said old man Merriweather saw him about 8:30 or so – said this guy named Johnny who gave him a ride bought the beers at the market.

"What do you think?" Jess asked.

"Just like I have from the start, I think he's either telling the truth or thinks he's telling the truth. Easy enough to check on," Rose responded.

"I'll go over and see the elders," Jesse volunteered. "How about you? Can you check out the other sources of booze in town? Make certain he didn't make any stops – although I don't know who'd sell to him up here."

"You bet," The deputy paused. ".... You gonna go see her?"

"Who?" Jesse asked, knowing darn well.

"You better do it. She's gotta be pretty upset, after all Sister did."

"A lot of people are upset including yours truly. But sure, right after I stop at the center, I'll swing by. Don't know what I'm going to say though."

"Meet back here at noon?" Rose asked.

"Fine. I have to get hold of Didion, too, and get a wrap up on the fire."

"I heard they put you to work. Also heard that little boy of yours made a hero of himself. You must be proud. Except for maybe the part about taking a kid into a situation like that in the first place." She gave him a playful wink and went out the door.

Jesse made his rounds, stopping first at the junkyard where Didion held an occasional day job. The man, more than once a recognized hero, seemed perfectly happy to be in the midst of the mountain's biggest junk pile, helping folks unload their pick-ups. Jesse knew his biggest thrill came in rescuing what other people thought of as trash and turning it into something useful. Didion wasn't dumb, nor was he lazy - just strangely satisfied with life's leftovers. Maybe some kind of post traumatic stress disorder, Jesse figured, aware that Didion was happier than most people 99 percent of the time. Just another one of the mountain misfits, like himself.

The fire investigators had been over the burn area throughout the morning, Didion said. "Wasn't too hard to find the point of origin - we were on it pretty quick. Looks like a tossed cigarette. Right there in the middle of the hot spot. Pretty stupid for a pack of nature lovers, huh?"

"How many acres?"

"We held it to about eighty, in spite of that dang wind that kicked up," Didion said smearing grime across his face with the back of his hand. "Already hot. Say - thanks for the help last night. My main man was down the hill and I really needed the extra muscle."

Jesse thought about that one cigarette and wondered how SOFTI would handle the bad publicity. He made a snap decision and, instead of driving over to the Tribal Center and then to Anna Sister's, he turned the Wrangler down the hill toward the County Justice Center. Before he made any judgments or decisions, he was going to talk to Hazlett. Look him eye to eye, man to man.

That proved difficult to do. Hazlettt was still on his back on the bunk in his cell. Blair sent Jesse back with a deputy who let him inside and slammed the door shut. He sat on the thin mattress opposite his ward and could see the pain in Hazlettt's face, feel it from somewhere deeper. Raising himself up on one elbow, Hazlett described the evening to Jesse in more eloquent words than Jesse thought him capable of. Hazlett talked about being visited that past evening by a messenger that spoke the truth to him, clearly for the first time ever. He talked about emerging from the council of elders into the early evening and feeling a sense of calm and self that was new, even intoxicating.

"I was still stupid," Hazlett admitted. "I'm not made for anything remotely related to alcohol -the taste, the smell, nothin' about it. And I had enough arrogance going that I opened the wrong door. I am sorry, Jesse. You gotta believe me."

Like Deputy Rose, he did. "Tell me about this guy, Johnny."

Hazlett recounted the short trip from beginning to end. Pleaded with Jesse to check out his story. Even cited Mr. Merriweather as a witness. Jesse promised he'd talk with the business man and also to Anna Sister, reassuring her that her nephew was on a new and better track. "Even after this, even after being stupid and gullible and God knows what else, I am walking a new path," he told Jesse.

A deputy arrived to let Jesse out of the cell and as he turned his back to leave, Hazlett marshaled the effort to sit up straight. His face was swollen like a prizefighter's on the losing end of the match. "You know, Jesse, I don't remember much of anything from the time I got out of the pick-up to when I woke up here. I don't have a clue how this," he passed his hand in front of his damaged body, "even happened. But I do have a picture in my mind of stashing those bottles somewhere that you wouldn't find them. Trouble is that I don't remember where. See, I knew you wouldn't approve of even non-alcohol beer - that's how dumb I was to drink it in the first place - and I hid the damn things somewhere that I'd get to them the next day. Find the bottles, Jesse. I think they were poisoned or bad or something."

Jesse met Deputy Rose at the *Timberline* office as the hot part of the afternoon was heaving a heavy sigh, like everyone in Redbud. At least the nights always cooled down and brought a welcome reminder that the mountains were far more merciful than the valley. Down below, the hardpan would hold the 100-degree heat for most of the night. Air conditioners would work overtime and hum like generating plants. Jesse looked at Rose, dressed in her starched brown uniform that gave no purchase to summer comfort. Not that Jesse ever slacked off in his own dress. He wore a short sleeved western cut shirt that still held creases from the professional laundry in nearby Sugarpine Grove where he dropped his laundry once a week.

Rose was sitting on the porch steps, darting glances back at the patrol car. A furry head and two upright ears popped up and a pair of eyes looked at her longingly. It was David Fossey's Queensland. "Got yourself a new dog?" Jesse asked, sitting beside her.

"Nope. Taking her to the vet. Told David I'd do it if her paw didn't get any better. Poor thing has got quite a limp." He noticed that she'd parked in the shade of a ponderosa and unrolled all the car windows. "Thing doesn't even want to jump out. Paw hurts too much. Her name is Lola – after Lola Montez, the Gold Rush actress."

"So, how many dogs do you have, not counting Lola here?" Asked Jesse, hoping to resolve at least one burning question about the mysterious deputy.

"You mean as of today?" Rose started counting on her fingers. "Shoot, I'd have to take my boots off to calculate that!" They laughed and Jesse figured this too would remain a mystery.

He told the deputy that, as frustrated as he was, he too believed that Hazlett was telling the truth about the previous night. They talked about the irony of the fire being started by a burning cigarette from the defenders of the forest and about the other complications surrounding the events of the past few weeks. Rose said there had been a number of things that had bothered her also. "That's why I decided to track down some information on Hazlett's big city lawyer."

"What did you find out? I had been meaning to go down that road myself."

"Interesting, but still doesn't tell me much. Seems she used to work for a prominent firm down in Orange County. Next thing she's at a scrappy nonprofit law group called Street Legal down the hill. I've been doing some digging on the O.C. firm, but it's one of those corporations with as many layers as an onion. I'm still peeling away."

"Should I even ask how you found this much out?"

"Had to pull in a favor. You know how it goes," she admitted. "I am trying to get back to some solid names behind all the holding companies and entities that are on the paperwork. I'll get it. It's just a matter of time."

They looked up the road toward the Eagle's Eye and saw Andy Winters stepping briskly toward them. Jesse gasped. ""What's wrong?" Rose asked.

"Nothing's wrong. It's just that the boy is carrying books under his arm. I've never seen that before." A smile crept across Jesse's chiseled face and Rose made herself look away.

"Hey!" Andy said to the two of them and then was distracted by Lola. He dropped his books on the ground and peered into the car window. The dog responded with licks instead of barks. "You ain't taking this old thing to jail are you?"

Rose laughed. "Nope. Taking her to the vet. Seems to have a hurt paw. She likes you. Barks at most people," Rose said.

"I like dogs. Wish I could have one. Someday I will." Andy looked at Jesse. "You know who came and saw me at the school today?"

"Nope. You gonna tell me?"

"Yup. Those fellas from the TV station down in the valley, that's who. And," he paused for effect. "The lady from the newspaper down there too. The big one that's got colored pictures on the front."

Andy had made the news again - local hero for rescuing the little girl. "That's great. You were mighty brave," Jesse said and heard Rose whisper so only he could hear, "And you were mighty dumb." Jesse nodded his head in agreement and motioned for Andy.

"Tell you what, since you are probably tired of being interviewed by now and I want the story from your point of view, how about you write something for the *Timberline*?"

"Me? I ain't so hot at writin'," Andy scuffed his boot around in the dirt. "You help me? I put some words on that tape recorder before I had to go get that girl."

"You bet. You wait here while I finish up my talk with the deputy. We'll go back to my cabin, barbecue burgers and write a front page story. How about it?"

"I guess. I ain't got nothin' better to do." Jesse and Rose both cringed.

It had been a full day. Burgers at home with an

eleven-year-old sounded almost peaceful. Jesse thought briefly about inviting the deputy, but discarded the idea as too complicated. And, the sad look in Anna Sister's eyes when he'd visited her earlier in the day, still haunted him. Andy would be plenty to handle.

16 / A DANGEROUS TURN

Choker sat at the bar of the Stag and drank steadily. Recently, when he'd been drowning his sorrows, he'd chosen to sit at a table in a corner, making his own solitude and not inviting any company. Tonight would be different. He knew what he had to do and hitched himself up to the bar for old time's sake. As a matter of fact, Choker was planning on making it his last time.

Rita noticed his change in attitude. "What's up with you Choker. First I see you too damned much, then not all and now here you are acting like it was the night before Christmas or something."

"I just made a few decisions, is all," Choker said ordering another beer. He looked around the room and took in the steady hum of activity. The crew from the mill had gotten off and the men were winding down. There was a handful of local women in the bar, flirting with the younger guys and earning free drinks. A friendly game of pool was on between Birdsong, another Tomah and a couple of guys who worked out in the woods. There weren't many who could beat Birdsong – his hand was steady and his eye could see a dozen angles at once. Choker grinned about the many twenties he'd bet on himself against the young Indian and lost. Lost, a word he didn't want to think about. He'd made a choice and at ten or so tonight, that'd be it.

One of the women dropped quarters in the jukebox and the duet between Tim McGraw and Faith Hill wrapped around the room. Pretty romantic stuff, Choker mused, for a basically gritty place. Not much of beauty happened in the Stag. Not much love. Not the kind that lasted anyway. But, it had been a second home to him for so many years. Where he could come to get lost when he needed to. Didn't want to take his anger home to Jenny. The place where he could bullshit with guys who were in as bad a shape as he was.

Choker tossed down the rest of his double shot of whiskey and chased it with a gulp of beer. He was feeling it, finally. One of the guys from the operation came over dragging along a girl wearing a too short skirt and too much make-up. Hugging the girl with his left arm, he tossed the right around Choker's shoulder. "This here's my buddy," he said by way of introduction. "Choker, this here's my new girl ... What was your name again, honey?" This made them both laugh and Choker wondered why he couldn't get silly drunk, like Ray, instead of mad drunk. "Let me buy you a drink. Where's the lovely owner?"

"You mean he don't own this whole dang bar?" She laughed to her date.

"I believe he is like me," Choker answered, "a major stockholder." This made everybody break up and Ray felt free to express himself. "This big man here," he said to the woman, now known as 'Honey,' this man is my brother." Ray waved his arm at Rita. "Bring my fren' Choker here a drink on me!" He looked woozily down at the Honey girl and slurred, "Les dance." They glided off to the clear spot in front of the giant rock fireplace and clutched at each other - for support as much as for dancing.

Choker looked down at the fresh boilermaker Rita had put in front of him and then up into her eyes. "You know I am not one to chase away business. I figure you're all grown men and can take care of yourselves," she said. "But maybe you better call it a night."

He held her stare. "This will be my last drink. Promise," he said and hesitated. "But thanks for giving a shit. I mean it." Rita wiped the bar with the damp towel in her hand and shook her head.

"Men."

The road was familiar, even on a moonless night, and Choker drove it without thinking - at least thinking about driving. He figured that he had everything in place, yet there was something eating away at the back of his mind. This was a move he had to make and he hoped that Jenny, dear strong Jenny would understand. The window was open and a soft wind slapped against his face. He was about to speed past the Jackass turnoff when it hit him - what he'd forgotten. Of all things.

"Shit," he said into the wind, slowly maneuvered the curve and pulled off the road. Cracking open his door a bit to get the light, he reached inside the glove compartment, removed the .357 Smith and Wesson, fished behind the pile of roadmaps and pulled out a little notebook that he used to keep track of oil changes and such. There in the solitude, the dome light casting a dim, improper glow on the scene, he pressed the pen to paper and thought. Choker wasn't much for writing and got stuck on the first line. He looked up and thought he heard something. Choker didn't want any surprises, so he gently shut the door and extinguished the light. For a moment the dark was as complete as in a mineshaft, but his eyes adjusted and soon shadows appeared. The sound erupted again - a flut -

tering disturbance in the trees not high up. Choker looked and locked on a branch where a great bird spread its wings, dipped from its perch and flew in front of the truck. It was an owl, a Snowy Owl. Beautiful sight, he thought, but bad luck. At least that's what everyone on the mountain said.

He grew impatient with his task, thinking that words should come so much easier to a guy who was all liquored up. He hoped like hell the rest of the night would go like he'd planned. He reviewed that night by Jackass Creek again. Had he been so drunk he wouldn't remember a brawl with that kid, Chris? Whatever had happened he would make it right tonight. Choker popped open the door again and decided to write the first words that came to mind.

Just as two sentences had flowed from his sluggish brain, to the ballpoint and onto the paper, a hauler carrying a load of firewood he intended to sell in the valley, roared around the curve. The driver had capped off his trip with five or six beers at the Stag and had popped open a bottle of Coors that lay tucked between his legs. He had the windows down to blow away the smell of alcohol that just might be on his breath and the radio was blaring a Neville Brothers tune. He was singing along and feeling no pain. The sudden appearance of light where it didn't belong drew the drunken driver like a moth to a flame and he broad-sided Choker. There was a cacophony of sound, the explosion of breaking glass and then silence. A thin hiss escaped from the engine of one of the trucks, like a rattler's warning. High above an owl sent its hollow cries into the night.

Fifteen minutes later the wail of the sirens carried faintly back to Choker's house and Jenny felt a chill. Jesse heard the sirens too, but was focused on getting his young guest tucked into bed. The story they'd done together was going to be a winner. He didn't feel like chasing ambulances, or whatever. The news would wait.

17 / UNFINISHED THOUGHT

Andy rose early the next morning but not early enough to beat Jesse, whom he found rummaging around in the brush alongside the driveway. "What're doin? I'm hungry. You ain't got no food."

Jesse apologized about the food and promised to take him to Eagle's Eye for a quick breakfast after he searched a little more. "What you lookin' for anyway?" Jesse knew the boy wouldn't be put off so he told him that two bottles that were evidence in a case might be hidden alongside the road. "I can help look." Of course, Jesse knew this would be next and he made Andy promise to holler if he found anything. Not to touch anything. "Cause that could compromise the evidence," Andy announced and Jesse stopped in his tracks. How the boy could go from "ain't" to "compromise the evidence" within one sentence amazed him.

"Right," Jesse said. "Fingerprints, stuff like that." But Andy wasn't done. He wanted Jesse to tell him who hid the bottles, when and why. Once briefed, he set about his task like a bloodhound, quickly finding the mound of carefully piled branches and leaves behind the cedar stump, right where Hazlett had arranged them.

"How?" Jesse began and then said. "Never mind. Thanks, you found them."

"Well, it weren't no bear that made that nice little pile there," he said by way of explanation.

Jesse had Andy run into the house and bring out a chopstick and two small paper bags. Jesse slipped the stick into the mouth of the bottle, careful not to lose any liquid that was left and placed each into a bag. He put both packages upright into an empty soda carton before making Andy go back inside the cabin and brush his teeth. They packed up and headed out to breakfast at the Eagle's Eye where they were met with a range of emotions.

Daisy came traipsing up to them and put her arm around Andy. "Well, aren't you the town hero ... and a TV star to boot." She wiped her hands on her apron. "By golly, I am going to buy you breakfast young man. What do you think about that?"

"Swell," Andy said, beaming.

"You, Mr. Publisher, will have to buy your own," she added to Jesse and hurried off to the kitchen.

There was no need, in Daisy's mind, to take orders. She knew what would suit them both best. And they would eat it, and like it.

Jesse and Andy settled in at the table next to the council's. Charlie dramatically picked up the valley newspaper and held it out at arm's length. "If my old eyes don't deceive me, I believe we have a celebrity in our presence." He turned the front page around so that Andy could see his own face, in full color, staring out just under the headline, "Young Hero Saves Tyke from Forest Blaze."

Herb took the paper from Charlie. "Here Andy, you might want to read this. And, maybe take it home for your Ma. She'll be proud." Charlie scowled. He'd bought that paper and hadn't finished the sports section.

"Cool," Andy said and set about slowly reading the article.

It was then that Mr. Merriweather marched in shaking his head. He focused first on Andy. "Saw you on the 11 o'clock news, young man. Good for you. Stop by the store later and I'll treat you to an ice cream bar." The hero stuff was getting better with each minute and Andy started to think what it might be like at school. He turned his attention back to the article.

"Guess you'll be talking to the sheriff again, Jesse? Nasty accident on the main road last night. About ten. You hear about it? Fatality." All eyes turned to Merriweather's – except for Andy's, being busy seeing his name in print so many

211

times. Merriweather explained that a fellow from the valley, driving a one-ton truck hit Choker's Dodge, and crushed the entire side of the local's pick-up. Merriweather paused for some dramatic affect. The guy in the wood truck was killed on impact – flew right through the front windshield - and Choker was down at Valley in critical condition.

There were lots of mutterings about Choker – "Poor guy." "As if he didn't have enough trouble" and from Charlie, "Jenny's the one I feel for. I swear Choker's been trying to kill himself with drink ever since that last layoff."

Before Jesse left the Eye to drop Andy off at school, he jotted a quick note, folded the paper and handed it to Mr. Merriweather. "Appreciate it if you could look into that for me, Mr. Merriweather." The old man unfolded the paper, read the message and tucked it into his shirt pocket. "I believe I can do that. I know the owner," he said to Jesse with a conspiratorial look. After the door of the café slammed shut, Mr. Merriweather's compatriots were all over him. But Merriweather refused to tell them what was in the note. "This is confidential press information. I would be violating a trust if I told you all what it says. Maybe even the Constitution," and that was that.

Jesse drove to the school and left Andy in the company of adoring classmates – mostly girls. He was confident the boy was going to have a very good academic day. Back at the *Timberline* office, he called Sheriff Blair. His headset on, he took notes about the crash for a story that would just make the current week's edition. Once the formal details were noted, Blair said, "Off the record." Jesse saved the notes he'd typed into the computer and sat back, picking up a pen and pad of paper. It was a journalist's inescapable habit.

Blair said that Choker had received very severe head injuries in the crash and was barely hanging on. Jenny was down there with her husband and suffering her own kind of pain. "That's why I didn't say anything to her about what I found in Choker's truck." Blair explained there was a .357 on the seat, right under Choker's battered body. "But what makes it worse, is that I also found the beginnings of a note," Blair said and took an audible breath. "It looks like he was thinking about taking his own life." Both men shared some silence over the phone line.

"The note was pretty clear about that?" Jesse asked.

"There were only a couple of sentences. It was to Jenny. I haven't told this to anybody so you keep it up close and personal, hear?"

"Got it."

"At this point it would serve nobody's good to let this out," Blair continued.

"Agreed," and Jesse heard the rustle of paper as Blair began to read.

" Jenny,

    First let me say that I am sorry I didn't talk to you about all this but I have made a decision and I have to do what I have to do. I have not had much courage in the recent weeks and I am about to change that ....'

And that's where it stops."

Jesse was relieved that he wouldn't be writing an obituary for Choker – although he'd only known the man as a local acquaintance. Tragedy in the mountain community was a shared experience, no matter what they relationships were. The men finished their conversation with updates about Hazlett and a brief discussion of the mysterious corporation that had first hired the Indian's lawyer. Jesse said he had some questions of his own that he was researching – Deputy Rose had started him thinking about a few more complexities in the case.

He hung up and mentally organized his day. A courtesy visit to Anna Sister was first on his list, then writing the stories – including an interview with Mark Kingsley from SOFTI about the fire - and getting the page layout going for electronic pagination. The rest of the day he planned to spend on the Internet and telephone. It promised to be a very long day, but then every Tuesday – the day he put the paper to bed – was a long one.

18 / FRONT PAGE HEADLINE

Anna Sister, having entirely returned to her elder being, was unmoved by the recent events in her nephew's life. "I know him now. The elder men have told me of the visit he had from his spirit and I am not worried," she had reassured Jesse. "I am thinking now about you." She gave Jesse a soft smile that told him nothing about what she meant.

Mark Kingsley turned out to be a more difficult conversation. He seemed to be a sincere young man and like most of the activists, was a transplant from metropolitan life. Being one himself, Jesse harbored no resentments or judgments about his immigrant status. Nonetheless, Mark was acting defensive about the findings of the fire investigators.

"Well, they'd just love that, wouldn't they? Environmentalists starting a forest fire," Kingsley had first responded. "After all, who's on that fire crew anyway? A bunch of good old boys, that's who."

Jesse had developed a decent rapport with Kingsley and just looked at him in silence. "Sorry. I'm just real upset. I've been under a lot of pressure about this," he darted a look at Jesse, "and that's not for publication."

Jesse told the young man he wanted to fairly represent the environmentalists' side of the story and he couldn't do that if Kingsley wouldn't open up a little bit.

"Okay. Let me take part of that first comment back. The fire fighters up here are super. We all owe them a debt of gratitude. And, I'd like to point out that about twenty people from our group were right on the lines with them. We worked together, no matter what the cause of the fire."

"What precautions did you take about fire up on the property?" Jesse asked.

"No open fires. Only contained ones in stoves and portable barbecues. There were buckets of water at every campsite and we ran two hoses out from the main building, where I live. We've been doing this for about five years and this is the first

216

time we ever had anything like this happen. We make it our business to be careful," Kingsley said. "Preserving the environment is our business."

Jesse took notes and probed further. "Do you find it surprising that someone from your group tossed a lit cigarette? Assuming that's what happened?"

"Assuming that - Yes, I find it completely unbelievable. We do orientation on the very first day. Fire safety is number one. Everybody who smoked cigarettes had a coffee can filled with sand on their site. It's not possible one of our people is that unaware."

They talked some more and Jesse went off-the-record with Mark. "This baffles me, truly," Kingsley said. "We have a lot at risk, media wise and according to our philosophy. I just can't believe one of our group did such a dumb thing." He paused and looked around at the charred acres that stretched in front of him. "Then again, I can't imagine anyone from town doing this either. I've been around here long enough to know what wildfire means to everybody." He kicked at the ground like an upset child and billows of blackened dust kicked up. "Shit. This is my home now and look at it!" He swept his arm across the landscape. The grasses that had turned golden only weeks before were gone and a brittle shell of charcoal covered the hillside. In the far distance, at the tree line, ponderosas stood like burned matchsticks, twisted black twigs protruding out from trunks like lethal needles.

"I'll be hearing about this from folks, for sure.

But on a personal level, I am very hurt." Mark's eyes filled momentarily with tears.

Jesse asked him more about the SOFTI's national affiliation and learned that headquarters were in New York and that there was an "advocate" office in Washington D.C. Jesse immediately translated "advocate" to "lobbying." It was due to someone from the national group, Kingsley explained, that he and the Northern California group had use of the land in Redbud. He didn't get much of a salary, only a stipend to keep the place up and for operations such as mailings and such. "But, that's all right with me," he said. "I love it up here and I don't really need money." He looked around quickly as if making sure they were alone, "And, I am writing a book. Almost half done," he added, "Off the record."

Jesse closed his spiral notebook and hurried back to the office where he spent the next six hours on the newspaper.

***

Andy's story was slated to run above the fold on page one. Jesse smiled as he highlighted the boy's byline to be in bold type, followed by "Special to the *Timberline*." Andy had done a pretty good job in *telling* the story, but had fallen a bit short in the writing. Jesse helped out, capturing the words Andy spoke into the tape recorder like the TV reporter he now wanted to be.

218

Mid-day, Deputy Rose swung by with Lola still in the back seat. She collected the beer bottles and put them inside a small red cooler. Rose explained that Lola had endured minor surgery, had stitches and needed a special diet for a while - something her owner David couldn't afford. So, for the time being, she had a foster dog. She peeled out of the parking lot, spraying Jesse with a coat of red dust. He figured it was intentional. He was right.

Jesse also grabbed a few minutes to call Emma, the County Clerk, a woman he knew well because of his profession, who did a manual search and came up with a parcel number and the name of the registered owner of SOFTI's mountain land. Then, he placed some strategic phone calls to old colleagues down south. After the close of normal business hours, he hit the Internet. Jesse went into the website for the Clerk Recorder in Orange County and started his search. Grateful for technology, he worked overtime, well into the early hours of the morning. One layer of information led to another and to yet another website. Unfortunately, Jesse came to a dead end when he hit the county in New York where the records he wanted to search were not available online. He'd have to wait for the morning and then call, hoping he'd get someone cooperative enough to help him over the phone. It was one thing to charm Emma over the counter in Goldrush, but quite another to do the same over a phone line. Driving home and musing about the power he seemed to have surrendered with the move to the mountains, he decided what to do. He'd engage one of his friends at the powerful L.A. Daily Sun to make the call and extract the information. If you can't use your ex-friends, he thought, who can you use?

He rose with a morning high. It was not all that unusual for Jesse to wake up almost euphoric in his mountain home, but this was different. His instincts were on alert. It had little to do with the natural environment but for a change, everything to do with his occupation. His skin tingled when he thought about the recent events in Redbud. His mind was working overtime. He stopped long enough to remember that when he'd had that feeling before. Then, he'd actually sought to heighten it with a thin white line. Build on the high. Just a little line to make it all happen faster. Thank you - he didn't feel that need anymore. Framed by his front door, Jesse looked out at the pine forest that embraced his cabin. He stepped outside and stared upward at the circle of soft blue sky framed by the peaks of the trees. He breathed deeply and knew. He knew a damned incredible story when it was happening. And it was his. Here in this little nowhere town, his sheltered workshop.

Ginny and Fred showed up at the *Timberline* office as they did every week that their pickup didn't break down, with bundles of papers, 200 to a bunch, tied together and tossed under the camper shell. Jesse tore open a bundle and nervously paged through the tabloid-sized paper. Though Jesse had no kids, he imagined each new paper like birth, intense and brand new. At first, he'd traveled to the valley and stood at the end of the press line, checking copies as they came off the whirling drums, still wet and new. He'd finally let go and trusted his printers - the fourth generation of Tatolians to run the business - to do the job right. It had been liberating for Jesse. He'd found that any mistakes in the paper were very likely his own.

19 / PLOTTING THE SCENE

Jenny sat by her husband night and day. Choker was in a coma and the doctor couldn't make any promises. "There's a great deal of swelling. With a head injury like that, we're lucky he's alive," he'd told Jenny. "I'm sorry, but this is all about waiting ... and praying - if you are so inclined."

So Jenny waited and, as she waited, she talked to her husband of thirty-two years. "Remember that first picnic you took me on?" she said, "and the bear that was more afraid of you than you were of him?" She laughed with the memory. "I was just terrified and making myself small while you stood up taller than tall and made this huge noise like no human being I'd ever heard. Then you turned over my tin of Apple Brown Betty that I'd made and banged on that tin like crazy. Hollering and banging ... And there I was, watching that dish I'd made just for you, scatter all over the ground and ... I fell head over heels in love with the man who dumped it out." Jenny drew a long, deep breath. "I didn't tell you then, but I wasn't much of a baker and I'd stayed up till three in the morning trying to get it right. I'd already fed two tries to my dog - who got sick." She simultaneously laughed and cried. Jenny went back to silently praying.

And so the next two days went by until Sheriff Blair showed up, holding his hat in his hands. He and Jenny exchanged a few quiet words and sat, one on each side of Choker. "You tell him that he's got to get well real quick," Blair said. "Logger's Jamboree is come'n up and he needs to teach those young bucks a lesson." Blair recognized what a foolish idea this was but was expressing an emotion, rather than making a suggestion. Jenny recognized love when she saw it.

"Thank you Sheriff," she said. "But I have already told him that he'll have to settle for being a coach this year. I want him right next to me. He'll have to root for our son, Cliff. He's gotten to be quite good." They fell silent. The sound of the monitor set a tenuous rhythm in the room, interrupted only by a woman's voice calling from the desk on the PA system. Blair knew it was a live person, but the voice sounded oddly disconnected and mechanical. Blair wondered what earthly good he could do sitting silently in this room, but he felt compelled to be there.

Choker made an audible sound. Jenny sat bolt upright, grasping the arms of the bedside chair. Blair saw her start and they both riveted their attention on Choker's face. His eyes flickered and his lips barely parted. Blair stood up and leaned toward Choker, his eyes locked with Jenny's in hope. Choker's tongue flicked over his lips, preparing to speak. Blair held his breath.

Choker tried out his voice for the first time since that night on the road, maybe realizing for the first time that he was alive. It began with a guttural growl. "Mine," he said, drawing out the vowel in a husky whisper. "I was on ... my ... way ..." And Choker's eyes and lips shut.

Jenny took her husband's words to mean that she was his - "mine." And that he was on his way home. Blair had a different take, knowing about the note and gun.

Blair headed back up the hill with a resolve. The tragedies that had hit Redbud would come to an end. To almost lose a man like Choker - a good man - to suicide, just plain didn't have to happen. Blair believed that Hazlett was innocent. Unlike some men wearing a badge, it was important - in fact, central to him that the guilty person, instead of a convenient person - be brought to justice.

Blair drove directly up to the *Timberline* office. He knew that Jesse had been putting in some extra hours on the case - as had Deputy Rose. It was time to compare notes. When he pulled into the parking lot he found that Rose was already there. This is good, he thought, a good omen, reminding himself that he didn't believe in omens. Blair also noticed there was an unauthorized dog poking its nose out from the back window of Deputy Rose's car. He wedged his hat on his head and trudged up the stairs.

It was supposed to be the "down day" when Jesse could plain take off or do whatever fed his fancy. It was an unusual Thursday that he sat inside his office - this time behind his desk instead of perched upon it - and faced two people on business.

Blair filled them in on his trip to the hospital. He said there was no need to tell anyone else about the note and the gun he'd found. "What good could be served?" he asked. "Except when Choker's back on his feet again, I may kill him myself!"

Jesse put a white board on a stand alongside the desk. He suggested they list the unanswered questions, throw out the handful of answers they'd found and try out some possible explanations. Try to create a chain of plausible, related events. They laid out the questions:

1. If the chain that was found wasn't Hazlett's - whose was it?

2. What was the point of the "set up" accident at the mill?

3. How did Hazlett get drunk on non-alcoholic beers?

4. Who called and tipped Gorring, if anyone did?

5. How did Hazlett end up with a hot shot lawyer? Luck of the draw or something else?

6. Who owns the property that SOFTI occupies?

Jesse thought of another question but didn't speak: Who else could possibly be involved—Gorring out of hate? Mac, for financial reasons? Choker, due to drinking way too much? He kept these speculations to himself.

Blair felt an obligation to point out that a whole new set of questions could be developed with the assumption that Hazlett was, indeed, guilty. Deputy Rose jumped on that suggestion.

"Well, if he is, we've got him," she said. "And since we are taking the position that he isn't, it's our obligation to think of alternatives, right?"

Blair grumbled a little but had to agree. They listed the evidence:

1. The chain
2. The severed latch
3. The remains of the cigarette
4. Hazlett's bottles

And, once again, Jesse added a piece. He remembered the embossed cigar band he'd found in the dust. "I don't know if it's related. I actually forgot about it. It's in a shirt pocket at home."

"Could be nothing," Blair said. "Lota guys up here enjoy a cigar now and again. Including yours truly."

Jesse reminded him that no one "enjoyed" a cigar in the mill. Smoking of any kind was prohibited for obvious reasons. And, the band he'd found was from a very expensive Cuban cigar. Jesse recognized it as the kind that used to be passed around in the cocaine crowd in L.A., but didn't add that piece of information. "A cigar like that could cost at least $80," Jesse added. "A little steep for the average mill guy." The band was added to the list and Jesse promised to give it to Blair first chance.

They then threw out theories, tried to make them fit the events and then tossed most of them - in whole or in part - away. Finally, after more than two hours of ideas and possible scenarios, they believed they'd found a thin thread running through each of the events. They parceled out assignments, sending Blair and Rose on the road and Jesse to the telephone and Internet for the balance of the day.

Blair dropped the bomb just before he left. "Hazlett is scheduled for a prelim next Wednesday. The deputy prosecutor is going all the way. He says that Hazlett's had plenty of chances. Murder One."

Rose looked at Jesse. "I might also point out

that this very same county official is planning on making a run for D.A. in November," she said. "Take a guess at what his platform is?"

"No mercy for repeat offenders? Three Strikes all the way?" Jesse answered.

"Got it on both counts," Rose said.

"It gets worse," Blair said. "He's got Fredrick Christiansen on the bench." Jesse and Rose simultaneously uttered the same four-letter word of regret. Blair shared their concern. "I swear, I wouldn't be surprised if the judge and Deputy Gorring share the same branch on the same family tree."

They would have less than a week to answer the questions that decorated the white board. Questions that, the deputy rightly observed, ought to be dealt with by Hazlett's lawyer. The need for immediate action pushed them back to the board, reconsidering the entire chain again and again as the sun moved across the blue steel roof of the Pole Building.

They divided up the tasks that needed doing. Jesse would use his familiarity with online searches and his expertise as an experienced journalist to go after information that probably resided in a dozen places across the country. Deputy Rose said she'd tap her own sources and call in some favors, leaving Jesse once again wondering about her background. Rose also said she'd make it her business to find out more about how and why Hazlett's attorney got a job so far from her big city home and her area of expertise which was corporate law. Blair would take charge of local information and physical evidence. It was early evening by the time they parted company. None of them was looking forward to a night of relaxation and fun.

It was Jesse who finally leaned back in his chair to suggest the common element. His years as a reporter allowed him to entertain the very worst of human failings. Unlike the kind of crimes that most often occurred in the mountains - those from blind rage or drunkenness or desperation - Jesse's hypothesis required cunning, manipulation and planning. The sheriff was surprised by Jesse's suggestion. Rose took it in stride, shaking her head as if she'd had the same suspicions.

20 / ANTICIPATION

The Jamboree was little more than a week away - starting Friday afternoon with a parade, then a program at the town hall and a dance - followed later by an enormous amount of drinking. The *Timberline* would enjoy more than its share of advertising dollars for the event. Jesse had even convinced some of the local shops to pool their money and buy ads in publications down in the valley. "It's like singing to the choir," he'd said to Jeeter at the hardware store. "Everybody up here will come anyway. You need some of those tourist dollars from the valley."

The next issue of the *Timberline* would pretty much write itself. Like all the stories done by daily newspapers on a seasonal basis – the dangers of the summer sun, families in need at Christmas, the risks of skiing off marked snow trails – the Jamboree varied little, except, occasionally, for the names of the winners. Jesse had his part time writer on full time duty for the event, and the inimitable Alice would be covering it from her perspective, Skipper had renewed interest in his job as a photographer and Jesse produced like a man possessed.

He was particularly proud of the current week's issue of the *Timberline Times*. Not only was Andy's story a big hit - getting even more raves than the professional story in the valley paper - but several of Skipper's remarkable photos were spread throughout.

The lead stories, written by Jesse, had painted the stark contrast between the peaceful gathering of protestors and the later fiery outbreak at the encampment. Together with Skipper's photographs, the paper offered a powerful account of the week in Redbud. His young photographer had surprised Jesse. Not only had he demonstrated uncharacteristic enthusiasm, but also talent that hadn't sparkled in his previous work. There was a shot of a group of young people gathered in a circle, playing music that could easily have been taken in the early 1970s. Skipper's portraits of faces spoke to a purity, an innocence and confidence of youth. Women's faces without make up, proudly wearing faint smiles and freckles.

Happy golden-haired children with dirt streaked across their cheeks. Intense, longhaired men looking like New Age philosophers.

They were, easily, the best photos published by the Timberline and were competitive with the majors in a daily market. Jesse made a note to himself to do something about that by the week's end. The Print Journalism Association's annual awards were coming up and Skipper's work belonged there.

Jesse had also written a news story about Choker's accident, tinged with hope that the local man would survive, and laced with regrets that the valley wood seller had not. In his editorial, Jesse had once again urged calm in the community and went on to uplift readers with thoughts about the upcoming Logger's Jamboree. It was the only annual celebration in the town, sponsored - as it had been since the early 1950s - by the Mac-Dougald logging operation.

Mac's father had started the tradition, proud of his men and the skills it took to make a living in the woods. People didn't fully appreciate what it took to saw a fifty-inch diameter log in half or throw a twenty-foot chain around a load of logs on a truck. People didn't know about the strength and precision it took to harvest trees that made houses, or paper and pencils for their kids and helped to fuel the region's economy. But Mac Mac-Dougald did and he wanted to spread the word.

The company's sponsorship of the event had some unanticipated results. The burley, red-haired Scottish immigrant had been genuinely proud of his crews - nothing more. But the competition had become part of the culture of the guys who worked in the mill, the loggers and the drivers. It had embraced their families and, eventually, the entire town.

As the date of the Jamboree drew closer, the workers taunted each other with challenges. Rita at the Stag, and the sheriff, turned a blind eye to casual bets that were placed on favorite competitors. Weekends and early evenings were reserved for practice and the men (along with a handful of women in recent years) hauled rounds of logs home to become bull's eyes for ax throwing practice. Business at the Stag even dropped off slightly while the participants were in training.

The Jamboree also had a public relations impact - which back in the 50s and 60s wasn't a concern for the industry. People from the densely populated valley made the annual excursion up the mountain to attend the event. The daily newspaper gave it front-page coverage and television reporters particularly enjoyed themselves. By the late 90s, women TV reporters were doing on-camera demonstrations of time-honored logging skills - locals jamming together in a pack to get their faces on the evening news. Of course, it was ludicrous for coiffured reporters to attempt feats that took years to learn, but it served a purpose. The valley was in love with the myth of the mountains, and its state and congressional representatives voted accordingly.

However, throughout the previous decade, the conservative element from the Central Valley had been in the political minority. The gradual rise of the environmental movement had amassed considerable power and financial resources, exerting a profound influence on forest management policies. "Green" lobbyists making six-figure salaries found the doors on Capitol Hill were wide open. At the bottom of the pyramid were thousands of idealists and volunteers, creating grass roots support.

At the same time, the timber industry was changing, discarding old - and destructive - ways of doing business. The evolution was fueled by the instinct to survive - and new environmental information. But, the activists' ball was rolling and gaining power. The environmental movement had developed an elite class of its own and a vested bureaucracy with lots to lose. Liberal politicians smelled the wind blowing from the West and wrote a suite of new laws. Without much clout, the political right fought a losing battle. Mills and logging operations shut down in droves and communities became extinct.

That's why the 49th Loggers' Jamboree was so important. Like a drowning crew holding their heads above the rising tide, the men and women from Red Mac Logging Company vowed - without a meeting or a vote - to take the tradition to its 50th anniversary, no matter what. Jesse had pledged the support of his newspaper toward this goal and signed on as

234

chairman of the publicity committee, using his practiced media skills to shine the spotlight on Redbud's Jamboree.

Alice Forester had been writing about the event for twenty-five years. Her column, usually devoted to births, illnesses and hospitalizations, and an account of who had visited whom during the previous week, focused on Redbud's quality of life. "Well, we can't go back to the old days, though I sometimes wish we could," she wrote. "And drinking too much won't solve our problems. What some young people of today don't understand is what it is like to grow older in this little town and all of a sudden think you might not have a job and maybe then you might have to move away." Jesse left the rambling sentences alone, having learned that editing Alice was a futile (and unpopular) effort. "Well, so many of our men have worked in the woods since they were teenagers, like their fathers did," she continued. "Suddenly, you're 50-something and you might lose your means of livelihood. Many of the old-timers (like me!) don't have the education or the future that some of the newcomers have, bless their hearts. Oh dear, I wish we could all just get along!"

With the paper distributed among the mountain's tiny communities and social centers, Jesse concentrated on his portion of the assignments in the investigation. He got an update about Choker's condition - sleeping most of the time only able to mumble unintelligible words. But, it looked as if the critical time had passed. Jesse spent a few hours on the phone talking to L.A. contacts and doing more investigation on the Web. By lunchtime, he felt that he was breaking through some barriers and could sense an answer within grasp. He walked down the street to the cafe, with a feeling of anticipation.

In the Eagle's Eye copies of the *Timberline* lay on tables and chairs. The council had convened for lunch and immediately declared to Jesse that the paper "was the best issue ever."

"I have to admit," said Charlie, "that I have done some travelin' and this here paper is as good as any I have ever seen."

"Yup, Charlie went to Bakersfield on the back of a mule once," Paul joked. "Weren't they still making newspapers on stone tablets back then?" Everybody laughed, including Charlie.

"Well, for a change, Charlie's right," pronounced Mr. Merriweather with authority. "We've finally got us a newspaper that makes us proud. Jesse, you are to be complimented."

The men nodded their heads and Daisy, who had slipped out from the kitchen gave Jesse one of her special smiles. Strangely uncomfortable with the attention, Jesse acknowledged their approval. At the same time, he wondered where this sudden dose of humility had come from. He'd never been reticent to receive prizes and accolades before.

"Matter of fact," Mr. Merriweather continued,

"I believe I'd like to have a private conversation with Mr. Publisher here. I'll be by your office soon as I finish my business." That "business," Jesse knew, consisted of no more than a couple more cups of coffee and pearls of wisdom.

Back at the *Timberline*, Jesse spent some more time on researching his part of the investigation. He thought about making a quick run over to the school to see how Andy was doing but decided it was better not to leave. There was no telling when Mr. Merriweather would show up – other than in his own good time.

Jesse's concentration was razor sharp as he made calls and pulled in some Southern California favors. He shot e-mails to his contacts and scribbled down random thoughts by hand. Though he was twenty-some years older now, the feeling of breaking a story was the same as it had been in his youth. The challenge of the story, the illusiveness of the information, the trail he built call-by-call and contact-by-contact developed into a picture of the truth. Truth that often had more than one face – such as the ongoing timber wars, where truth resided on all sides.

There was fire in the belly of a journalist, Jesse recognized, much like that which drove guys like Didion to chase danger; and cops who could go from bored at the donut shop one second to peak performance in the next. The focus and commitment, the living in the moment had been Jesse's natural high – until that other chemical high had dimmed his instincts. But the pure, good feeling was back and Jesse experienced it fully for the first time since he'd come to the mountain. There was a story to be unwound, uncovered and told and the stakes were high.

Merriweather didn't bother to knock. He shuffled straight in and took a seat, looking curiously at the newspaper's electronics. "I never will get the hang of those things," he said shaking his head. "But I guess there's no going back. The computer is here to stay."

Jesse agreed and said it was a great tool in his business, particularly helpful to small newspapers in mountain communities where modern resources tended to be scarce. He sensed the old man had started the computer conversation not as idle gossip, but for a reason. That was Merriweather's style.

"Yep, I don't touch the things myself but I do recognize good business ... that's why we're computerized at the store. Saves me money, gives me better records and all." Merriweather paused and Jesse remained silent, waiting for the punch line. "That's why I can tell you with total confidence that whatever knocked Hazlett out didn't come from my market. Not only do I have a record of the purchase made by that young man in the pick-up with Hazlett, two cold bottles of Coors and nothing else, but our records show we've been outta that non-alcohol stuff for more than a week. Not much call for it around here."

238

Merriweather said he'd been able to pinpoint the time the purchase was made because he'd seen Hazlett in the parking lot. Being a stickler about keeping his wind-up watch totally accurate and making sure that nothing illegal was going to happen in his parking lot, Merriweather had checked the time, in case he'd have to talk to the sheriff later.

This was the first opportunity to talk to Hazlett's witness to about the ride and Jesse gently asked the merchant some questions to see if his answers corroborated the Indian's story. Merriweather's description of the pick-up truck was a match. He was even able to add some critical information about the license plate. His eyes weren't good enough to read the numbers even if he'd wanted to, but the plates were clearly from out of state – Oregon, he guessed, but couldn't swear to it.

"The kid looked like the rest of them. Kinda scrawny, hair a little over the ears, dirty blond. Think he had a short beard going too. He didn't stand up real straight, I remember that. Wore a green jacket – one of those light ones - and had a backpack over his left shoulder. I saw him mostly from the back coming out of the store. I had my eyes on Hazlett most of the time. That boy has caused his people some grief. Hope his aunt is all right. Good woman." Merriweather said the stranger had come out of the store carrying one paper bag and had handed bottles through the window into Hazlett. "I have to admit, that's when I got worried. Hell, I should have called the sheriff."

"You didn't?" Jesse asked, assuming it was the businessman's call that had alerted Gorring.

"Naw, I didn't want to go back in the store and I figured, with the fire and all, the sheriff would be plenty occupied."

Merriweather left, walking the short distance from the Pole Building to the market. Somewhere in his seventies, he still kept regular but flexible hours in his tiny office, looking over papers and occasionally strolling the aisles like a Lord surveying his people and holdings. For all Merriweather's pretended rural simplicity, Jesse knew the man had an innate sense for good business – installing computerized checkouts and inventory tracking belied the "simplicity" that many mountain people purported to have.

The phone rang just as Jesse was scrolling through his emails. He opened up a message from an editor buddy down south and stared at the screen as he answered the phone. It was Deputy Rose on the other end, telling him that she'd found the source of Hazlett's attorney – an East Coast corporation named "LL Ltd."

"That is how the corporation is registered but I read further down into the whereases and wherefore's and found "Landing Leisure Development Corporation," Rose reported. "I have the officers' names – none of which means diddley to me. It's privately held and I've got folks working on a list." Jesse glanced at his computer screen. It was a trail of company and corporate names. He scrolled down while listening to Rose and came to the end. "LL Ltd" appeared at the bottom. The ancestor of all the entities above it and a match to the deputy's findings.

They sat in silence over the phone, knowing that something very important had been discovered, yet not knowing the significance. Rose said she would use police resources to get more information about the officers and email her list to him. Jesse told the deputy about Merriweather's visit and his description of the man who'd probably set Hazlett up. "The sheriff's been all over the lab in the Bay Area to get the analysis of what was inside those bottles, out as quick as possible," Rose reported. "But, they're like all labs – overloaded with emergency projects."

"I think it's smart to assume that Hazlett was drugged," Jesse said. "Once we find out by what, it might lead to by whom, but we can't wait. Another thing ... when Merriweather told me how much he saw, I assumed he'd made the call to Gorring since Blair was up on the fire. But, he says he didn't. What does Gorring say?"

"Says he got a call that Hazlett was violating the terms of his bail from some male who wouldn't give his name," Rose answered. "He was down here at County and said he drove right up to your place and waited."

"Interesting. It takes a good thirty minutes minimum to get to my cabin from headquarters, if all goes well. Merriweather was very certain about what time he saw Hazlett in the parking lot. Gorring would have had to drive like a maniac – or fly like a bird to get there before Hazlett. It's only about eight minutes from town to the turnoff. Walking time from the main road to my place ... about twelve to fifteen minutes. What time did Gorring get the call?" Rose was uncharacteristically quiet.

"It didn't say in the report he wrote up," she answered, aware she had missed an important detail. "I'm sorry, but I let my dislike for the man get in the way. I haven't actually talked to him. I just read the report. He's due on at three today." Rose said she'd get back to Jesse with the time of the call. "Better yet, I'll stop by after I take Lola to the vet. She's still limping." The compact little Queensland had become a near partner for Deputy Rose over the past days and Jesse suspected the woman was looking for reasons to keep the dog just a little longer.

They hung up. Jesse continued to look at the chain of companies, five in all that stood in front of LL Ltd., burying the source to all but the most curious and persistent. He did an Internet search on the company and found nothing. Being privately held, there was no requirement to file with the Securities and Exchange Commission. LL Ltd. would be accountable only to its shareholders, whomever they might be. He heard the "ping" of Outlook receiving a message. That would be the list from Deputy Rose. Jesse printed out the list, glanced at it and recognized no one. He laid the paper alongside his keyboard and picked up a plastic baggie that held the cigar band. For a moment, he let himself recall the parties, rooms filled with the rich and sweet aromas of contraband Cuban cigars. The air, hanging heavy with curls of smoke wrapped around beautiful people snorting coke from Sterling spoons and drinking in the promise of uninhibited sex with willing women. He looked at the colorful embossed label accented with gold decorations and put in a call to a Southern California contact who once worked for a cocaine kingpin in Colombia.

21 / JAMBOREE HIGH

Keeping with tradition, the mill closed early on Friday to allow the workers to prepare for the weekend's festivities. Most of the women, however, remained behind, busy on last minute details of the forty-two-foot long float. The parade would start at six p.m. that night, attracting nearly everyone from a twenty-five-mile radius for Redbud's half-hour on Main Street. The only phone line to cross the thoroughfare had been removed for the event by a crew wearing what looked like, at least, official phone company uniforms. There was a rumor the mill's annual entry in the float division would be breathtaking and also very tall.

People stood in friendly groups along both sides of the street. The blue and white patrol cars sat at each end of the eight-block long route, flashing lights closing down the only road through Redbud. The porch surrounding the Stag's Leap was thick with men in clean Levi's and women wearing lady's western blouses who were eager to get an early start on the night. From his post on the railing of his office, Jesse looked up and down the street. He smiled to himself as he remembered the parades of his past. The Rose Bowl, Macy's Thanksgiving Day Parade – events he'd covered as a young and rising journalist star. Oddly, none was as meaningful as the heartfelt procession that would roll, dance and march by his office this night.

Andy had joined him for the evening and Jesse tried to keep an eye out to track the boy's whereabouts. Two television stations and a photographer from the daily newspaper were on the scene, being trailed by Andy who had already made friends with the reporters. Jesse was amused to see it was the TV cameras hoisted on the shoulders of burley men that Andy followed. The boy showed less interest in the newspaper team. Jesse spotted Deputies Rose and Gorring working the lines of people back from the street. Rose had come by (dog-less) and said that Gorring had gotten the anonymous call about an hour before he'd arrested Hazlett, confirming what they'd thought. Rose had seemed a little down, less spunky. Jesse owned it up to her having to leave the dog behind for some minor surgery on her paw.

The parade began with the blast of powerful hollow whistle from the mill, followed by the shriek of the siren from Sheriff Blair's official car leading the parade. The parade's Marshall, this year Tommy Thompson, rode in Mr. Herb's vintage convertible Hudson – brought out only once or twice a year.

As always, the high school band provided the marching music, followed at a great distance by a group of young Tomah dancers wanting to keep time with the rhythm of their own drums. The Boy Scouts, Girl Scouts and 4H Club tripped along in uniform waving to their families on the sidelines - the Lion's Club from nearby Ashbury ran alongside the same float they'd shown for years, the Lions wearing the costumes of bears and bobcats. Not to be outdone, the Finegold Elks threw candy from a float decorated with flowers made from white plastic bags. The Church of the Everlasting Convenant rolled down the street with churchwomen kneeling atop the float, clutching bibles and handsaws and toy log trucks to thematically unite their entry. A giant styrofoam cross leaned against the cab of the truck, threatening to topple each time the driver braked.

But, as Alice Forester had predicted in her column, none could compare with the mill's entry. The mill had won the float competition for more than fifteen consecutive years and was now competing against itself. As it rounded the curve into town, people gasped. The cherry red rig, shined to a gemlike finish, pulled an entire forest on its bed. Trees towered twenty feet into the air, boulders that looked real enough to hold gold were artfully arranged on the rolling landscape. "How did they do that?" whispers rose from the crowd. Had they read the *Timberline*, they might have guessed. According to columnist Forester, the mill's secret weapon was an administrative assistant who had gone to valley once a week, for six months, to learn faux painting at an adult school class. Topping it off, two of the mill's best climbers hung, suspended by ropes, pretending to clutch the trees. The mystery of the downed phone lines was solved.

There was one entry that didn't make it to the street. As they had in past years, protestors had gathered to make their comments about the event. This year, they'd wanted to have their own float in the parade. The organizers – consisting of a hometown committee, had denied the application. On behalf of the entrants, SOFTI filed suit in court but was too late to get an injunction or a decision about the group's right to march in the parade. Consequently, the entry sat like a losing contestant on the road leading to Town Hall for all to see and few to admire. It was a paper-mache gravestone, painted to look like redwood (even though redwood had never been harvested in the area), pulled on a wagon by a young man in the garb of the Grim Reaper. A small band of "mourners" surrounded him. Jesse noted that it was still early enough for townspeople to walk on by without comment. Later in the evening, as the drinking and revelry heated up, the young objectors would not be ignored. He took comfort in knowing that Mark Kingsley also knew this and was generally able to control his minions. The whole Jamboree parade had taken little more than a half-hour from start to finish. The crowd disbursed, some families heading home and others to Town Hall where an award program and dance would later be held.

Jesse looked for Andy, planning to scoop the boy up and head over to hear the speeches and a few tunes by local musicians. Most specifically, he wanted to be there to applaud his delivery team, Ginny and Fred, who were doing a karaoke duet in the opening program. Then, he planned to hustle himself and Andy out of town and away from the action that characterized the first night of the Jamboree. He silently prayed that he wouldn't get a late night phone call about some tragedy at the Stag or on the many winding roads to home.

Late that night when there was nothing but darkness and the sound of the wind in the trees, after Andy was deep in sleep, Jesse sat at his desk and stared at the list he and Blair and Deputy Rose had made. He memorized the corporate chain of ownership that ultimately led to LL Ltd. And read, once again, the notes he'd taken during the talk he'd had with his SoCal drug contact. The cigar band had once wrapped around a Cohiba.

It wasn't, as Jesse had suspected, an eighty-dollar cigar. It cost at least one-fifty, way out of the league of Redbud's working man. He booted up the laptop he kept at home and began his Internet journey to the land of cigar aficionados.

It was nearly two a.m. by the time Jesse was satisfied that no resident of Redbud could come by a Cohiba honestly. The pressure for information was mounting. Hazlett's first appearance before Judge Christiansen was only five days away.

Saturday dawned hot – day two of the Jamboree feeling as if the sun was already high in the sky and it was August, though it was only early June. Across the quilted patches of Redbud, loggers had gone to bed entirely sober and awakened early – forsaking the usual Friday night socializing. They showered and lingered a moment in front of their bathroom mirrors, feeling self-conscious as if someone were watching. Later in the day thousands would in fact, be watching. Even Don Dyke, who'd competed and won in many events, but now, served as an organizer and judge, did what many of the loggers throughout the mountain were doing. He flexed his biceps, twisted his wrists to see if the sinewy muscles still made contours on his arms, and smiled at his reflection. Even at his age, Dyke thought, he looked pretty damned good. Others, filled with the vanity of youth, spewed forth into the morning driven by hormones and history.

At the community park, civic leaders were already

at work. Jeff, the pharmacist, had laid out sites for vendors by trailing a bag of flour to mark out the fifteen-foot wide spaces. Daisy had set up a booth to sell her cinnamon buns. The marketing guy, who had created her slogan in a drunken moment, also told her that food sold "through the nose – like popcorn. And what smelled better than fresh baked cinnamon buns?" The Tribal Council had several booths – one selling intricately beaded jewelry made by locals and the other offering crates of faux turquoise adornments made in China. There was a small stand for the traditional Tomah drink made from ground acorns – geared pretty much to the Indian community where the drink was a treat - and the few brave white people who tried to choke it down with dignity.

Yet another stand would enjoy nonstop business throughout the weekend. Indian Tacos were, of course, a recent invention. But some entrepreneurial Tomah women had made the dish more than the expected concoction. Weeks before, they mixed up dough that was frozen and then thawed during the day of the event. As it thawed, it rose slightly and then was fried until it puffed up like pastry. Marinated beef that was rubbed with a secret blend of spices, topped with shredded greens and cheese, tomatoes, cilantro, local herbs and a salsa were wrapped inside and guaranteed to dribble down chins and onto clothing. Rumor was that the Indian Taco had been invented in Redbud and later spread across California. However, the old women whispered that the version that escaped from the kitchens of the Redbud Rancheria, was lacking a "secret something." Anna Sister herself had told Jesse the essential flavor had been passed down from grandmothers since the "coyote's first walk." That is to say, since the first meal around a fire.

The announcer's stand had been assembled and the audio team from the local high school was on hand to manage the sound. A radio station from the valley was also set up to do live broadcasts throughout the day with on-air personalities standing by to sign autographs. Accommodations had also been made for the television crews, including a media tent sponsored by industry giants like Stihl and Husqvarna.

But the focus would be on the events arena. There, twenty-foot logs were laid out, giant rounds of pine had been decorated with targets, and forty-foot poles jutted from the ground waiting to be climbed. A log truck, shined and polished like a piece of jewelry, was parked to the side and loaded with logs, each no more than thirty inches in diameter. Regulations passed in the mid-90s prohibited the cutting of anything bigger on public lands and, although the timber for the Jamboree had been donated from privately owned forestland, Mac thought it was a good idea to show how the letter of the law was being followed. However, for some of the competitions, much larger logs had to be used. The regulation size was no challenge for the experts.

After a quick and early breakfast at the Eye, Jesse left Andy in the keeping of Herb who promised to get the boy home for a change of clothes and to check in with his mother. Once the events started, Andy would be working in the media tent, thanks to Jesse, helping the reporters and, no doubt, following the cameras around.

At the *Timberline* office, Jesse pulled up the blinds and looked down on the street that, for the moment, was quiet. In a half-hour, the road would see more traffic in one day than it did throughout the entire year. Although he'd had only four hours of sleep, Jesse felt invigorated and excited – as though he was standing on the edge of a cliff and contemplating flying. It was, he knew, the adrenaline rush of a great story in the making. He was only waiting for more pieces to come together and, as planned, answers walked in the door with Sheriff Blair and Deputy Rose.

Blair arrived with verification that the bolt had been cut with an ordinary, handheld hacksaw. It had been a rough cut and whoever did it took more than a little time on the job and didn't appear to be experienced with such tools. Hazlett's toxicology report from the lab in the Bay Area had been waiting for Blair when he checked in this morning – emailed to him after the sheriff convinced the lab to make the tox report a priority the day before. Hazlett had indeed been drinking non-alcohol beer – laced with a benzodiazepine and an opioid to cause the effect of downing pure alcohol. The chemists said that Hazlett's reaction had been severe, probably because he'd been clean for two weeks, and the toxins threw a major shock to his system. They also said the concoction was not the work of a professional – it was a crude but effective mix.

Rose had produced a very short list of investors in the parent company that lay behind the layers of corporations. The majority owner was a name that Jesse immediately recognized – the illusive Tyler Wentworth. He drew in an audible breath. "I'm going to make one quick call and if the answer to my question is what I think it will be ...," he said to the sheriff, "this is a whole lot bigger than any of us anticipated."

After Blair and Rose left, Jesse checked his watch and decided that it was not too early to call. Mac would already have been up for a couple of hours, getting ready for the Jamboree. When he finally locked up the office to drive over to the Jamboree, he had a very clear picture in his mind of what had been happening in Redbud. He even knew the name of the person who was orchestrating the events. However, knowing the name wasn't all that much help when the perpetrator was not using it, but hiding under another identity.

Veterans of Jamborees past arrived two hours early for the afternoon's event, visiting the booths, standing in the queue for Indian Tacos and staking out shady spots on the bleachers that surrounded the main arena. By high noon the competition was about to begin. Dirk Dixon, the announcer from the local high school sports department put on his best microphone voice and opened the show, welcoming visitors, promising feats of "bygone glory" from the men and women who would demonstrate their skills. This, he announced, was the biggest crowd he'd seen in his years of emceeing the event. He introduced the dignitaries, starting with Mac and Tommy Thompson, thanked the sponsors and introduced the soloist, a gospel singer that had come all the way from the south end of the valley to sing the National Anthem. Jesse listened from his post near the entrance to the park. Closing his eyes, he could hear strains of the great gospel singer Mahalia Jackson in the woman's voice. The decision to pay a professional, he figured, had been a good one.

The anthem was followed by "America the Beautiful" from Big Don's wife, Elaine, who whistled the piece like a virtuoso. What had first, years ago, seemed ridiculous to Jesse, was now a treat for the ears. By the end of the rendition, the crowd was singing along and Dyke was beaming with pride. Reminding people that logging was serious – and often dangerous – business, Dixon then called for a minute of silence "let it be in prayer, if you are so inclined, to remember all the men who lost their lives in woods, working hard for a living and caring for their families and their community." Only the wind in the tall pines made the music, and folks stopped and bowed their heads. A blast from

254

the trumpet section of the high school band broke the silence. The crowd chorused a sigh and Dirk shouted, "Let the Games Begin!"

Jesse's eyes were not on the arena, however. They were surveying the crowd. Just outside the entrance, the SOFTI contingent sat under an Oak tree, their protest signs lying on the ground. The Grim Reaper showed up and positioned his headstone like a marker alongside the entrance. But, overall, the protestors seemed mellow. Mark Kingsley, on the other hand, appeared to be uncharacteristically nervous - pacing and walking down to the main road frequently.

Blair and his people were scattered throughout the crowd and at the entrance. Police presence was more obvious than in other years although the tone of the day seemed non-threatening. Mac was in the arena near the judge's stand. He liked to watch from up close but never took part in the timing or judging. People said he looked like the ghost of his father, cheering his people on and throwing his great arms over his head when competitors from the mill placed or won.

Loggers came from all over the West - much like riders in the rodeo circuit. Oregon and Washington were the most represented states after California. Many of those who traveled to logging competitions were near-pros and some of the locals didn't stand a chance against them. But, some did and town pride swelled like a tide when the local favorites showed up the out-of-towners. The events also inspired much booing when the visitors were up, but they were used to it. Jesse had interviewed them in the past and the out-of-town competitors played the same role as the nemesis characters in the World Wrestling Federation. It was all in a day's work.

The afternoon moved on through ax throwing, with a Birdsong man standing up against an Oregon logger and winning. The pole climbing competition brought the crowd to its feet as two men scrambled up a ninety-foot pole, rang a bell at the top and made their way back to the ground as fast as possible. The best of the bunch made the climb and descent in 20-some seconds. It was a photo finish with a Washington logger beating the local man by a half-second. The tie-down competition saw the first female entrants - amazingly lithe women throwing the massive, heavy chains across a fully loaded truck and leveraging the lock in place. They'd had the choice to compete against one another, but the four women had decided to take on the men, pretty much knowing they'd lose. Still, their efforts were impressive and much appreciated by the crowd who cheered them on with boisterous enthusiasm.

Choker-setting was next on the program and Dirk introduced the event by announcing that Redbud's favorite "Choker" was conscious and expected to make it through. "Our friend is being moved out of intensive care tomorrow and sent his wife Jenny to join us today, as a sign of sup -

port," Dirk said, motioning for Jenny to stand. "She thanks you all for your prayers and support." There was abundant cheering before the competitors lined up alongside logs four-feet thick. A signal gun started the chainsaws screaming and the loggers dug tunnels underneath the fallen logs like manic gophers. Once clear to the opposite side, a chain was tossed though the hole, the competitor leapt over the log whipping the other end of the chain with him, clamped a lock in place and threw the choker chain to the ground. Timers clocked the seconds on a stopwatch. When the dust cleared and the victor's arm was raised in triumph, more than few tears were shed. Choker's son, Cliff Anderson, took the trophy.

The heat rose along with the dust in the arena. A county water truck rolled in and wet the dirt. Snow cones and cotton candy stained the faces and fronts of kids, spectators folded their programs into fans and beat at the hot air. The men and women in the arena glistened with sweat and drank from jugs of water donated by the Sparklett's outlet in the valley. It was mid-afternoon and time for the Hot Saw competition. The timer's gun erupted, its echo quickly drowned out by the revving up of powerful chainsaws. Young children buried their heads in some soft spot on their parents and most people in the crowd cupped their hands over their ears. The scream of the fine tuned engines was fierce. It still amazed Jesse that men were able to harness such remarkable power in their hands and command it to slice through logs as if they were made of butter. Just the right angle here, the right pressure there, manipulating the saw bar for maximum speed until three perfect slices of log rounds fell to the ground. Ten burley men lined up, some pumped with massive muscles and the strength of youth. But, when the timers checked their clocks, it was a middle-aged sawyer from the mill who won by a margin of a quarter second. His wife stood grasping the railing shouting, while tears streamed down her cheeks with pride in her aging logger.

The final event of the day took the crowd from the arena to the pond near the foot of the hill. Halfway down the slope was a solemn event that had already begun under the roar of the chainsaws. Tomahs had gathered, men in a tight circle, handmade drums sitting between their knees. Some were in traditional dress, others wore blue jeans and tattered tee-shirts. All had tied headbands around their jet-black hair. Their heads bent toward the drums as they rhythmically pounded the skins with leatherwrapped mallets. The crowd milled on the edges to listen, curious kids inching up close. The singers sat inside the circle, an elder leading with cries that seemed to come more from the mountain than from the man. His young acolyte sang next, with words from the language of his ancestors that almost no one but the elders understood. Yet, Jesse, standing under an oak, strangely felt the meaning of the words as his mind drifted. It seemed like only a moment in time, but he had been filled up, his thoughts taken away and replaced with a pure feeling he would later try to bring back. His eyes had been closed and when the drumming stopped, he opened them to see Anna Sister standing in the shade near him, watching. They didn't speak.

The last event was a crowd-pleasing favorite. It had it all – comedy, hot competition and cool water. Two competitors stood on a floating log, trying to spin the log in unpredictable directions that would knock the other man – or woman – off and into the pond. There was a little more "equality" in logrolling since it didn't absolutely require strength. Balance and agility counted for a lot. Everyone pitied the poor man who got dumped into the drink by a woman. But it happened more than once that afternoon. Susan Shaughnessy, in fact, placed in the top three spots, winning because she was very fast, athletic and smart, but also because she was a knockout looker and knew how to distract men from the task at hand. At the end of the event, she stood on the massive stump of a long dead tree and pumped her arm in the air as Skipper eagerly shot pictures for the *Timberline*. Shaughnessy basked in the spotlight.

It had been an excellent afternoon, passing with appropriate excitement and without any unpleasant surprises. Back around the edges of the clearing where the event was held, there had been the customary drinking but it hadn't gotten out of hand. Jesse smelled the faint aroma of pot in the air as he passed by Kingsley's group. No one cared. Andy had done a "stand up" for one of the TV stations and was eager to get to a television to watch himself on the evening news. And, Deputy Rose was deep in discussion with the vet, Dr. Nobel, their foreheads nearly touching as they looked at something in his hand. Jesse felt a little surge of emotion and then laughed at himself. Actually, those two would make a very good pair, he thought, and went to fetch Andy.

With the competitions won and lost, the visitors wound slowly down the hill - creating the only traffic jam that Redbud would see all year. Reserves from the sheriff's Department and the Civilian Corps were called out to direct the swarm of cars and campers trying to be the first out of the gate and on the road. The evening would belong to the locals.

Winners would be honored at the annual dance at Town Hall with a live band, a bake sale by the local churchwomen and no alcohol, athough everyone knew that plenty of alcohol would be consumed. Back at his cabin, Jesse dressed for the evening and explored the uneasy feeling that wouldn't leave him. He was missing something important in his calculations of what was going on. It was why he hadn't immediately shared his theory with Blair or Rose. It was also his instinct as a reporter to hold something back, play out the possibilities until he felt as if he was dealing with facts instead of suppositions.

There were contradictions in the information he was compiling. After backtracking the name of the entity behind Hazlett's lawyer, Jesse found it led to

LL Ltd. The same group that owned the property adjacent to Thompson's, where SOFTI folks camped. Even more surprising was his discovery – several layers down the chain – that LL Ltd was ultimately behind the offers to Mac for his properties. There was a connection among the seemingly separate events - one that currently made no logical sense to Jesse. Why would a company that supported the likes of a far-left environmental movement pay for the defense of someone who allegedly killed one of their own? And, why try to acquire MacDougald's property with a very competitive offer? And, finally, where was the elusive Tyler Wentworth, activist-dropout who still pulled the strings of the radicals while owning a sixty-five percent interest in LL Ltd.?

Passing his office and rounding the curve of the hill leading to Town Hall, Jesse was met by an unexpected gathering of the environmental clan. Behind the small group of familiar faces, including Mark Kingsley's, was a throng of people milling around old yellow school buses. Jesse estimated the group to number about one hundred. He pulled over and caught Mark's eye, got out of the Wrangler and met the young man on the edge of the road, slightly distancing himself from the gathering. Jesse immediately noticed the new flock of protestors was not the same folk who came to the annual spring gathering. These people looked more intense, perhaps a little older than the campers had been. He felt an edginess in the air as Mark looked at him. This, calculated Jesse, was why

261

Mark had been periodically dashing down to the main road earlier in the day, looking nervous.

They nodded and Mark waited for the questions he knew were coming. He said that SOFTI National Headquarters had been concerned about the potential fallout from the fire – that his people might get blamed just to distract the media from the real issue. The real issue being the rape and destruction of the forest.

"This is a pretty big contingent for damage control," Jesse observed.

"I guess the whole thing picked up momentum when they realized the Jamboree was this weekend. They figured it would be an opportunity to make an even bigger statement," Mark explained. "To be honest – and this is off the record – I recommended against it."

As they talked, Jesse looked more closely at individuals in the crowd. Many simply looked like city versions of Mark and his usual contingent. But, here and there, were people with sharp eyes surveying the area. There was nothing relaxed in the demeanor of these men and women. They looked ready to spring into action. Jesse asked Mark what the plan was.

"You know I can't tell you that, Jesse. You and the sheriff are like that," he said, crossing his fingers. "Then again, I am not looking for any trouble. Certainly no violence. That's not SOFTI's way, as you well know." Just as he was about to say more, a tall man with broad shoulders and collar length black hair sauntered over. He nodded at Jesse and looked him up and down.

"Mark, man, you're needed by your people," he said with only the faintest hint of an order in his tone. "Unless your friend here wants to join us?"

"This is Jesse Kilgore, publisher of the local paper," Mark said. "He's been real fair. Jesse, this is Mike Jones from our branch in Idaho." When Jones (if that was his name) shook hands with Jesse, he noticed a slight unnecessary pressure in the newcomer's grasp. 'A challenge?' Jesse wondered.

They parted company and Jesse continued on to Town Hall where, at some point in the evening, he fully expected the protestors to join the locals. Walking up to the big shake and shingle building that served many purposes for the townspeople, Jesse saw the mood was not as celebratory as it might have been. Clearly, people had seen the gathering at the base of the hill.

The council of men from the Eagle's Eye, seldom seen all together outside the café, had convened around a picnic table near the entrance. Charlie let out a piercing whistle and motioned Jesse over. "You seen that down there, I assume?" he asked, and Jesse half nodded and half shook his head.

"You know what that means?" Charlie continued and proceeded to articulate his answer. "It means this here night is going to be a rough one. The one night that Redbud gets together and really puts it on, is gonna be ruined."

"Oh don't be such a damned old pessimist," Paul said. "We've had those kids up here before and they've never been more than mosquitoes."

Merriweather, thinking like a businessman, looked on the positive side. "My clerks said a bunch of 'em came in the store and was just as polite as could be. Said they weren't even buying liquor – like the rest of the town had been since 5 p.m. I'd worry more about our guys."

Flip, who had been one of those "guys" that Merriweather had been referring to echoed Charlie, as he usually did. "Hell, this is a time for cele-bratin'. And it's our celebration, not that pack of rejects' down on the road. If I was younger ..." Flip's voice trailed off and it was clear the old timer had already put down his share of beer.

"Well you ain't!" Charlie snapped. He hated it when Flip really tied one on. "You just stay with us and keep it buttoned."

Herb, who was as pressed and pleated as ever, was sporting a new western shirt and nails so clean they looked as if they'd been manicured. He folded his hands on the table. "My advice is simply to expect the best and behave as if it were happen-ing," he said. "Nobody can take away the pride we all feel about this day – no matter how hard or far they march."

264

"Can I quote you on that?" Jesse asked with a smile. It was the kind of thing that only Herb could get away with saying.

"If you are so inclined," the gentleman said. "And Jesse, just a heads-up. Andy's mom, bless her, brought the boy with her to the dance. Now, I know we support that, but I suggest we keep an eye out for him later – just in case ol' Marsha finds another ride home. Know what I mean?"

Jesse agreed and moved on to Sheriff Blair's cruiser where about six deputies and twenty-some reserves were gathered around. The sheriff was giving them marching orders for the night – saying to fully expect a certain amount of drunk and disorderly, to handle it with a firm – but gentle – hand. Not to tolerate any fighting at all, to haul off everybody involved and be brutal about drunk drivers.

"This year, unfortunately, we have a new element to deal with. Now, I don't know what their plan is," Blair said about the protestors, "but I don't think they came up here to dance and eat oatmeal raison cookies. Some of you have had training in crowd control – hold up your hands ..." About eight people, including Deputy Gorring and Deputy Rose responded. "I want you eight to make teams with the rest. If anything comes down, the teams meet and follow every order from the designated leaders," Blair said. "Get in groups now before the night really gets going. Decide where to reconvene later, if that becomes necessary. And,

Rose, come back here when you're done. You too, Gorring." He turned and faced Jesse. "I got a bad feeling about this."

Jesse nodded in agreement. "That's not the same crowd that I met up with at the camp before the fire broke out," Jesse said. "Matter of fact, I think that even Kingsley has some concerns. Did your people have trouble with them yet?"

"Nope. In a way, I wish we could have written a traffic ticket or something - just to check a couple of ID's, but so far they've followed the letter of the law."

The two agreed they could expect visitors at Town Hall later that night. Probably after dark. If it came to pass, the results could be very bad. The combination of logger's pride, copious alcohol consumption and the dark could be explosive, perhaps lethal. Blair considered calling the sheriff in a neighboring county to bring in reinforcements, just in case. "If I don't call Joe up in Blue Lake County now, it'll do no good to call him later." Blair stroked his chin and wrinkled his forehead. "On one hand it could be nothing. Then again ... damn! Those kids could cost the county a bundle tonight!"

Before leaving the sheriff to make his decision, Jesse briefed him on what he'd discovered and suspected. "None of that means much if I can't find the source. But I'm convinced it's just one person," he said. "I think this is way bigger than logger verses activist. That's what really scares me."

"Maybe tomorrow we can focus more on this," Blair said impatiently. "Right now I've got myself a situation that's pretty immediate and, so far as I can see, unrelated."

"I'm not so sure," Jesse said as he walked up to the steps of Town Hall. Inside, the program was about to begin and Dixon was attempting to quiet the crowd down. Once the chatter had ceased, the only sounds left were of ice falling into glasses of homemade lemonade and the voices of small children wanting to be noticed. Dixon kicked off the program by introducing the winners' circle – a dozen local men and Susan Shaughnessy, who had won or placed in the day's competitions. As each name was read, the electric guitarist in the band struck a Hendrix-style riff and the crowd roared. Pride was palpable in the room, like something that could be grabbed and held.

Dixon then introduced MacDougald – who "needed no introduction" and the Jamboree committee, including Jesse, who declined to walk up on stage. Finally, before letting the musicians loose, he introduced the Jamboree's Marshall, Tommy Thompson. "Tommy has asked for just a couple of minutes of our time and, after all he's done for us, don't you think he deserves it?" Applause flooded the hall and then quiet resumed.

"I'm not much of a speaker," Thompson began, "but tonight is special and I know we all want to keep it that way. I am privileged to be here but I feel the need to ask each and every one of you a favor – a favor that will benefit us all. As you know, we've got ourselves some visitors." Boos and hisses rumbled the room. Thompson held his hand up. "I know, I know. And that's just what we can't do. The sheriff will make sure they keep their distance and we all have to make sure that we keep our cool," he said, looking over the room like a diplomat. "Cool heads, no confrontations. No aggression from any one of us. If they taunt, we remain silent. If they threaten, we walk away. This is our town, not theirs. We must remain in control. Remember, tomorrow, they'll all be gone and we'll still be here, feeling as much pride as we do tonight." Applause began softly and then erupted. The people were with Tommy. He held up his hands one last time. "I want to thank you for the great honor you have given me. God bless Redbud and each and every one of you." Thompson exited stage right, not wanting to stand still for the applause that exploded and shook the rafters. MacDougald was right behind him. Neither man really liked the public spotlight.

***

Dixon jumped up and shouted, "Let the music begin!"

Jesse worked his way back to the door, out of the range of the blaring speakers and the full dance floor. Deputy Rose was leaning against the door jam, looking out at the perimeter of the parking lot and into the trees. They stood in silence for a while and then she looked up at him. Her green eyes sparkled in the last of the day's sunlight – looking much like the color of leaves on a poplar tree. Jesse heard himself asking a nonsensical question. "How's your dog?"

"It's not my dog. It's Fossey's dog. And, why do you ask?"

"Why do you ask, why do I ask?" he answered and they both smiled.

"I had the distinct impression that you are not a dog lover," she said. "I can always tell."

"Was it something I did?"

"It was something you didn't do," she answered. "Most people who like dogs have the urge to pet them. Never once have you reached out to pet Lola, though you've had many chances."

Jesse laughed. "Old habits die hard, I guess." He reached out his right hand. "See that tiny little set of scars between my thumb and index finger? That came from an encounter with a dog when I was six years old. I reached out to pet it, and this is what I got. Stitches and a rabies shot. Pretty memorable."

"I'm sorry – but a lifetime of afraid?" she said.

"I'm not so much afraid as cautious," Jesse said, "and, of course, embarrassed."

"Embarrassed? There's nothing to be embarrassed about when you get bitten by a dog!"

"There is when the dog is a Chihuahua," Jesse replied. They both laughed out loud. "Seriously, I saw you in consultation with the vet and thought something might be wrong." Quite unintentionally, Jesse had placed a slight emphasis on the word "consultation."

Rose, who missed little, lowered her eyes. "He was showing me what he pulled out of Lola's paw," she said. "It was a very nasty piece of metal about a half inch long, sharp as a needle and just as bright. Poor thing. She's going to be fine now. He's a really good vet."

Jesse paused a beat, recognizing a piece to the puzzle had just been found. "Rose, the bolt on the gate at the mill was a half-inch wide," he said.

"Jeez, you're right!" Rose slapped her head. "I can't believe I didn't make the connection!"

On the tip of Jesse's tongue was a comment like, "maybe you were too distracted," but he swallowed it. "I think Lola's owner needs to be talked to again," he said instead. "Have you seen him?"

"David would never come to anything like this. He's far too – intellectual? preoccupied? My guess is that he's working."

They stood on the front porch and chatted as the sun disappeared behind Eagle Eye Mountain. The music pounded and people danced. There were shadows in the pine trees skirting the parking lot and Rose knew what was going on. All the officers did and had decided, in the interest of peaceful community relations to let the drinking go on unless it got out of hand. Mostly, folks would just sleep it off at home or in their cars. No harm done.

"Wonder what time they'll come," the deputy said.

"The longer they wait, the worse the consequences could be," Jesse responded. "Matter of fact, I think I'll take this lull to run over to the mill and have a little talk with Fossey. Take him one of those famous oatmeal raisin cookies."

"Okay, sounds like a plan. But I won't be able to reach you if something comes down here," Rose said. "Blair's got a handheld in his cruiser, let me give it to you, just in case. Since I know what you're thinking."

Jesse was worried. If the deputy truly did know what he was thinking, he'd have to be embarrassed all over again. "You do?"

"Yeah, I know you're thinking all these things – the protests, the land deals, the killing – are somehow connected ... and that David is maybe a part of it." She paused. "And, I agree. Just can't put it together. Frustrating."

Jesse was relieved and impressed. "Right – and between you and me, I'm a little worried about the make-up of that new crowd I saw down there with SOFTI's folks. There's something about a few of them. Like maybe I've seen them before. "

"Me too," Rose said handing him the two-way radio. "Only difference is, I've *actually* seen a couple of those same faces." Just as Jesse was about to ask the obvious question, Rose spun on the heel of her boot, gave him a quick salute and dashed over to the sheriff who was shaking his finger in Deputy Gorring's face.

22 / BURNING AGENDA

Jesse rolled down the hill and onto the main road. He peered to the left toward town and saw the muted glow of a few headlamps and the bobbing of flashlights. SOFTI's people seemed to be where they'd been an hour earlier. What are they waiting for he wondered and worried.

He turned right and headed up the hill that climbed to the mill and far beyond, to the mountain's crest. He passed the Rancheria. Between there and the mill was a mile of darkness that he once would have found disturbing. But, exiled to life in Redbud, Jesse had grown to be at ease with nights so dark they could never be duplicated in the electrified city jungles. His eyes adapted quickly to the absence of artificial light and what he could not see, he'd learned to hear. Over the past year or so, there had even been moments when he'd been alerted to things in the dark from pure feeling – a sensation he couldn't locate or explain.

It was this feeling that spoke to him now as he pulled into the dimly lit parking lot of the mill. The tires of the Wrangler sounding like firecrackers on the loose gravel. He stopped just inside the open gate instead of driving into the lot next to the main office building. He peered along its side. He wasn't sure why, but he was careful to walk softly as he approached the building. In the rear of the building there was a single light burning in the office that David used during his night duty – on working days it was occupied by the bookkeeper. Jesse walked to the window and looked inside. There were two desks crammed in the small space. An old-fashioned black telephone and a paper bag that looked as if it might contain a midnight lunch sat on Fossey's wooden desk, a jacket with the emblem of the mill on the back was draped over the chair. On the floor next to the chair was a black duffel bag, unzipped.

Jesse backed away from the building and headed for the operations center of the mill, walking on the balls of his feet and silently cursing his decision to wear Western boots. They were not made for stealth. He thought how lucky it was the Queensland, with its keen upright ears, was elsewhere. At the same time, Jesse wondered at his caution – he didn't think the security guard had masterminded the events in Redbud. Still, he was convinced of a connection and grateful the dog was convalescing with Deputy Rose.

An eight-foot high chain link fence surrounded the milling operation. The gate, however, had been broken years ago and never entirely shut. Impenetrable security had never been Mac's concern since, for decades the company had been the lifeblood of the region. There had been few threats to worry about. Security guards had only been brought on since the protestors had become more than an annoyance. The SOFTI group was well organized and great with the media, but not in the league of eco-terrorists that acted out violent threats. For a moment, Jesse worried that this was all about to change. Mac had told him that the day the mill would have to be barricaded - would be the day he'd move off the mountain. Life in Redbud was as much about trust and community as it was about business for the MacDougald family.

Conscious of every step, Jesse slipped through the leaning gate and approached the cavernous main building that housed scores of saws, planers and tools that made lumber out of logs. He eased into a door at the side of the building, stepping silently on the wood chips and sawdust blanketing the floor. Dim, bare light bulbs hung suspended from wooden rafters throughout the vast space. Sections were defined by activity, with sunken and elevated areas encased by four-foot walls that housed steel machinery.

He saw no activity, no David Fossey. Strangely, he thought back to a month ago when he would not have hesitated to holler "David!" Tonight he proceeded with stealth, his feet falling like a bobcat stalking quail. His eyes surveyed the area and his ears picked up subtle sounds. As he moved he felt an instinctive knowing course through his body, and he headed to the far wall where rough-cut logs were stacked waiting to be pulled through the planer.

Jesse grabbed hold of the half-walls as he moved through the labyrinth of work areas, leveraging the weight on his feet. He tried to recall the deafening screams of saws that filled the day, penetrating the protective ear guards all the employees wore. How diametrically opposite now, he thought, as hushed silence hung heavy from the tin roof to the concrete floor. He heard pine chips buckle and break beneath his boots, muffled sounds he hoped only his ears could hear. Jesse stopped and listened, closing his eyes and stilling his own breath. From the pit that held the conveyor belts and planer saws, Jesse heard muted shuffling noises, then the sound of metal scraping on concrete.

In a low crouch, Jesse continued toward the great stack of lumber that fed onto the belts and through the saws. Willing himself to creep like a predator, he touched the wooden wall around the pit. Holding his breath, he eased his head up and looked over the edge. David Fossey was on his knees, his back partly to Jesse. With his left hand, Fossey was making a bed of wood chips at the base of the stacked lumber. In his right was a bottle of clear liquid, a wick snaked out into a coil that Fossey grasped in his palm.

Wishing he had accepted Blair's offer of a firearm, Jesse sunk down on his haunches. It would not be good to surprise Fossey while he had a flammable liquid in his hands. Not knowing what it was, Jesse couldn't take a chance of guessing if the bottle contained something innate until lit – like kerosene – or explosive, like nitroglycerin. An explosive liquid in Fossey's hands could become a weapon. Jesse decided to keep very still until he heard more from the guard. Odds were, Jesse figured, that the bottle held a highly flammable liquid. A hot fire at the mill could be explained. An explosion would look too much like sabotage. So far, the perpetrators had done pretty well at disguising their motives – turning blame on neither the protestors nor the loggers. However, what Fossey had planned was clear. Why, was still the question.

Jesse heard the sound of glass scraping against the concrete floor. He figured that Fossey had placed the bottle under its nest of wood chips and sawdust. He waited until he heard the shuffling sounds of feet moving on the uneven surface of the floor. He eased his head to eye level over the wall. Fossey was crouched over and backing out of the space, trailing the wick along the floor. It was coiled in Fossey's hand and long enough to put considerable distance between the arsonist and the fire that was to follow. Jesse figured the wick had been soaked, maybe treated with a chemical to slow the burning. He waited until Fossey backed out of the pit that housed the equipment. Jesse stood up and stepped toward the guard, timing each footfall with Fossey's own backwards shuffle. They were not six feet apart when Fossey suddenly stood and said, "Shit!" dropping the wick and stomping forward back into the pit. He'd left something behind and Jesse stood exposed. He tried to duck back behind the wall but Fossey heard the deliberate move and spun on his heel. "SHIT, DAMN!" he shouted again much louder, and swiftly reached inside his leather vest and pulled out a Sig Sauer. "Don't move, Jesse. I swear. I mean it!"

Jesse raised both his hands about chest high. "Hang on Dave. No need for that. You're not in so deep that I can't help you," Jesse said in the calming tones of a counselor. At the same time, he took a step forward to the edge of the pit. "It'll be okay, I promise you."

"Just stop right there. Not another step or I'll use it." Fossey held the pistol with both hands, as if he knew what he was doing. "I don't want to shoot you, Jesse. It would make things more difficult." Fossey eased his left hand to the back of his belt. "Tell you what I want you to do. I want you to step very slowly down, Jesse. One step. And then move to your left, clear into the corner by that post." Jesse did as he was told, all the time standing tall and not revealing the doubt that was creeping into his mind. Fossey, the mild-mannered poet was taking on a whole new persona. His pale face was glistening with sweat and his eyes sparked like hot embers. Jesse stopped at the post and faced the guard. A pair of police issue handcuffs was in Fossey's left hand.

"You see, I can't shoot you because that would cause unforeseen problems. However, if you burn up in the fire that's going to erupt tonight, well, who's to explain? Maybe they'll think that you started it. Like, for a good headline?" Fossey half smiled at the thought.

He was not the kind of hostage taker that Jesse knew about from his reporting experience. Fossey didn't seem frightened or panicked. There was a cold spot inside the man that appeared to be unreachable, but Jess tried, nonetheless. "What about your family?" Jesse asked. "What are they going to do when they find out? They depend on you."

"A: they won't find out. I have it all planned," Fossey answered. "B: they have plenty of blood money to survive on, straight from the Man."

"Man?" Jesse asked.

"Yeah, the Man. The same one who destroyed my father. Your pal, everybody's pal, Mr. Mac Mac-Dougald, son of the timber baron who put my father in a wheelchair and financed his gambling addiction. That one. The one who sent my mother over the edge and out of town. The one who let my baby brother go to jail. The MAN," Fossey's voice had risen and Jesse saw him check himself. The guard paused to regain his composure. "Please don't think that you can get me talking and I'll forget what I'm doing Mr. Publisher. I'm far too smart for that. Didn't anyone tell you – that cute Deputy Rose for example, that I'm the intellectual of the family? I got ALL the brains!"

"I never doubted your intelligence, David. What I am questioning is your judgment. You are making a very big mistake. A man with your abilities could have a real future."

"It's too damn late for that!" Fossey snapped. "Too much water already running through the creek." He smiled at his own sorry metaphor and Jesse knew who had killed Chris Lance.

"Please don't think I slipped there, Jesse. At this point, I don't care what you know. And, I'd like you to fully appreciate the ambiguity we've created. No one knows who to blame. Of course, while everyone is wondering, no one is wondering about me. I'm just a sorry poet with a pitiful family who likes dogs and pigeons."

Jesse didn't think for a minute that Fossey had "slipped" with an admission he'd murdered Lance. But, Fossey had slipped when he'd said "we." It wasn't at all surprising to Jesse who knew enough about details of the crime to know that Fossey wasn't alone or, for that matter, hadn't been the master planner. Fossey smiled. "Because I'm sure you'll want to know how this plays out – and you won't be around to appreciate it, I'll tell you that the fire will be another unfortunate conundrum – I like that word, don't you?" Fossey was clearly enjoying himself and Jesse's instincts heightened as Fossey's focus drifted. "Of course, they'll discover arson. And, bad luck, you. Of course, they'll look first to the new pack of enviros that showed up to join the SOFTIs tonight – I always thought that was an unfortunate acronym ... They won't think it's me because I am going to be the victim of a harmless, but discernable, blow to my noggin and be out-cold in my office. Snoring while the metaphorical Rome burns." Fossey bunched the handcuffs up and held them out at arm's length. "Enough," he announced. "I am going to toss you these cuffs and you are going to wrap them around that handy steel pole behind you and lock your wrists inside."

"Why would I do that when I know I am going to die anyway?"

"Because you think you are very smart. Being left alone here while the little ember on the wick burns its way to the big bang will give you time – to think, to act. Whatever! It's less final than being shot right now, isn't it? And, look at the bright side, you'll probably die from smoke inhalation before you fry like a slab of bacon – at least that's what 'they' say."

Fossey reached back in an underarm pitch and lobbed the cuffs to Jesse. The arc of the throw peaked as if in slow motion and Jesse felt himself reach out with his right hand and grab the cuffs in a collected ball. But time accelerated when Jesse ratcheted back his arm with lightning speed and launched the cuffs like a missile, back into Fossey's grinning face where it torpedoed into flesh and bone. The guard automatically reached up to cradle his damaged face and Jesse moved in like a street warrior.

It wasn't much of a contest. Smart, Fossey was, but strong, no. Jesse's mountain-man size and natural speed made the struggle for the gun a short one. Fossey lay on the floor, sawdust clinging to his wet cheeks. A deep gash where the cuffs had caught him on the ridge of his cheekbone was leaking blood. Jesse grabbed the guard's arms and twisted them back, pushing up to the point of breaking.

"What's this about?" Jesse demanded. "Tell me. Tell me now!" He yanked up hard on Fossey's arms. There was a sharp "pop" from somewhere around the guard's shoulder. Fossey screamed. Jesse let up the pressure. "Now!" he shouted.

Fossey sputtered and spit sawdust from his mouth. "It won't matter," he half-laughed and cried. "It's too late. ...." He stopped and Jesse ratcheted up the pressure, slowly, to give Fossey room to make a choice.

"He's as good as dead. We took care of him an hour ago ..." Fossey snickered. "Too bad, you two could have fried up together." Jesse shoved the guard's face hard against the concrete one more time and Fossey whimpered. Jesse then picked him up and dropped him in the corner. He took Fossey's arms and stretched them backwards, tying them around the same pole that was to have been Jesse's stake. The poet guard no longer had strength in his arms. Something, Jesse didn't care what, had been either broken or dislocated.

"You sit tight, Fossey," Jesse heard himself saying, not at all liking the threatening tone of his own voice. "Someone will be right here. But, in case you figure you can use your intellect to get out of this – since your arms don't seem to be working too well ..." Jesse reached back and delivered a knock-out punch to Fosse's jaw. The guard hung like a broken, forgotten puppet.

Jesse picked up the bottle of accelerant and the coiled wick. He ran full-bent for the Jeep and as he spun out of the parking lot, grabbed the police radio and shouted orders. Blair got on the horn and hollered back that the protestors had descended on the dance. "Hands full!" the sheriff shouted. "That mob moved in on the hall and all hell broke loose!"

"Send Rose then and Didion too. Now! Up to Mac's ... Have Didion bring the water truck up and his medic's bag! And get somebody over to the mill to pick up Fossey – he's tied up by the rough-cut stacks. He's our killer. Read him his rights and throw his ass in jail."

"Fossey? Damn!!" Blair answered. "I'll get up there as soon as I can ... I'm trying to find Thompson to calm this thing down ... SHIT!" The sheriff was off the radio and Jesse was speeding like a bullet to Mac's sprawling home. He swerved onto the main road and counted precious minutes to Mac's driveway that was firm with newly laid gravel. The car windows were down and he smelled the smoke before he saw the fire. The winding drive seemed longer than ever and Jesse took the turns like an Indy driver until the house was in sight. The west wing of the cedar home was fully engulfed in flames. Smoke billowing out from the center where the main door was located and tongues of fire danced from the back slope of the roof. Just inside and to the left, he knew, was Mac's study where they had met just the other day.

He leapt from the Jeep and raced to the front door, feeling the surface with the palm of his hand. Hot, but not scorching. Jesse ripped off his shirt and shoved it under the water spigot by the front porch. He wadded it up and twisted the doorknob. Locked. Mac never locked his door.

Jesse stood back and pulled out the Sig Sauer that he'd taken from Fossey. He aimed at the lock and fired. Please, he intoned, don't let Mac be behind that door. Jesse's body slammed the hot door. Black smoke escaped as if it too were running from death, its fingers traveling up and out the top of the door jam. Jesse dropped down to a low crouch, bracing himself with one hand and covering his

284

face with the wetted wad of shirt. He moved by memory to the door of the den, his eyes stinging and watering. He squinted, making them slits that barely saw definition in the walls or furniture of the once-fine house.

At the carved oak door that opened to Mac's den, he didn't even stop to test the heat. The fire was moving too quickly from the back of the house to the front. He stood and turned the searing hot knob of the study door with the damp shirt. He thrust his shoulder into it, cracking the door violently open. Smoke hung like black fog in the room and Jesse crouched, moving toward Mac's desk, the smoke so intense it was only through instinct that he continued to push forward and put his trembling hand on Mac. The big logger lay sprawled out on the carpet, arms forward as if reaching for escape.

Forgetting the man's greater bulk and not stopping to feel for a pulse, Jesse buried his face one last time in the now-acrid shirt and tried to inhale as deeply as possible. He dropped it to the floor. As he reached down for Mac's still body, there was no thought in Jesse's mind. No will. No plan. There was only the purest power of spirit that lifted the fallen man to his shoulder and carried them both through the study door; past the paintings and antiques that now danced with little flames; under the glowing chunks of ceiling that fell to the floor like confetti; through the dragon breath of smoke that billowed and roiled at their bodies and, finally, out onto the cool, blessed earth.

Jesse cleared Mac's mouth and throat with his fingers and immediately started mouth-to-mouth resuscitation. In the distance he heard the wail of sirens – the screaming, fast vibrato of a squad car and the lower, undulating tones of Didion's fire truck.

Although it seemed like an eternity, it was only seconds before Jesse felt a firm hand on his shoulder. Deputy Rose pulled him away from Mac as Didion swept over the mill owner like an angel of mercy, simultaneously feeling Mac's neck for a pulse and strapping an oxygen mask on his face.

"You okay?" He asked Jesse looking him up and down for obvious injuries.

"Fine, fine," Jesse gasped and started to cough.

"Mac's breathing, and his heartbeat is strong. I think he's going to be all right," Didion said. "You did a good job."

Rose handed Jesse a bottle of water and he gulped it, grateful for the immediate relief it brought. He tossed his head back and cleared his throat. In the distance, more sirens were blaring. The back of the house and west wing, where Mac had fallen, were now totally engulfed in flames. It was no longer a matter of saving the house, but keeping the blaze from jumping into the pines. Thankfully, Mac had cleared a generous swath of landscape around his house – a 'defensible zone', giving the fire fighters a chance. But it wasn't the fire that concerned Jesse as the smoke cleared from his head.

"We've got to get back to town – to the Hall," he told Deputy Rose as he started to stride toward his car. "I know who's behind this now!"

"Not Fossey?" Rose asked, running to keep up with him.

"Not nearly. The guy might be bright but he doesn't have the sophistication to pull this off."

"You going let me in on who it is?" Rose asked as she headed toward the patrol car.

The first of the bigger fire trucks came speeding onto the scene, their sirens howling. Jesse had said something to Rose and she'd missed it in the din. "Shit!" she said turning the key and spinning out behind Jesse. Had she heard, however, Rose would not have been enlightened because all Jesse had said was, "You wouldn't believe it."

***

Town Hall was the scene of near-pandemonium. People had started to leave for home but were distracted by the parade of patrol cars racing to the mill and fire trucks speeding off to Mac's house. Fire made people feel like animals trapped in a burning forest, wanting to run but not knowing where. Coupled with the band of protestors putting a halt to the dance and facing off with some angry locals, it was a night of confusion. Jesse left his vehicle at the bottom of the driveway and ran up the hill, anxiously looking for the sheriff. Deputy Rose was right behind him.

Blair looked relieved. "Damn, you all right?" Jesse nodded and Blair continued. "Just when you think things can't get worse. The sirens started up and everybody panicked! Headed for their cars. That pack of kids scattered like rats on sinking ship – ran like hell down the drive! And, to top it off, I can't find Thompson anywhere – I needed him to calm down the situation. Too late for that now."

"When did you see him last? Jesse asked.

"Thompson? ... guess when he and Mac got sick of being on stage and snuck off!"

Jesse grimaced and shook his head. "That's what I thought. Listen, I don't have time to explain so you're going to have to trust me here." Blair and Rose looked intently at him, as if sensing what was to come. "We have to find Thompson. He's it. He's the key. And, he's got nothing to lose at this point." Jesse handed Blair the gun he'd taken from Fossey . "You'll want to check this out. I think it'll trace back to Thompson."

"Shee-uuut!" Blair spit out. He put the radio up to his lips and sent out the word to grab Tommy Thompson if anyone saw him. "He may be armed and I am given to understand that he is dangerous," the sheriff concluded. "I can barely believe it," he said to Jesse.

"That was the whole point," Jesse said. "I'm going off to find him. I've got an idea."

Rose looked at him and nodded. "I've got the same one. That new gang of folks. Most of their vehicles were parked down by the turnoff to Kingsley's camp. Let's take my car. I'll use the siren."

Blair said he'd check the crowd leaving the hall and flood the driveway with lights so his people could get a better look at those leaving the area. He called Deputy Gorring and told him to establish a roadblock on the north and south exits out of Redbud. "You only let locals who you recognize past, you got it?" There was a pause and Blair shouted, "Of course, I don't mean to let Thompson out! You see him, you arrest him!" There was a pause before Blair bellowed, "I don't care how rich he is!!!"

Jesse jumped into the car with Rose behind the wheel. The blare of the siren got people to move out of the road and they sped the short distance to where the protestors had first gathered. They had regrouped there for some purpose – whether to flee or to strike again, Jesse didn't know or care. He only cared that Tommy Thompson had used them toward his own ends and was using them again – to hide.

"How'd you figure it out?" Rose shouted above the siren.

"It was too big for Redbud," he shouted back, bracing his hand on the dashboard. "Debrief later!"

They skidded to a stop at the fringe of a crowd of about sixty protestors. The rest had apparently fled. Kingsley was trying to calm them down, shouting through a bullhorn like an uncertain commander. "It won't get the movement where we want it to go if we get physical ..." he was saying. But the throng wasn't responding. They seemed angry and ready for action. Jesse noticed it was mostly comprised of the strangers – not the usual SOFTI crowd but the newcomers he'd spotted earlier. A big burley man wearing a black leather vest shoved his fist into the air "I say we push 'em to the limit!" he shouted. There were cries of support along with murmurs of disapproval.

"I know that guy," Rose said, and wove her way into the crowd. Jesse followed, looking at faces as he passed the restless men and women. They got to the edge of the circle surrounding Kingsley and the vocal protestor. Rose didn't say anything. She hooked her thumbs into her belt just above the holster of the gun she carried and stared into the tall man's eyes. Flashlights and car beams illuminated the circle. As if compelled by her gaze, the man's eyes fell on Rose. He had been about to speak again but shut his mouth instead. Seizing the moment, Kingsley made another appeal for calm. "We appreciate your support. We really do – but these are just not the right tactics up here. It's time for everybody to head back home – the opportunity to get our message out has been lost. This won't make for good headlines. I know for a fact that Tyler wouldn't want any more action tonight."

Extolling the name of Tyler Wentworth, the leader of the national movement, brought the crowd down. Though no one had actually met the man, his influence hung heavy over the crowd. They mumbled softly to each other and started to move away. The big guy who'd been hoping to rile up the group, took another look at Rose, turned and headed toward his Harley. She followed, asking Jesse to stay behind. Off at the edges of the light, the deputy and the biker talked briefly, ending with his kicking the motorcycle to life. Rose put the radio up to her lips and cleared the way for the biker to leave town. The low rumble of the Harley faded as it disappeared around the curve to town. Rose went up to Kingsley and took the bullhorn from his hands.

"Listen up," she ordered. "We're gonna let all of you out of here in an orderly fashion – car by car or whatever. We have a crime scene up here tonight and I'll want some identification from everybody. Then, you're free to go." The crowd made angry grumbling noises and a couple of men shouted, "Bullshit!" Jesse had been whispering something to Kingsley who raised his hands to quiet everyone down. Rose handed him the horn.

"People – this isn't about us or our cause," he said. "It's about the murder of Chris Lance – one of our own. It's very important we cooperate and not obstruct justice in this case. Please, for a moment. Think about how it would look in the papers. Let's just do as the deputy asks. It's in our best interests." The mumbling continued but it had an acquiescent tone and people began to move toward the cars, vans and motorcycles parked alongside the road. Rose had moved her car across half the driveway. She and Jesse stood like sentinels and ushered each vehicle out. Jesse stood silently at her right, looking over her shoulder at the occupants of the vehicles.

Rose was polite and officious – checking identification cards, writing names and contact information down in her notebook. There were about twenty vehicles to check. Most people had car pooled or ridden double on a motorcycle. Jesse looked carefully at each person as Rose asked that the interior lights of the vehicles be switched on. There were slightly more men than women. None looked like Tommy Thompson – but then, Jesse didn't expect him to look like his familiar self. Down to the last five cars, Jesse wondered if he'd guessed wrong. But, it had all happened so fast that Thompson couldn't have planned a getaway. He had to be improvising a way out of town. A Ford Explorer pulled up and a young woman glared out the driver's window.

"This is unconstitutional, you know," she said. "You have no right."

"Yes Ma'am I do," Rose answered. "And we'll have you on your way just as soon as I see some ID from you and your two passengers. Please switch on your interior lights. I appreciate it."

292

Grumbling, the woman did as told and fished in her purse for her driver's license. The other passengers, a woman in the front and a man in the back, did the same search. Rose shined her flashlight on the documents as they were handed over, returning them with a polite "Thank you." The man in the rear seat passed his license forward. He was one of the agitators that Jesse had found disturbing earlier in the night. He had dirty blond hair and beard; dark glasses covered his eyes. He was encased in a black motorcycle jacket. A beam from the flashlight caught the reflection of gold on the breast pocket, like an insignia pin.

Rose accepted the license. "Mr. Womack? You're licensed to drive a cycle. Lose your bike?" Rose smiled and handed back the ID. Jesse whispered in her ear. She returned her attention to the car's driver. "If you'd just wait a moment, Miss," she said. Rose listened to Jesse and stiffened her composure. "If I could ask the three of you to step out of the car, please?"

"WHAT?!!!" This is outrageous!" The driver hollered. "I'll have my daddy's lawyer after you!" The car doors opened as Rose and Jesse walked around to the passenger side. They waited for Mr. Womack to put his feet on the ground. He was tall, way too tall to be Thompson. A black motorcycle helmet hung from his right hand and he wore a set of leathers on his legs. From the breast pocket of his denim shirt, protruded a gold-banded cigar.

"I want to ask you again – this time, seriously,

Rose said in a low, commanding tone. "Where is your machine?" Womack spun on his heel and faced the few vehicles remaining. He cupped his hands around his mouth and shouted urgently into the darkness. "Go! Go! Now!!!"

From the edges of the forested darkness a motorcycle exploded to life – a fast Suzuki GS1000. Its driver, helmeted and suited up in bright yellow and black leathers, flew toward the makeshift roadblock. Jesse knew it was Thompson – a changed and determined Thompson. The motorcycle sped toward the small opening and Rose aimed her Smith & Wesson, knowing she couldn't shoot without endangering a bystander.

Jesse acted instinctively and scooped up one of the round rocks– the size of a softball - that lined the driveway. In a blur, Thompson was upon them and exactly as he flew by, Jesse pitched the rock at warp speed, hitting the spokes of the front wheel with the force of a guided missile. The bike lurched violently forward and Thompson lost control. He was thrown from the bike as it somersaulted and skidded onto the road. Thompson curled up and rolled across the rock and gravel, landing in a thicket of short Manzanita like a stunned wasp. He didn't move.

Jesse ran toward Thompson and hoped the rough landing hadn't killed him. It hadn't. Thompson pushed himself up to a seated position and faced Jesse with a sleek Smith and Wesson.

"Back off!"

Jesse heard the distant voice of Deputy Rose as he froze in his tracks. Thompson slowly rose to his feet, shaking his free arm and legs to check for damage. He reached up and pulled the helmet from his head and smirked. "I always was in favor of helmet laws."

Thompson had done a good job of disguising himself. His hair was dark and he wore a short beard. His nose seemed to be enhanced and his cheeks, fuller. "Now – let me tell you what," he said. "I am going to back away from you and you're going to let me go." Thompson continued to grin, enjoying the moment. "The reason you are going to let me go is that I have a little insurance. I am, if nothing else, a good business man." The smile grew wider. "That little redheaded boy you are so fond of is up at my place, waiting to be barbecued."

"Andy! You took Andy?!"

"Like I said. A little insurance. When I found out you got the best of that sissy Fossey, I talked your boy into coming up to my secret little hideaway – where I go to plan and think. He's tied up there - literally. I have the propane valve on and windows closed. At some critical time, I predict an explosion. But don't worry – by then he won't feel a thing."

Jesse didn't argue or answer. If what Thompson said was true, there wasn't time for words. "Now, I can give you the exact location and you could possibly prevent the disaster – or you could try to catch me and consequently lose the boy. It's entirely up to you." It seemed unnaturally quiet, even the wind-born voice of the pines was still.

From out of the dark shadows somewhere behind Thompson, Deputy Rose broke the silence. "Drop it, Thompson," she barked. "Now!" As Thompson looked right and left to see where the voice was coming from, Jesse rushed forward and tackled him, wrenching the gun from his hand. Rose ran forward and quickly cuffed Thompson. "He's got Andy," Jesse said urgently.

"Bull," Rose responded.

"Bull?"

"You know. Opposite of a heifer? Andy's with Mr. Herb. His so-called mom went off with a friend from the dance and she put him in Herb's hands. He's waiting for you to come get the boy. They're both down at the gas station. I forgot to tell you. Got busy."

She put her mouth close to Thompson's right ear. "Nice try," she hissed and placed him under arrest. She advised the handcuffed man of his rights and pushed him toward the crowd that had become a mixed audience of townspeople and protestors. The sheriff arrived with two more men who deposited Thompson's motorcycle accomplice in the back of a patrol car. Mark Kingsley stepped forward.

"You know this guy?" Jesse asked, pointing to

Thompson in his new identity,

"Never saw him before. Not even earlier."

The sheriff unholstered his gun and took Rose's place. She moved around in front of Thompson.

"How about now?" Rose peeled the fake beard from Thompson's face and lifted a corner of latex that had altered his facial characteristics. "Think blond hair."

Mark was in shock. "Mr. Thompson?! I don't understand. Why were you running away?" Kingsley looked from his neighbor to Rose and Jesse. "He helped us out! Mr. Thompson was just good to everybody!" Rumbles of amazement rolled through the crowd like a wave.

"I believe that was the point," Rose said. "The last person you'd suspect of murder, arson and, so far as you and your friends are concerned, betrayal.

"Betrayal?" Kingsley asked.

"You tell," Rose said to Jesse.

"Truth is, Mark, this isn't Thompson. Thompson is someone this man made up just for us, all of us," Jesse said, making his voice gentle. "This man's name is Tyler Wentworth. You know him as the founder of your movement. The man who disappeared years ago but still fuels SOFTI's ideology." There was an audible gasp from Kingsley and the group of people that had surrounded him. "I don't want to say too much until the sheriff has this man tucked away. But that's what the deputy meant when she said 'betrayal.'"

The handful of protestors who were left began mumbling as word spread, and the sheriff moved the prisoner toward the patrol car. People were demanding an explanation, recognizing Thompson but not yet fully grasping the truth. Moment by moment the realization set in and the young people let their feelings soar with angry words. Locals murmured in disbelief. Just as the sheriff opened the car door for Thompson he spun around and bared his teeth like a dog.

"What do you know?!! Just what do you know!" he shouted. "I know. I lived it. I AM the movement. And, do you know what? I am right. It is money and corporate greed that run the world, just like my faithful followers say! And you – all of you," he waved an arm at the shocked group of protestors, "are just so easy to use!" Thompson started to laugh like a madman and Blair shoved down on his head to urge him into the back seat of the car. The door slammed shut, muting the voice that all of Redbud would forever think of as Tommy Thompson's. Blair fired up the siren and drove out while the crowd stood stunned in disbelieving silence.

Rose sent everybody home. Cars, campers and motorcycles crawled through town and down the hill. A host of locals went to the Stag to discuss the unbelievable night, the culmination of the 49th Annual Logger's Jamboree.

In the end, only she and Jesse remained in

the halo of light from the yellow street lamp above. Just outside the circle atop a boulder sat Mark Kingsley, his shoulders slumped forward and head hanging low. "Poor kid," Rose said.

"It's hard to have a hero fall," Jesse responded. They stood saying nothing. Rose broke the stillness. "We'll have to sort this out, you know. Tomorrow? Looks like you might be needed at the moment."

"That'd be good. I've about had enough action for one day." He turned to the deputy. Even in the streetlight, face smeared with dirt and damp with beads of perspiration, she was darned pretty to him. "Good work," he said, extending his right hand.

"You too," she said, responding to the offer to shake. "I had it too, you know, but not all of it. Can't wait to hear how you put all the pieces together. I'm not easy to beat, you know."

"Don't know why anyone would want to," Jesse said easing into his famous smile. He took her hand, but instead of shaking, just held it. "It's enough just being your partner in crime."

The glow of the streetlamp subdued the blush that rose on the deputy's face, but Jesse recognized that they were having 'a moment.'

"See you early – I'll drive down to the center about eight?"

"Eight," she repeated, looking reluctantly into his eyes. "It's a date ... I mean. Oh, hell," she muttered and headed for her car. Jesse watched her go and let the smile linger on his lips until he turned to talk with the betrayed and idealistic young man who'd been disillusioned.

23 / REVELATIONS

Although most of the Eagle's Eye regulars had stayed up later than usual on Saturday night, owing to all the action and talk that followed, a few made it to the cafe by nine o'clock. They had their breakfast and coffee by the time the place started filling up. Herb had been among the first since Jesse had dropped Andy off with him at a little past seven. The boy was sitting at the men's table beside him. Merriweather had been next, followed by Paul who'd missed the previous night's shebang. The men were delighted to be able to tell the story as best they knew it. It was a story with vast craters of information missing, based solely on rumors that Charlie, accompanied by Flip, was happy to share.

"I hear they grabbed Thompson. What do you think about that?" he said.

"He'll be out by noon. Got the wrong man. Not possible, that's what I say," Merriweather answered. "It was one of them damned agitators from down south. Mark my word. Tommy Thompson. Pillar of the community!" He closed with a grunt.

"Well, I been around some and had an uncle in law enforcement," Charlie challenged. "Don't seem to me that the sheriff would take a chance on arresting somebody like Thompson if he didn't have cause to do so."

"Doc Holiday – that's who his uncle was," laughed Paul.

"It was a set up. You wait and see," Merriweather said. "Instead of besmirching a man who's been up here with us for five good years, I think we should just be thankful that Mac is gonna make it." He looked around the table with satisfaction, and beyond to the other folks from town who had gathered for breakfast, anticipating that this would be the place to come for news. They listened and the men raised their voices appropriately. They were not, after all, known as the Council for nothing. Merriweather was pleased to be the bearer of factual information.

"I talked to the hospital today – you all know his nephew is married to my niece and that makes me some kind of relative? Well, they said he had smoke inhalation real bad, some third degree burns on his hands and knees and stomach, but he was awake and fine. Should be able to see visitors early as tomorrow!"

"Jesus be thanked," Daisy chimed in. "I prayed all night long." She stopped pouring coffee for customers and gave the discussion her complete attention.

"Didion was down there when I called," he added and held out his cup, enjoying the silence he'd commanded. He dumped two packets of sugar in the hot coffee and started to stir.

"Oh, for heaven's sake, Merriweather, get on with it!" Charlie commanded, knowing precisely what his colleague was doing.

"Didion took Mac down there last night. Figured he could do it faster than waiting for the MediVac copter. Said he knew the injuries weren't life threatening, once he got him breathing on his own."

"We are lucky to have that boy," Herb said, even though Didion was well into middle age.

"He also said that if our Jesse hadn't gotten to Mac when he did, it would have all been over. Pulled him out just as the house imploded on itself – or something like that." Merriweather sipped his coffee and looked around.

"God bless our Jesse," Daisy said.

"Said something else, too." Merriweather was making too much of the moment and all the men turned on him with protests and grumbles.

"I don't suppose this should get around, but he said he's pretty sure the fire was set," Merriweather announced. "In fact, Didion thinks it was some kinda a bomb." The news had the desired effect, setting the Council and the rest of the Eye's patrons buzzing with speculation. Andy's jaw dropped open as he silently mouthed "a bomb?"

"A small one, a simple one," Merriweather continued. "They have a name for things like that."

"Incendiary device," Paul offered. "Easy and cheap to make. Can learn how on the Internet."

It was into this pitch of excitement that Jesse walked, knowing there would be a curious gathering at the café. He nodded to the men, shot Daisy a smile with the gesture for coffee and sat at the counter next to the men's table. "Mornin'," he said.

Charlie took the floor. "Well, Mr. Jesse, we all hear that you are some kind of hero. That was mighty fine of you to pull Mac outta that fire."

Jesse glanced up at Daisy who poured his coffee and beamed at him. Uncomfortable with the personal attention, he tried to move past the topic. "It's nothing anyone of you wouldn't have done. Heck, it was done and over with so fast, I barely remember. And, I hear Mac's fine. I'm just grateful I was there," he said.

"Which of course, begs explaining," Paul interjected. "We understand you were there for it all. You gonna make us wait to read about it in the newspaper?"

"That wouldn't be very neighborly," Charlie urged.

"No, of course not. I'll tell you what I told the sheriff, if you all promise not to tell anyone else." He looked at the men and then around the room and laughed aloud. "There's no secret. The whole story will be on the news by tonight so – seeing as how it's our story, you should hear it first, I'd say."

It may as well have been a church service for the silence that fell on the room. Silverware stopped clinking against plates and coffee mugs were put down. The townspeople who had been pretending not to listen to the conversation, turned to openly take it in. Daisy took a seat at the end of the counter and her son took a break from the grill and peered over the galley pass-through.

"This all started here in Redbud about two years ago. Isn't that when Mac first started getting offers on his property?" Jesse said, directing his question to Mr. Merriweather who nodded. "Well, that offer and the ones that followed are related to this. Behind everything that's happened here is one complicated land grab that was managed all the way from Washington, DC then to Orange County and finally to our own backyard.

That's when Tommy Thompson, alias Wentworth, started to implement his plan to make Redbud a very high-end resort community. We – that's Deputy Rose and me – started using the Internet and some of our contacts to track down the source of offers on the mill – and, at the same time, find out who owned the property next to Thompson and who actually paid for Hazlett's hot shot attorney. When we dug back far enough through a trail of related corporations, we found they all traced back to LL Ltd. – Leisure Lands, Limited, a privately held corporation registered in Nevada. Interestingly, the majority stockholder is Tyler Wentworth, but he's not on the Board of Directors and not easily identified. Also, the Board is composed of five very deceased people, resurrected for Mr. Wentworth's protection."

"So why didn't Thompson know who owned that piece of land next to him?" Flip asked and Charlie swatted him on the arm.

"Of course he knew! He owns it!" Charlie barked.

"Oh," said Flip.

"Yes, he knew," Jessie continued, "but didn't want anyone else to know that he was amassing land. He didn't want to raise suspicions or alter his reputation in the community," Jesse explained. "He figured that letting the protestors camp next to his 'official' property would serve his purposes, make him look like a peace maker in town. Down the road he figured he would need all the support he could muster if he succeeded in driving the mill out and getting Mac's land for development. In fact, he had it calculated that he could rise up as a local hero to rescue the town from economic death once the mill collapsed."

"Why did that boy have to die?" Charlie asked.

"Things weren't moving fast enough for Thompson. He'd underestimated Mac's loyalty and disinterest in large sums of money. He'd already investigated all the potential weak spots and when he found out about the Fossey family, he used it. He befriended David and fed his hatred of Mac's family. Promised David final retribution for what had happened to his mother and father and younger brother. Thompson was very good at manipulating people, I discovered. He got David to do his dirtiest work, never had to get his own hands bloody. Together, Thompson figured he and Fossey could make things so bad that Mac would fold his hand and leave. And they had to keep the focus on Hazlett being guilty."

"So tell me why Thompson hired him that lawyer?" Charlie demanded.

"To make darn sure the attention and presumption of guilt was on Hazlett," Jesse said. "She was guaranteed to make procedural blunders and to alienate our judges up here. Thompson, er, Wentworth, was payin' her well to build a smoke screen. He figured he's covered all the bases. People with messianic tendencies are often guilty of underestimating people."

"Like how he figured he could just slip outta town, huh?" Flip offered.

"Yeah, how did you know what he'd do," Charlie asked.

"I didn't," Jesse admitted, "even though the big clue was right in my face. Deputy Rose was looking at the ID of this biker without a bike – that should have been enough. But, I only made the connection when I saw a hundred dollar Cuban cigar sticking out of the man's pocket. It was the exact same gold band that I'd found at the mill after Begae almost died there. I knew then that Thompson -Wentworth would be on two-wheels."

"I heard you done knocked him off that bike with a big ol' rock," Andy added with obvious pride.

"It was a lucky throw, that's all."

Merriweather was still choking on the fact that he'd been wrong about Thompson. "But why kill Mac? How was he gonna get his hands on the property then?"

"Mac has a secret. He's got an heir that he never talked about – one he never found, although he certainly tried. It's not up to me to speculate about that. It will have to come from him. But, Thompson was one hundred percent certain Mac's heir would sell to him," he paused. "I'm sorry, but it's the part I'll have to leave out until Mac decides how to handle it."

"You tell me why a guy like this Wentworth fella – a hard core environmentalist – would change so much," Merriweather challenged, still grappling with Thompson's guilt.

"For starters, young Wentworth was always a rebel, denouncing his father's wealth, yet willing to live on a family allowance. But when he went underground in the late 80s, the family disowned

308

and disinherited him. He found out what it was like to live without financial resources and he didn't like it one bit," Jesse explained. "Wentworth, as Thompson, wanted a shortcut back to affluence and used his ever-loyal following to become a land baron. Wentworth pulled the strings and SOFTI danced. He owns more than a hundred thousand acres around communities like Redbud."

The intake of a communal breath was audible and Charlie was about to launch into a comment when the bell on the door of the café made its familiar music. Hazlett pushed the door in and held it while his Aunt walked past. She held her head high and seemed to have regained some of the vibrancy Jesse had seen in her the day of their memorable mission. She paused just inside the door, looking around as if she might be an intruder, perhaps an unwelcome one. It was true that Anna Sister, and very few of her people, made the café a regular spot to socialize. She lifted her chin and nodded a greeting to Daisy, but walked straight to Jesse who rose to meet her.

Looking up at him, she spoke softly. "We are in your debt. You are a friend. My nephew has something to say to you." She looked back at Hazlett whose eyes were slightly cast down before they rose to meet Jesse's.

"I will not betray your trust," he said. "I know I've behaved stupidly. I give you my word and my thanks." He reached out in the gesture of a handshake but grasped Jesse's arm instead of his hand.

309

The men locked their arms in the special gesture used among Hazlett's people.

"I had a lot of help. Many people believed in you," Jesse answered.

"I know, including Mr. Merriweather, and I thank him also," Hazlett said respectfully, lowering his eyes then briefly looking at the old man. "You watch and you will see the belief has not been misplaced."

The café was quiet to the point of discomfort until Daisy broke the silence by beaming at the cluster and saying, "Well, God bless you all."

Anna Sister and Hazlett made signs they were about to leave. Jesse stood and walked them out the door. One of the elders sat in the driver's seat of a rusted, old pick-up truck, waiting. He gave Jesse a nod. Hazlett leapt like a deer into the bed of the truck and Jesse opened the door for Anna Sister, gently touching her elbow to help her make the step up into the cab. He shut the door. "You all take care, now."

The old Indian woman reached out the window. "This is yours," she said, opening her hand to reveal a small leather bag. "You left this behind and it was given to me to return to you."

The truck backed away and turned toward the Rancheria. Jesse stood in the bright morning sun and felt the object in the bag. Mostly, and surprisingly, it felt warm, as if the object were giving off heat. He closed his fingers around the bag and eased it into the front pocket of his denim jacket. There would come a time when he would explore its contents. A time when he would understand. He returned to the Eye to pay for his coffee, politely brushed off any more questions and drove back to his cabin, stopping at Jackass Creek along the way, to sit and listen to its song.

24 / RELATIONSHIPS

Deputy Rose had made herself scarce since she'd been in that uncomfortable, personal moment with Jesse, under the street lamp. From Jesse's perspective, the mystery of Rose was getting even more alluring. He was not vain, but was accustomed to women finding him attractive. This, he told himself, meant nothing other than agreeable physical genetics and nothing more. He'd known murderers as handsome as movie stars. Jesse didn't put much stock in physical beauty. Nonetheless, he was momentarily puzzled by how the deputy had been able to ignore a fairly obvious invitation. That's why, when she came bursting through the door of his office, he felt a rush of excitement.

She was leading Lola on a harness, like the ones used for police dogs. "Meet my new partner," she announced. "Lieutenant Lola. My former partner, Deputy Gorring, is on extended leave while he figures out whether to resign or be fired." She smiled, clearly pleased with the turn of events.

"That bad?" Jesse asked.

"Blair tore into him about that phone call – just a minute." She looked down at Lola and said, "Sit!" The dog plopped its bottom to the floor. "Stay!" She made a hand signal in front of the dog's face, dropped the leash and walked to sit in the chair by Jesse's desk. "She's in training. Bright, much brighter than Gorring. And, I might add, Lola has better breath!" Again she smiled with amusement, making Jesse's heart beat a little faster. "Anyway, the sheriff – he can be very tough when he wants to – pushed Gorring until he admitted it had been the Fossey boy on the phone, setting Hazlett up to get busted after the stop at the market. And, get this, that piece of work in the back seat that we took in? Same guy that gave Hazlett the laced "non-alcohol" beer. Small world." She looked at the dog who sat frozen to the spot. "Come," she said. Lola approached her. "Lie down." She dropped her index finger toward the floor and the Queensland complied. "Too bad you can't train men like that."

"Well, somebody's feeling very feisty today," Jesse observed, hoping he was wearing one of those smiles that so thoroughly melted Daisy. If it affected the deputy, she didn't let on.

"I have one unresolved question," she said. "What was the point of bringing in that out-of-town hotshot attorney? Why would Thompson want Hazlett off the hook?"

"Same reason as he had to give shelter to SOFTI's folks. It was just a diversion and – as you discovered – she may have been high-priced but she didn't have the credentials to win the case. The hometown justice in this county would have eaten her alive, especially after Hazlett got busted for violating the terms of his bail. Either way, Thompson would have won."

"Oh well, the mountain is a better place today than it was last week," she replied. "We got rid of some environmental pollution. How about you? Anything new?"

"Matter of fact, I'm doing a feature story. One that will make A. Forester and Daisy and her church friends weep tears of joy."

"Feel like sharing?"

"That depends," he answered.

"On what?"

Jesse took the chance. "On whether you'll have a picnic with me this coming weekend, down at the base of Eagle's Eye Rock."

She hesitated for a split second. "Can Lieutenant Lola come?"

"Lola can come. How about it?"

"Depends on how good the story is."

Jesse laughed. "You are tough. A tough woman with no first name. Okay, I'll take a chance." Jesse told her how, in researching the offers on Mac's property, he'd run across some information about the man himself. As a very young man, just twenty-one, he'd taken off for Washington state, hadn't wanted to take on the responsibilities of the family business. But timber was in his blood and the only way he knew to make decent money. Mac went to work at a major mill just outside an Indian reservation.

"It was there he met a young woman, barely eighteen. They fell in love but it was cursed from the start. She was a full-blooded tribe member and they had to hide, meet in secret. Long story short, the girl found out she was pregnant, told her family and they spirited her away to another state. One day she was there, the next gone. The worse thing was that Mac didn't know why. He was heartbroken, even got sick. Eventually, he gave up and went home."

"Why didn't he try to find her?"

"He says he did, but her family said she'd gotten married and moved away. You see, he didn't know about the pregnancy. He thought he'd been rejected, mostly because he was white."

"Tough, poor Mac," Rose said.

"It wasn't until ten years later, when Mac was

315

deep into his daddy's operation that he traveled to Washington on business – they had bought some timber property there – that he learned the true story, from his lover's sister who had, ironically, married a white man."

"That must have just about killed Mac," Rose said, reaching down to stroke the dog. "Mac is such a responsible guy."

"It did," Jesse answered. "He put all his resources and efforts into finding the mother and child. He tried for years, private investigators, lawyers, tracers - nothing worked. It was like they'd vanished from the face of the Earth. Finally, he said he just had to quit."

"So, what changed?"

"Honestly, if all this hadn't happened, I think he still wouldn't know. But Tommy Thompson unwittingly did one good thing. He found Mac's child. Not a child really, a young adult now." Jesse explained that Thompson's plan to buy off the mill and lumbering operations required that he know everything about Mac's finances and his life. Redbud's "no-locked-doors" policy made it easy. Thompson simply combed through Mac's records, found out about the search for a child, and got lucky. He found Mac's offspring living in Oregon, the product of foster homes. The kind of kid who needs a financial and emotional hand.

"Thompson was good at it. He did a full-fledged rescue. Got the kid a paying job in the environmental movement (that he, of course, secretly ran) - and built up tremendous loyalty over a period of about five years, never revealing anything about Mac."

"And this was supposed to end how? I mean, what would have happened if Mac had agreed to sell?" Rose was thinking like a reporter now, covering the angles. Jesse found that darned appealing.

"Since we've established that Thompson is perfectly capable of murder, I would guess it would have ended very badly for Mac's child. Thompson figured he had it made either way. Mac dead – the relationship is a big surprise that Thompson can cleverly reveal and then manipulate the kid to sell his inheritance to LL Ltd. Or, with Mac alive and agreeing to sell, the child is made to disappear."

"Please don't think I haven't noticed the vague nouns you are using in reference to this child. Are we talking a he or a she?"

"Join me at the window?" Jesse asked and walked to the bank of windows that overlooked the entrance to the community park. The same park that had recently teemed with joyful competition, and then been the staging area for the protestors. Rose instructed Lola to 'stay' and stood beside Jesse.

"My God," she gasped. "This is …. Amazing."

Mac's company truck was parked with the bed facing the newspaper office. The tailgate was down and there, sharing bottles of Pepsi, sat Mac and Mark Kingsley, laughing together and glancing tenuously at each other.

The publisher and deputy stood quietly side-by-side until they felt like intruders watching the father and son exchange their first words as family. They turned away. "What do you say to that? How about that picnic?" Jesse asked.

Rose looked serious. "I say, do you want mustard or mayo on your sandwiches?"

Jesse's smile was as spontaneous as his question. "Can I pet your dog?"